"Mr. Carr can lead us away from the small, artificial, brightly-lit stage of the ordinary detective plot into the menace of outer darkness. He can create atmosphere with an adjective, and make a picture from a wet iron railing, a dusty table, a gas-lamp blurred by the fog. He can alarm with an alusion or delight with a rollicking absurdity—in short, he can write—not merely in the negative sense of observing the rules of syntax, but in the sense that every sentence gives a thrill of positive pleasure."

—Dorothy L. Sayers

"You can argue as you will about which was the most enjoyable period for a reader of detective stories: My allegiance remains irrevocably fixed to the 1930's, when you could count on four new novels a year by John Dickson Carr."

—Anthony Boucher

"If Agatha Christie was the queen of the murder mystery, Carr was certainly its king. . . . She's fine in her way (I've read all 80 of her mysteries), but when you're looking for an intricate plot and a ghostly atmosphere, you can't do better than John Dickson Carr."

—Walter Kendrick
Village Voice

D1571059

By **John Dickson Carr**
available in Library of Crime Classics® Editions:

Dr. Fell Novels:
DEATH TURNS THE TABLES
HAG'S NOOK*
THE SLEEPING SPHINX
TILL DEATH DO US PART

Other:
THE BURNING COURT*

Series Consultant: Douglas G. Greene

forthcoming

JOHN DICKSON CARR

THE SLEEPING SPHINX

INTERNATIONAL POLYGONICS, LTD.
NEW YORK CITY

Library of Congress Card Catalog No. 84-81895
ISBN: 0-930330-24-2

Printed and manufactured in the United States of America
First IPL printing April 1985.
10 9 8 7 6 5 4 3 2 1

THE road, so long that it looked narrow, had on its left the thick greenery of Regent's Park and on its right the tall iron railings around St. Katharine's Precinct of St. Katharine's Church. Just beyond, next to St. Katharine's, you could see the line of trees which screened from the road a terrace of tall, stately houses looming white through the dusk.

Number 1, Gloucester Gate. He could see it now.

It was the turn of the evening: faintly blue and white, with birds bickering from the direction of the park. The heat of the day still lingered in this avenue which seemed no less rural for being in the middle of London. Donald Holden stopped in his slow walk, and gripped his hand around one of the bars of the fence. Panic? Something very like it, at least.

Of all the ways in which he had pictured his home coming —and there had been many of them—he had never pictured it as anything like this.

Things were much too altered in seven years. You might have hoped they were not ruined; but at least they were altered.

He thought he had appreciated the full force of it that afternoon. He had been wrong. He was only beginning to appreciate it now. Major Sir Donald Holden, late (theoretically) of the Fourth Glebeshires, seemed to have gone through eternity since the afternoon. What he saw now was not the white house, with its Regency pillars, where Celia might be waiting. What he saw was room 307 at the War Office, and Warrender sitting behind the desk.

"Do you mean," Holden heard himself saying again, "that for over a year I'm supposed to have been dead?"

Warrender did not shrug his shoulders. That would have been too elaborate a gesture. But a twitch of his underlip conveyed the same effect.

1

" 'Fraid so, old boy," Warrender admitted.

Holden stared at him.

"But—Celia . . . !"

"Good God," Warrender said flatly. "Don't tell me you're married?"

During a silence, while they looked at each other, Warrender displayed emphasis by unscrewing the cap of a fountain pen and holding the pen as though he were going to sign something.

"You know as well as I do," said Warrender, "that if anybody gets a job like yours, where we've got to pretend he's still with his regiment and kill him in the line of duty, he's *allowed* to tell his wife. And we inform his solicitor. The other thing only happens in books and films. We may be a peculiar lot here," his khaki-covered arm indicated the War Office, "but that's understood."

"I'm not married," said Holden.

"Engaged, then?"

"No. Not even engaged. I never asked her."

"Oh!" murmured Warrender. With an air of finality, with a curt breath of relief, he screwed the cap back on the fountain pen. "That's different. I was afraid I'd been remiss."

"You haven't been remiss. When am I supposed to have died?"

"As far as I remember, you were killed with the Glebes during the attack on . . . well, I forget the name of the place; I can look it up in the file in half a tick . . . but it was in April just before the war ended. A year and three months and something today. Didn't Kappelman ever tell you?"

"No."

"Damn careless of him. You were supposed to have got a decoration. It was in all the newspapers. Quite a to-do."

"Thanks."

"Look here," Warrender began abruptly, and checked himself. Warrender rose to his feet: very lean, very tired looking, hardly half a dozen years older than Holden himself. He stood with his knuckles pressed against the top of the desk, supporting his weight.

"When Jerry started cracking up," he added, "it was the signal for the big boys to hare for cover. Von Steuben bolted to Italy; we had to get Steuben; and you were the man to get him. But they had an intelligence service too. So you had to 'die,' like several other people, to give you a better chance. Well, you got Steuben. The old man's very pleased about

2

that. Look here: you wouldn't really like a decoration of some kind, would you?"

"Great Scott, no!"

Warrender's tone grew bitter.

"It doesn't matter now," he said, and nodded toward the windows overlooking Whitehall. "The war's been over for a year and three months. You're out of the army; out of MI 5; out of everything. But can't you get it through your head that there was a time, not very long ago, when it did matter a devil of a lot?"

Holden shook his head.

"I wasn't complaining," he answered, with his eyes fixed on his companion. "I was only . . . trying to get used to it."

"You'll get used to it," said Warrender. He broke off. "Look here, what are you staring at?"

"You," said Holden. "Your hair's gray. I never noticed it until this minute."

Both of them were silent for a moment, while the noise of traffic rose up from Whitehall. Warrender instinctively put up a bony hand to his hair; his mouth seemed twisted.

"Neither did I," said Warrender, "until the war was over."

"Well, good-by," Holden said awkwardly. He stretched out his hand, and the other took it.

"Good-by, old son. All the best. Ring me up one day, and we'll—er—have lunch or something."

"Thanks. I will."

Remembering not to salute, since he was now in civilian clothes, Holden turned toward the door. He had his hand on the knob when Warrender, hesitating, abruptly spoke in a different voice.

"I say. Don."

"Yes?"

"Damn it all," exploded Warrender, "I'm not your superior officer any longer. Can't you tell an old pal anything?"

"There isn't anything to tell."

"The hell there isn't. Come back here. Sit down. Have a cigarette."

Holden slowly returned, with an inner breath of relief he would never have allowed even Warrender to hear. He sank down in a battered chair beside Warrender's desk. Warrender, glowering, pushed forward a cigarette box as he himself sat down; the smoke of two cigarettes rose in heavy, office-stagnant air.

"Your hair's not gray," Warrender said accusingly. "You're

3

perfectly fit, except maybe your nerves. You've got a brain like . . . like . . . well, I've often envied you. What's more, wait a minute!" Again Warrender broke off, his eyes narrowing. "By George, I've got so much on my mind"—his cigarette indicated the filing-cabinets—"I forgot that too! Two years ago! Or thereabouts! Didn't you come into a title or something?"

"Yes. Baronetcy."

Warrender whistled.

"Any money attached to it?"

"Quite a lot, I believe. Which reminds me," said Holden. blowing out smoke, "that I'm supposed to be dead. I suppose somebody else has got it now."

"How many times have I got to tell you," groaned Warrender, in a sort of official agony, "that this idea you've got —about the War Office not telling solicitors, when an Intelligence bloke is supposed to be dead—only happens in plays and films? You're all right. Your solicitor knows."

"Ah!" said Holden.

"Then that's off your mind," Warrender said soothingly. He eyed Holden with refreshed interest. "So you're Sir Donald now, eh? Congratulations. How does it feel?"

"Oh, I don't know. It's all right."

Warrender stared at him.

"My dear chap, you're crackers," he said with real concern. "This last job in Italy has turned your brain. Why aren't you dancing the fandango? Eh? Why aren't—" He paused. "Is it this Celia?"

"Yes."

"What's her other name?"

"Devereux. Celia Devereux."

By twisting sideways at Warrender's desk, Holden could see the little desk calendar with the staring red figure 10. Wednesday, July tenth. It was a reminder so sharp pointed that for a moment he closed his eyes. Then, suddenly, he got to his feet and went to one window, where he stood staring down.

Despite the comparative coolness of the office, heat danced in shimmers down stolid Whitehall. After the rainiest June in a quarter of a century, July had come in with a blaze of sun which heated the blood and dazzled the eye. A red bus rumbled past, its new paint glaring after wartime shabbiness. Sandbags, barbed wire in Whitehall, had all been swept away as traffic thickened and thundered. Seven years.

Exactly seven years ago yesterday—the ninth of July—

4

Margot Devereux, Celia's sister, had been married to Thorley Marsh in the little church of Caswall St. Giles. All Holden's thoughts and emotions centered round that wedding, as a kind of symbol.

It had been, he could not help remembering, another such hot day as this. The thick grass blazing in that remote corner of Wiltshire; the shining water round Caswall Moat House; the cool little cave of the church, in whose dimness white and blue and lavender dresses mingled with the colors of flowers.

The rustling, the occasional cough, all came from the pews of spectators behind his back. As Thorley's best man, he stood a few paces behind Thorley and to the right: with Celia, as maid of honor (how well he could remember the light of painted windows through the transparent brim of her large hat!) standing over on the other side of Margot.

Who was it who had said that churches were like "the treasure-caves of pirates?" Confound these literary associations, which always kept twining into his mind. Yet the place had a cavelike smell and atmosphere, too, with its glimmer of stained glass and brass candlesticks. And . . .

He couldn't see Thorley Marsh's face: only Thorley's broad, thick back, straight in black broadcloth, radiating good nature like that rising young stockbroker's whole personality. Yet Thorley was desperately nervous. And Holden could see, past the gauzy white of the veil, a part of Margot's profile— the healthy, hearty, laughing Margot, acknowledged as the beauty of the family, to whom Celia's delicacy formed a marked contrast—with her head a little lowered, and color under her eyes.

How fond he was of both Margot and Thorley! How he knew, in his bones and soul, that this was going to be the happiest of marriages!

"I, Margot, take thee, Thorley," the husky contralto voice could barely be heard, "to my wedded husband." It was in little gasps, after the clergyman's urban utterance. "To have and to hold from this day forward. For better, for worse. For richer, for poorer. In sickness, and in health . . ."

A wave of emotion, as palpable as the scent of flowers, flowed out from the little group of spectators in the pews. Everything was emotion, catching at the throat. He had not dared to look at Celia.

How afraid he had been, with that disquiet which always haunts the best man, that he was going to drop the ring! Or that Thorley would drop it when he handed it over. And that they would both have to scramble all over the floor for it, in front of all those people! Then the shock of astonishment at the ease with which it could be managed, when Mr. Reid in his white surplice bent forward and in a ventriloquial sort of voice murmured: "Place the ring on the book, please."

So neither of them could fumble it. He and Thorley had looked at each other in surprise, as though this were a special new bit of business ingeniously devised by the church for their benefit.

When it was all over, after what seemed an interminable amount of kneeling on hassocks—yes, that had been the high point of emotion—everybody ran forward, in a whirl of colors, and began kissing everybody else. He remembered the grandmother, Mammy Two (eighty years old, her face so whitened with age that it looked powdered) sniffing, with her handkerchief at her pale-blue eyes. He remembered Obey, in a funny hat—Obey, who had nursed both Celia and Margot—hovering in the background. And Sir Danvers Locke, who had given the bride away. And old Dr. Shepton looking on dubiously through his pince-nez. And little Doris Locke, aged twelve, one of the flower girls, for some reason suddenly bursting into tears and refusing even to attend the reception afterward.

As for Celia . . .

It was at this point that Frank Warrender's patient, common-sense voice roused him out of a dream.

"Well, old son?"

"Sorry," said Holden. He swung around from the window, smiling, and crushed out his cigarette on the edge of the sill. Warrender, with concern, watched that lean figure against the light from the window: the thin, intellectual face, brown from an Italian sun, with its narrow line of moustache and inscrutable eyes.

"I was thinking," Holden continued, "about Margot's wedding to a friend of mine named Thorley Marsh. Seven years ago, just before the war broke out."

Warrender's eyebrows went up. "Margot?"

"Celia's elder sister. Margot was twenty-eight; Celia maybe twenty-one. There were only three of the family left: Celia, and Margot, and the old grandmother they called Mammy Two." Holden laughed, not loudly. "Weddings, in retrospect, are always supposed to be funny. I wonder why."

"God knows, old boy. But . . ."

"I suppose," Holden went on thoughtfully, "because anything that involves strong emotion is afterward considered funny, from matrimony to having high explosives dropped

6

on you. But in weddings there's a sort of (what's the word I want?) a sort of *kindliness* mixed up with the emotion, and it's always remembered with a shout of laughter. 'Do you remember when you—?' And so on."

He was silent for a moment, opening and shutting his hands.

"Margot is beautiful," he added suddenly, as though Warrender had doubted it. "I never saw her so beautiful as then: all colored up, so to speak. Rather tall for a woman; chestnut-colored hair under the white veil; brown eyes set wide apart; dimples when she laughed, which was often. And likeable. The sort of girl who's captain of the hockey team at her school: you know? But Celia—my God, Celia!"

"Look here, Don. Why are you harping so much on this wedding?"

"Because it's the keynote of everything. It went to my head with a romantic bang. And I lost my chance with Celia."

"How do you mean, you lost your chance with Celia?"

Again Holden was silent for a moment.

"I met Celia in the evening," he answered. "Alone. In the path, under the trees, beside that same little church. I . . ."

And again there returned, poignant in vividness, every aspect of that day: every tinge of the sky, every fragrance of grass. The wedding reception at Caswall Moat House—with the sun making a hot cuirass of black broadcloth and starched shirt, and the dun-colored building mirrored in burning water. There had been a Devereux at Caswall ever since it had been known as Caswall Abbey, and one William Devereux bought it from the eighth Henry.

He remembered the tables set out in the great hall, which had been remodeled in the eighteenth century. The toasts, the reading of telegrams, the haste and fuss in one throb of excitement. Then, afterward, the departure of bride and groom, wearing soberer clothes, in Thorley's car. . . .

All over.

"Just as it was getting toward twilight," said Holden, "I went for a walk in the fields. I didn't expect to meet anybody: I didn't want to meet anybody. Emotion, you see! I went toward the church, which is between Caswall Moat House and Caswall village. There's a little back gate, and a little path that goes past the side of the church between it and the churchyard, with beech trees arching over it. And there I met Celia.

"I was tired. I was—a little crazy, I think. Anyway, for a second we just stood there looking at each other, maybe

7

twenty feet apart. Then I walked straight up to her and said . . ."

"Go on," prompted Warrender, glowering down at the desk.

"I said to Celia, 'I'm in love with you, and I'll always be in love with you, but I haven't got anything to offer you.' She cried out, 'I don't care! I don't care!' And I said, 'Let's never speak of it again, shall we?' She looked at me as though I'd hit her, and said, 'All right, if you insist.' And I hurried away from there as though the devil were after me."

Warrender sat up straight, crushing out his cigarette in an ash tray.

"You blithering ass!" he almost shouted.

Ten seconds in time! Holden was reflecting. Ten seconds in time, that conversation with Celia, and the repressed emotion of months pouring out of it. The green twilight of the trees, damp and fragrant. Celia with her hands pressed together, slender and gray-eyed; with brown hair like Margot, but otherwise utterly unlike her vivacious sister. Ten seconds —and then everything torn away. He became aware that Warrender was cursing him very comprehensively.

"You blithering ass!" Warrender ended, on a note of mania.

"Yes," Holden assented calmly. "I think so now. And yet," he shook his head, staring at the desk as Warrender did, "and yet, you know, I'm not altogether sure I wasn't right."

"Pfaa!" said Warrender.

"Think for a minute, Frank. In 1939 the Devereuxs had Caswall with umpteen-hundred acres. They had a big house here in town, out Regent's Park way. And money. Plenty of money." He reflected. "I don't know how well off they are now. Rather better off, I should think; because Thorley was an up-and-coming man in the city, and I understand he's made a good thing out of the war.—In honest business, of course!" he added hastily, as he saw Warrender's eyebrows draw together.

"Oh, ah? Maybe, I'm cynical. Well?"

"And, in 1939, what was I? A languages master at Lupton, with three hundred a year and my keep. Fine old public school, yes. Cosseted life, nothing to worry about. But a wife? I think not."

"But now you're Sir Donald Holden, with a bucketful of cash!"

"Yes." Holden's tone was bitter. "And not very glad to have two brothers, far better men than I'll ever be, die in

8

action so that I could come into the title. Anyway, about Celia . . ."

"Well?"

"I'm older now. I suppose, on the whole, I did make an ass of myself. But it's no good debating that. I've lost her, Frank, and serves me damn well right."

Warrender jumped to his feet.

"Don't talk such blithering rubbish! What do you mean, you've lost her? Is she married?"

"I don't know. Very probably, yes."

"These other people: are they—still about?"

"Still about, I believe. Except Mammy Two; she died in the winter of '41. But the rest are well, so far as I know. And happy."

"When was the last time you saw Celia?"

"Three years ago."

"Or wrote to her?"

Holden looked at him.

"As you yourself pointed out, Frank," he replied carefully, "from the time Jerry started cracking up you had a number of jobs for me. I was in Germany in '44. In '45 you sent me straight to Italy after Steuben. And, in case it's escaped your memory, for the past fifteen months—fifteen months, mind! —I've been supposed to be dead."

"Hang it all, I've apologized! It was damn careless of Kappelman not to . . ."

"Never mind the official side, Frank. Let's face it."

Perhaps it was the blazing sun at the window that made Holden's scalp feel thick and hot. He moved away from the window, his thin brown face—reserved, moody, dogged—as unfathomable as the eyes. He stood knocking his knuckles, over and over, restlessly, on Warrender's desk.

"When we're in the services," he said. "we get the mistaken idea that people and things at home always stay the same. But they don't stay the same. They can't be expected to. It's an odd thing, too. Last night, my first night in London, I went to see a play . . ."

"A play!" scoffed Warrender.

"No; but wait a minute. It was about a man who returned after they supposed he was dead. He raised merry blazes, and cut up all kinds of a row, because his wife wasn't still cherishing him with a grand passion.

"But how could she be expected to? Changes, new faces, the passage of years—! This grand passion is a notion out of the *Roman de la Rose*; it died with the Middle Ages, if it

9

ever existed. When one man's gone, a woman eventually finds she can be just as comfortable with another; and that's —well, it's only sensible. As for Celia, after the thundering fool I made of myself all that time ago . . ."

He paused for a moment, and then added:

"Last night, of course, I didn't know I was supposed to be dead. But I did know there'd been a severance, a blind gap of years. Not a word on either side. I got up and crept out of that theater like a ghost. And now I've had it." He started to laugh. "By George, I've had it!"

"Nonsense!" observed Warrender. "Are you still—er— keen about the girl?"

Holden nearly exploded.

"Am I still. . . !"

"All right," Warrender said coolly. "Where is she? Is she still living with Margot and this What's-his-name, or where is she?"

"When I last heard of her, she was still with Margot and Thorley."

"Well, we'll assume she's still there. And where are they now? In town, or at Caswall?"

"They're in town," answered Holden. "The first thing I picked up in the lounge of my hotel last night, when I got back from that infernal play, was a copy of the Tatler. There was a photograph of Thorley, looking as sleek as his own Rolls Royce, stepping out in front of the Gloucester Gatehouse."

"Good!" Warrender nodded briskly. He pointed to the battery of telephones on his desk. "There's the phone. Ring her up."

There was a long silence.

"Frank, I can't do it."

"Why not?"

"How many times must I remind you," inquired Holden, "that I'm supposed to be dead? D-e-a-d, dead. Celia isn't a strapping, uninhibited girl like Margot. She's—excitable. Mammy Two used to say . . ."

"Say what?"

"Never mind. The point is, suppose Celia answers the phone? She's probably married and not there anyway," Holden added, a little wildly and irrationally, "but suppose she answers the phone?"

"All right," said Warrender. "This Thorley bloke, I presume, has got an office in the city? Good! Ring him there, and explain the situation. Now look here, Don!" Warrender glared at him, the gray hair over the worn face. "This thing is getting you down. You're already thinking of yourself as a bloody outcast and Enoch Arden. And it's got to stop. If you don't ring, I will."

"No! Frank! Wait a minute!"

But Warrender had already reached for the telephone directory.

CHAPTER II

AND now, in the evening, with the last faint light beyond the trees of Regent's Park, and on the other side of the street—as he passed St. Katharine's Precinct—the tall Regency houses looming up whitish in gloom, Donald Holden still could not feel any less apprehensive, or consider that anything had been settled.

For a time he stood gripping one of the iron bars of the railing round St. Katharine's. Then he moved forward, his heart beating heavily.

A little paved drive, shut off from the main road by trees and a wickerwork fence which had replaced the old iron railings, curved in a crescent past these houses. The house where Celia probably was, and where Margot and Thorley certainly were, was Number 1: the house nearest him at the corner.

Massive, solid as ever! Towering up in smooth white stone, its two storeys above the ground floor buttressed by fluted Corinthian columns set massively into the façade, and supporting a shallow roof peak on which were a few battered statues. Any change here?

Yes. Though even in the dusk its lightless windows shone, new glass clean polished, across one edge of the façade ran a tiny zigzag crack. One of the roof statues stood a little askew against the darkening sky. Regent's Park had got it rather badly in the blitz, but he couldn't remember seeing that crack before. It was probably . . .

Well? Go on!

It was certain, as certain as anything could be in this world, that the whole family now knew he was alive. Yet Frank Warrender's telephone call to Thorley's office in the city couldn't have been called an unmitigated success. Again Holden pictured Warrender, with that portentous and stuffed air Frank always assumed at the telephone, dictatorily attacking the staff. The information that Colonel Warrender, of the War Office, wished to speak to Mr. Thorley Marsh on a matter of vital importance, had brought first a scurry of voices and then the ultrarefined tones of a male secretary, obviously perturbed.

"I'm sorry, sir," the secretary replied. "Mr. Marsh is not at the office." (Holden's heart sank.) "He phoned that he would be at home all day. You could reach him there, if the matter is urgent. Is there anything *I* can do?"

Warrender cleared his throat.

"I believe," he said, tapping his fountain pen on the desk to emphasize each word, "I believe Mr. Marsh has a sister-in-law named Miss Celia Devereux." Whereupon, officialdom being what it is, he could not help rapping out: "Have you any data on Miss Devereux?"

"Data, sir?"

"Precisely."

So great has become our terror of regulations in this free age that the secretary was clearly confusing the War Office with the Home Office, perhaps even with Scotland Yard, and wondering who was in trouble.

"During the war, sir, Miss Devereux was parliamentary secretary to Mr. Derek Hurst-Gore. The M.P., you know. I—I don't think she is employed at present. If you could give me a little more information as to the sort of—er—data you want?"

"I mean," said Warrender, in a startlingly more human tone, "is she married?"

The secretary's voice seemed to jump. Holden, who was bending forward to catch each word out of the telephone, gripped the edge of the desk.

"Married, sir? Not to my knowledge."

"Ah!" observed Warrender. "Or engaged?"

The voice hedged. "I believe, sir, there *has* been some talk of an engagement to Mr. Hurst-Gore. But whether anything has been officially announced. . . ."

"Thank you," said Warrender, and hung up. His official face relaxed.

"The only thing for you to do, old boy," Warrender added, "is to send a long telegram to this Thorley What's-it, at his home address. Even if it falls into the wrong hands, it'll break things gently. You hang about until the telegram's certain to have been delivered, and then just go out and see the girl. And . . . well, you know. Good luck."

Now there was an end of hanging about.

Over the Park, over Number 1 Gloucester Gate, warm dusk deepened. Distantly a taxi honked; otherwise it was so still that you might have been at Caswall in the country. Holden heard his own footsteps ring on asphalt as he walked into the little crescent of the drive. A short distance, only a short distance from the flight of stone steps leading up to the front door, he stopped again.

Perhaps the unlighted windows daunted him, the sense that nobody was there. But that couldn't be. Perhaps the front door would be opened by fat Obey, the old nurse. Perhaps it would be opened by Celia herself.

"Mr. Derek Hurst-Gore. M.P."

At the right-hand side of the house, a little stone-flagged path, enclosed by a rose trellis on the other side, led to a back garden surrounded by a high brick wall. Holden, hesitating, made for that path. He told himself (at least, on the surface of his mind) that it was past dinnertime; that they would probably all be in the drawing room; and that the drawing room was at the back of the house, up one floor from the ground with its little iron balcony and staircase. So, of course, it would be best to go straight there.

And, as he walked down that path, a rush of memories returned bittersweet. In that back garden he had often had tea with Celia. He could see Margot there, too; in a deck chair, with a fashion magazine or else (her only kind of reading matter) a thriller or a book of trials. In that same garden, during the blitz days which now seemed so far off as to be prewar, Mammy Two—wrinkled-white of face, insatiably curious, her shawl round her shoulders—had stood night after night, watching the raiders under a sky white with gunfire.

Since their part of Wiltshire was a safe area, Thorley had thought it only prudent to take Margot to Caswall during the blitz. But Mammy Two refused to go.

"My dear child," Holden could hear her husky indomitable voice saying, in an utterly bewildered tone, "it's so silly of them to think they can browbeat us with this nonsense." (Bam went a battery of three-point-nines in Regent's Park; and the glass lusters of the chandelier jumped and clanked and tingled.) "It makes me really angry. That's why I'm here. I hate London otherwise, y'know."

And again:

"Die?" said Mammy Two. "Well, my dear child, I only hope when my time comes they'll have finished the new vault in Caswall churchyard. The old one is so crowded it's a sin and a shame." Her old eyes, pale blue in a white face, hardened and grew apprehensive. "But I don't want to die yet. I've got to look out for—things."

"Things?"

"There's a funny streak in our family, y'know. One of my granddaughters is all right, but I've been worried about the other ever since she was a little child. No, I don't want to be taken yet."

And so, in the bitter winter of '41, when high explosives showered down amid drifting snowflakes, she stayed too long in that garden watching the searchlights, and she died of pneumonia within a week. Celia, they said, had cried for days. Celia wouldn't leave town either.

Celia. . . .

Pushing away these memories, which brought a lump into his throat in spite of himself, Holden hurried past scratching tendrils of rose trees into the garden. Again the utter stillness oppressed him. The cropped lawn, the sundial, the plum trees against the east wall, swam in a thin whitish dusk which made outlines just visible.

And there were no lights at the back of the house, either.

But this wasn't possible! There must be somebody at home! Besides, the full-length windows of the drawing room were standing wide open.

Holden stared at the back of the house. Across it, about fifteen feet above the ground, ran a narrow balcony with a wrought-iron balustrade; a flight of iron stairs led down into the garden. On the left were the tall door-windows of the drawing room; on the right, if he remembered correctly, a similar pair of door-windows led to the dining room. No sign of life anywhere. The ground-floor windows, even, were shuttered; the back door was closed.

Holden, now so puzzled that his self-assurance was returning, ran quickly up the iron stairs. It was as though, in the vividness of those memories, he had never been away. The balcony still rattled underfoot, just as it used to do. Fishing out his pocket lighter, he walked to the nearer of the open drawing-room windows. He put his head inside, and snapped on the flame of the lighter.

"Hullo!" he called. "Is anybody at home? I . . ."

Inside the room, a woman screamed.

That scream went piercing up with such suddenness, out

14

of the dim drawing room, that in the shock of it the lighter slipped through Holden's fingers and clattered on the polished hardwood floor. At the same time the realization flooded his wits—ass! fool! imbecile!—that he had done precisely the thing he had been trying so hard to avoid.

It was the same drawing room, very large and lofty, its walls painted dark green, the arabesque gold of the Venetian mirror above a white marble mantelpiece, the white slip covers on the furniture showing ghostly against dusk. Not a single glass prism seemed missing from its chandelier. And the room was very much occupied.

Holden could make out the shadowy figure of Thorley Marsh, and of a girl who—thank God!—certainly wasn't either Celia or Margot. They appeared to have been standing rather close together, but they had jumped apart. Holden's brain seemed to ring with the intensity of that moment of silence.

"I'm Don Holden, Thorley! I'm alive! I . . . Didn't you get my telegram?"

Thorley's voice, usually full throated, quavered out of gloom.

"Who—?"

"I tell you, Thorley, I'm Don Holden! It was all a mistake about my being killed! Or at least . . . Didn't you get my telegram?"

"Tele . . ." began Thorley, and stopped. His hand moved toward the side pocket of his coat. Then, clearing his throat, he enunciated very slowly and clearly, but still shakily: "Telegram."

"It's true, Thorley!" breathed the girl. (Who was she? Holden couldn't distinguish her face. She had a young, soft voice.) "You—you did get a telegram!" She gulped. "It got here just as I did. We—we landed on the doorstep together. But you didn't open it. You put it in your pocket."

"Don!" muttered Thorley.

And he walked forward hesitantly, at his slow moving and heavy tread on the hardwood floor.

Holden bent over and picked up the fallen lighter. He could have kicked himself. In his pleasure at seeing Thorley, in the radiance of good nature and kindliness which always surrounded Thorley, he had not quite realized the shock this would be. But in that case (swift-prompting thought) what about Celia? Thorley hadn't opened the telegram! Then Celia didn't know either.

Thorley, wearing a dark suit, had been only a blur of black

and white until he emerged into the after glow from the windows. He stood there for a moment, staring. He had changed very little. He had perhaps put on weight, making the bulky body thicker, and gained in the face as well: a handsome face, though the tendency to weight made his fine features seem a little too small. There were tiny horizontal lines across his forehead. But the black hair, shining and plastered down to a nicety, showed no tinge of gray. Then Thorley woke up.

"My dear old boy!" he cried. It was as though icicles tinkled and fell. He threw an arm across Holden's shoulder, and began to wallop him on the back with real affection. He added, hastily and rather incoherently: "Unexpectedness . . . you must forgive . . . under the circumstances . . . things that have been happening—"

(Things that have been happening?)

"Anyway," said Thorley, with all the charm and kindliness radiant in his smile, "anyway, my dear fellow, how are you?"

"I'm fine, thanks. Never better. But listen, Thorley! Celia . . ."

"Oh, yes, Celia." A new thought came to Thorley; there was a slight pause. His dark eyes grew evasive. "Celia . . . isn't here just now."

Holden's heart sank. Wasn't he ever to see her, then? Probably she was out with Mr. Derek Hurst-Gore, M.P. Still, maybe it was better like this.

Across the room there was a slight click, and a light went on.

The girl, hovering, had been standing at the far side of a white-covered sofa where there was a little table and a table lamp with a buff-colored shade. Both Thorley and Holden swung round as she pressed the button of the lamp. Standing just over that lamp, with the light from its open top shining up strongly across her face, the girl tried to keep a cool and assured air.

She was perhaps nineteen, though with a hair style and make-up designed for one considerably older, and she was not very tall. That core of light, brilliant in the midst of green-painted walls, showed her dark-blue frock trimmed with white, and the blonde hair drawn above her ears, under a white hat. A stranger? Apparently. Yet to Holden that pretty face, with its rather angry blue eyes and spoiled mouth, suggested . . .

Yes! It suggested the background of a church, never very

far from his thoughts, and a little flower girl, aged twelve, who . . .

"You're Sir Danvers Locke's daughter," he said flatly. "You're little Doris Locke!"

The girl stiffened. That word "little" had obviously annoyed her. She stood turning her head slowly from one side to the other, either in keeping her eyes away from the light or in deliberately posing.

"How terribly clever of you to remember me," she murmured. Then, in a different voice, she burst out: "I think it was an awfully mean trick of you to pop up like that!"

"It was unpardonable, Miss Locke. I deeply apologize."

His formal courtesy and grave bearing, for some reason, made her flush.

"Oh, that's all right. It—it doesn't matter." She took up gloves and a handbag from the table. "Anyway, I'm afraid I must be pushing off now."

"You're not going?" Thorley cried incredulously.

"Oh, didn't I tell you?" said Doris. "I promised to meet Ronnie Merrick at the Café Royal, and then we're going on somewhere to dance." Doris looked at Holden. "Ronnie's nice. Probably I shall marry him, because my father wants me to, and they say he's going to be a great painter one day: I mean Ronnie, of course, not my father. But he's so young."

"He's a year older than you," said Thorley.

"I always say," observed Doris, elaborately turning her eyes away, "that a person is as old as they feel." Again her tone changed. "Go on, Mr. Holden! Say 'as old as they feel' is shocking grammar. You were always like that. Go on! Say it!"

Holden laughed.

"It's bad grammar, Miss Locke. I don't know about the 'shocking' part."

But the girl was regarding him strangely. Something different, something straightforward and likable, looked out of the blue eyes.

"You—you were the one," she added suddenly, "who was so keen about Celia. And thought you were keeping your secret so well, only everybody knew it. And she was absolutely scatty about you. And now, things being what they are . . . oh, God!" said Doris, her fingers tightening round her handbag. "I must go. Excuse me."

And, startlingly, she almost ran for the door.

"Wait!" cried Thorley, a bulky figure coming to life. "Let me send you in the car! Let me . . ."

But the door had closed. They heard a quick, agitated rapping of high-heeled shoes fading away down the hall; then the hollow slam of the front door, which made one or two prisms tingle in the chandelier.

("Things being what they are." Mr. Derek Hurst-Gore, M.P.?)

Thorley, solid and stolid looking, took half a dozen indecisive paces toward the door. Then he swung round, the lamp light sleek on his black hair, and stood jingling coins deep in his pockets. He began talking in a very hurried way.

"Er—that was Doris Locke," he explained rapidly. "Daughter of old Danvers Locke. He's got a big place down in the country near Caswall. Fellow collects masks; all sorts of masks; even got a metal one worn by a German executioner hundreds of years ago; crazy hobby. But filthy with money—absolutely filthy—and, of course, in with all the right people in the business world. He . . ."

"Thorley! *Oi!*"

Thorley broke off. "What did you say, old man?"

"I know all that," Holden said gently. "I'm acquainted with Locke too, you know."

"Yes. Of course. So you are." Thorley passed a hand across his forehead. "It's damn difficult," he complained. "Putting things back in their places again."

"Yes. I've found that out."

"Then you weren't killed in that famous attack? And didn't get a DSO?"

"I'm afraid not."

"You've rather let me down, young fellow," said Thorley, with the ghost of his jovial laugh. "I've been bragging about you all over the place." He frowned. "But look here: what *did* happen to you? Were you a prisoner of war or something? Even so, why did you stop writing? And why turn up like this when the war's been over for so long?"

"I was in Intelligence, Thorley."

"Intelligence?"

"Yes. Certain things had to be done, and certain other things printed in the newspapers. I'll explain later. The point is . . ."

"I suppose," Thorley said gloomily, "it was all eyewash, too, about your getting that baronetcy. Ah, well! Doesn't matter now. I remember thinking, though, it was a bit of bad luck: getting knocked off in the field only a couple of months after you'd come into a pot of cash, and could arrange your life in any way you liked. Poor old Celia . . ."

"For Christ's sake, stop talking about it!"

Thorley, startled and hurt, opened his eyes wide. For a moment he looked like an overgrown child.

"I beg your pardon," said Holden, instantly getting a grip on himself. "I seem always, from the best of motives, to be doing or saying the wrong thing. No offense?"

"Lord, no! Of course not!"

"As you say, Thorley, that doesn't matter now. My story can wait. The point is, how are things with you?"

For a moment Thorley did not reply. He wandered over to the large sofa beside which the lamp was burning, and sat down. He put his hands on his knees, and contemplated the floor. His face, with the handsome features rather too small for it, was as blank as the dark eyes. The house seemed very still, uncannily still. Not a breath of wind stirred in from the darkening garden.

Holden laughed. "As I came in here tonight," he remarked, suddenly conscious that he was trying to make light conversation and wondering why, "as I came in here tonight, I was thinking about Mammy Two."

"Oh?" Thorley glanced quickly sideways. "Why?"

"Well," smiled Holden, "have you and Margot got any children yet? I think it was always a source of disappointment to Mammy Two that you didn't at least begin a family. Hang it all, Thorley, how's Margot? And, by the way, where *is* Margot?"

Thorley's glance rested on him for a moment, and then moved across to the white marble mantelpiece on the other side of the room.

"Margot's dead," he answered.

CHAPTER III

THE shock of that announcement, the vague sense that Thorley had really said something else and that he had misheard the word, kept Holden dumb.

No clock ticked in the room. There was an ormolu clock on the mantelpiece, in front of the great dim Venetian mirror with its arabesques of tarnished goldwork, but that clock had been silent for many years. Holden's eyes moved over to the mirror, and across to a cabinet of Sèvres porcelain against another wall, and then back again to Thorley sitting there—his hands flat on his knees, his head again lowered—under the light of the buff-colored lamp.

And now for the first time Holden noticed something else. Thorley's dark suit was a black suit; and his necktie, against the shiny white collar and white shirt, was also black.

"Dead?"

"Yes." Thorley did not look up.

"But that's impossible!" cried Holden, as though desperately trying to persuade him out of an unreasonable attitude. "Margot never had a day's illness in her life. How . . . when. . . ?"

Thorley cleared his throat.

"At Caswall. More than six months ago. Just before Christmas. We were all down at Caswall for Christmas."

"But—what. . . ?"

"Cerebral hemorrhage."

"Cerebral hemorrhage? What's that?"

"I don't know," Thorley said querulously. "It's something you die of." Holden could see that Thorley was moved, deeply moved, and his voice had thickened; but what sounded in that voice was a kind of irritation. "Confound it, talk to Dr. Shepton! You remember old Dr. Shepton? He attended her. I did all I could." He paused. "God knows I did."

"I'm sorry, Thorley." Holden also spoke after a pause. "I know you don't want to talk about it. So I won't say anything more, except that I haven't any words to express how . . . how . . ."

"No, it's all right!" For the first time Thorley looked up. He said huskily: "Margot and I were—very happy."

"Yes. I know."

"Very happy," insisted Thorley, his fist clenched on his knee. "But it's all over now, and I don't see any practical good to be gained by brooding on the matter." After breathing heavily for a few seconds, breathing noisily through small nostrils, he added: "I don't mind talking about it now. Only: don't ask me too much."

"But what was it all about, Thorley? What happened?"

Thorley hesitated.

"It was at Caswall; did I tell you? Two days before Christmas. Margot and Celia and I, and a very fine chap named Derek Hurst-Gore—did you say something?"

"No. Go on."

"Anyway, the four of us drove over in the evening to Wide-stairs—that's Danvers Locke's house—for dinner and a bit of a paity. There was Locke, and his wife, and Doris; and, by the way, an insufferably self-opinionated young ass who thinks he can make a living by slinging paint on canvas. His name's Ronald Merrick. He's got a calf-love for Doris; and, for some reason or other, Locke wants her to marry him."

"Never mind about that, Thorley! What about Margot?" Thorley's fist clenched tighter.

"Well, we were a bit late in getting there; because the good old hot-water heater at Caswall, as usual in cold weather, went on strike; and Obey didn't get it repaired until next day. But the party was grand fun. We played games." Again he hesitated. "I didn't notice anything wrong with Margot. She was excited and overhearty, but that usually happened when she got involved in games. You know?"

Holden nodded.

The image in his mind of Margot—brown eyed, with the dimples in her cheeks—grew achingly clear. In his philosophy Margot was one of those simple souls, easily moved to laughter or tears, always blurting out something that shouldn't be blurted out, in connection with whom the idea of death is utterly incongruous.

"Anyway," muttered Thorley, "we left the party very early. Eleven o'clock or thereabouts. We were all stone-cold sober; or near enough, at least. By half-past eleven we'd all turned in, or I thought we had. . . . Have—have you been to Caswall since the war?"

"No. Not since your wedding. Somebody told me, in the summer after the blitz, it was to be taken over by the military."

Thorley shook his head.

"Oh, no," he said. He did not exactly smile, but a curious expression of complacency, almost of smugness, crept round his jowls; Holden had never seen it there before. "Oh, no. *I* saw to that. None of my relatives got hoicked into the services, either. You can wangle anything, my boy, if you know your way about.

"But I was telling you. You remember the Long Gallery at Caswall? Margot and I," he moistened his lips, "had the suite of rooms on the floor above that. A bedroom and a sitting room each, with a bathroom between the two bedrooms, all in a line. That's where—that's where we were.

"I didn't sleep very well that night. I kept dozing off, and waking up again. About two o'clock in the morning I thought

21

I heard somebody calling, or moaning and groaning, from the direction of Margot's rooms. I got up, and looked in the bathroom. But it was dark. I turned on the light there, and looked in her bedroom; but that was dark too and the bed hadn't been slept in. Then I saw a light under the door to her sitting room.

"I went in there," said Thorley, "and found Margot, still dressed in her evening gown, lying all sprawled on her back across one of those chaise-longue things. She wasn't conscious, but she was sort of moving and raving. She was a funny color, too."

Thorley paused, staring at the floor.

"It scared me," he confessed. "I didn't want to wake anybody else up, so I nipped downstairs and phoned the doctor. Dr. Shepton was there in fifteen minutes. By that time Margot was partly conscious, but with throat constriction; and there was rigidity, you know; and she didn't seem to know much what was going on.

"The doctor said it was brought on by nervous excitement, and probably not serious. We got her to bed. The doctor gave her a sedative, and said he'd be back in the morning. I sat and held her hand all night.

"But Margot didn't get better: she was worse. At half-past eight the doctor came back; I nipped down again and let him in. Poor old Shepton was looking pretty grim. He said he was afraid of cerebral hemorrhage: breaking of blood vessels in the brain, I think it is. It was very cold. Still nobody in the house was awake yet. At nine o'clock, as the sun was coming up, she just . . . died."

There was a long silence.

Thorley's last word fell piteously, with a small and plaintive simplicity. He looked very hard at his companion, as though longing to add something else; but Thorley decided against it. Lifting his thick shoulders, he rose to his feet and went to one of the windows, where he stood staring out into the garden.

"Shepton," he added, "wrote out the death certificate."

"Oh?"

"Never saw one of 'em before," remarked Thorley, jingling coins in his pocket. "It's a thing like a gigantic check, with a counterfoil that the doctor keeps when he tears the certificate out and gives it to you. You're supposed to post it on to the registrar, but I forgot to."

"I see," said Holden, who didn't see in the least.

Had he experienced, ever since he first entered this house tonight, a vague feeling of disquiet? A subconscious sense that something was wrong? Nonsense! Yet there it was: an instinct of black waters swirling, of dangerous images just out of view, and—what was worst and most irrational—the feeling that Celia was involved in it.

"I see," he repeated. "And is that all you have to tell me?"

"Yes. Except that poor Margot was buried in the new family vault in Caswall churchyard. It was two days after Christmas. We . . ."

Some strange note in Holden's voice, faintly jarring, had caught Thorley's attention in the midst of his absorption. Thorley stopped jingling coins in his pocket and turned around from the window.

"What exactly do you mean, is that all I have to tell you?"

Holden made a despairing gesture. "Thorley, I don't know! It's only . . . I never had any idea Margot's health was as bad as that!"

"She wasn't in bad health. She was in good health. The thing might have happened to anybody. Shepton said so."

"Death from overexcitement at a party?"

"Look here, Don. Have you any reason to doubt Dr. Shepton's ability, or his good faith?"

"No, no, of course not! It's only that . . . that . . ."

"You're shocked, old chap," said Thorley in a commiserating voice. "Of course you are. So were all of us, at first. It was sudden. It was tragic. It made us remember that," there was almost a blink of tears in his eyes, "that in the midst of life we are in death, and all that sort of business."

Thorley shifted, as though hesitating to approach some fact that must be approached.

"And there's another thing, Don," he went on, "I've arranged to go down to Caswall tomorrow. Only for a short visit, of course. This will be the first time any of us has been there since it happened. As a matter of fact, my boy, I'm thinking of selling the place."

Holden stared at him.

"Selling Caswall? When you've got the money to keep it up?"

"Why not?" Thorley demanded.

"There are four hundred years of reasons why not."

"That's just the point," said Thorley in a different voice. "The place is unhealthy. It's unhealthy with age. All those portraits in the Long Gallery—they're unhealthy." He did

23

not explain the reason for this last extraordinary statement. "Besides, it can't be staffed properly. And we'll never get as good a price for the place as we'll get now."

"How does Celia feel about it?"

Thorley ignored this.

"So, as I say," he persisted, "Celia and I are going down to Caswall tomorrow." He took a deep breath. "Under any other circumstances, my dear fellow, I'd be only too delighted to invite you to go along with us . . ."

There was a long silence.

"Under any other circumstances?"

"Yes."

"Then I gather," Holden said with great politeness, "I am not invited to Caswall."

"Don, for heaven's sake don't misunderstand!"

"What is there to misunderstand? But if Celia's going with you . . ."

"Don, that's just it!". Thorley paused. "The fact is, I'd rather you didn't meet Celia."

"Oh? Why not?"

"Not just at the moment, anyway. Afterward, maybe—"

"Thorley," said Holden, putting his hands in his pockets, "I'm quite aware that for the past few minutes, in your highly diplomatic way, you've been trying to tell me something. What are you trying to tell me? Why don't you want me to meet Celia?"

"It's nothing, really. It's only . . ."

"*Answer me! Why don't you want me to meet Celia?*"

"Well, if you must know," Thorley replied calmly, "we're a little disturbed about the balance of her mind."

Now the silence stretched out unendurably.

Outside the circle of light thrown by the table lamp, the radiance across white-covered sofa and edges of rugs on a polished floor, the rest of the big drawing room had retreated into darkness. The mirror brought back from Italy by a seventeenth-century Devereux, the Sèvres porcelain cabinet from the palace of Versailles, the little First Empire settee against another wall, had all faded into shadows. Up over the garden outside, seen through long door-windows, were a few bright stars and the hint of a rising moon.

Donald Holden turned away and walked slowly round the room, inspecting each article without seeing it. His footsteps sounded with great distinctness. Thorley watched him. Still without speaking, Holden circled around until he faced Thorley from beside the lamp.

"Are you trying to tell me," he said, "that Celia is insane?"

"No, no, no!" scoffed Thorley, with cheery, false heartiness. "Not as serious as that, of course. Nothing, I'm sure, that a good psychiatrist couldn't cure; that is, if she'd only go to one. At least," he hesitated, "I hope it's no more serious than that."

Then Holden did what Thorley perhaps least expected. He started to laugh. Thorley was shocked.

"If you see anything funny in this!" Thorley said reproachfully.

"Yes. I do see something funny in it."

"Oh?"

"In the first place," said Holden, "I don't believe a word of it." The idea of the gentle, gray-eyed Celia as mentally incompetent was so grotesque that he laughed again. "In the second place . . ."

"Well?"

"When you started all these devious cat-footed tactics of approach, I thought you were trying to get rid of me so as to leave a clear field for the excellent Mr. Derek Hurst-Gore."

"I never had any such idea!" cried Thorley, in obviously genuine astonishment. "Though, mind you," he added on reflection, "Celia might do worse if—if she were in a state to marry anybody. He kept his seat when the Conservatives went out, and he's going to go far. Whereas (if you'll excuse my saying so, old man) you're not much of a catch; now are you?"

"Agreed," said Holden. A cold shock had gone through him at those words, "if she were in a state to marry anybody." The shock cleared his wits; it stung him alert, and made him very steady. "But never mind Mr. Derek Hurst-Gore. Let's get back to this question of Celia's insanity."

Thorley made a fussed gesture.

"Don't say that word! I don't like it!"

"Well, let's call it her mental disturbance. What form does that disturbance take?"

Thorley let his glance stray away; as though he were trying, without turning around, to look out of the window behind him.

"She's—saying things."

"Saying what things?"

"Things that are impossible. And crazy. And—well, pretty horrible," muttered Thorley. Suddenly he looked back at Holden, his face whitish in gloom. "I'm very fond of Celia, Don. More so than you'll ever guess, if you only knew the whole facts of this business. There mustn't be any scandal.

There must never be any scandal. But, if she keeps on talking as she's been talking . . ."

"Saying what?"

"Sorry, old chap. I haven't got time to go into it now."

"Then shall I tell you?"

"What's that?"

"Has she by any chance been saying," asked Holden, "that Margot's death wasn't a natural death?"

The stars, hitherto bright over a dark garden, were paling with the rising moon. Neither Thorley nor Holden moved.

"You see," continued the latter, "even if Celia were completely out of her mind"—Holden could not help a shudder going through him—"why are you so anxious I shouldn't meet her? After all, I'm an old friend. I couldn't hurt her. Is it because you knew very well she's as sane as you are, and she's got at the truth that Margot didn't die a natural death; and you're afraid I'd back her up?"

Holden took a few steps forward: short, shuffling steps.

"Listen, Thorley," he said, gently. "You're quite right. I will back her up. And if you're trying any games against Celia, or even thinking of trying any games against Celia"—his hands opened and shut—"then God help you. That's just a little warning."

Thorley, catching the expression of his eyes, stared back at him. Thorley's next remark sounded almost grotesque.

"You've—you've changed," he complained.

"*I've* changed? What about yourself?"

"Changed?" Thorley was equally surprised. "No, I think not. I'm still doing business at the same old stand. And if it comes to any—er—argument between us, we'll see who wins: the old maestro," he tapped himself on the chest complacently "or you." Then his expression grew strained again. "But I think you ought to know, for old friendship's sake, that you're doing me an injustice."

"Am I? I wish to heaven I could think so!"

"It's true, Don." Thorley hesitated. "Do you want to hear the real reason why I don't want you to meet Celia yet? Can you take it?"

"Of course I can take it. Well?"

"Well! Celia's practically forgotten you."

It was the one thing which could knock the props out from under him. And it did. Thorley was sympathetic.

"Now let's face it, Don," he said. He came over and put his hand on Holden's arm. "At one time Celia was very much in love with you. You, as I understand it—I've only heard this through Margot—once started to make love to her, and then suddenly said you never wanted the subject mentioned again."

"I was a blazing fool!"

"Well," Thorley shrugged his shoulders, "that's as it may be. I think you weren't, myself. The point is, you've given her plenty of time to forget it. What happens if you turn up now?"

"Why should anything happen?"

"Celia's in a very dangerous mental state. Wait a minute! You don't seem to believe that. But you can at least believe Margot's death was a very great blow to her. She adored Margot. You agree?"

He could not help admitting it. "Yes. Margot was always a kind of idol."

"And how many times have you seen Celia since the beginning of the war?"

"Only twice, since 1940. The Glebes were sent wherever there was trouble going: Africa. Then, in '43, I was drafted for special training with Intelligence. Languages, you see. And . . ."

"Only twice, since 1940," mocked Thorley, in a sympathetic voice. "Celia isn't well, Don. Mammy Two (do you remember?) always said she'd been worried about her, ever since Celia was a child. I tell you straight, Don: if you turn up from the dead now, and reopen that old emotional business when she's almost forgotten it, I won't be responsible for the consequences. Can't you see that?"

"In a way. Yes."

"Fortunately, as I told you, Celia isn't here this evening. But look at that door to the hall there! What do you think the effect would be, if Celia came back and suddenly saw you here now? If you have any feeling for her, Don—any feeling at all —you can't risk that. Now can you?"

Holden pressed his hands to his forehead.

"But . . . what do you want me to do?"

"Go away," answered Thorley firmly.

"Go away?"

"Go back down those balcony stairs," Thorley pointed, "the way you came. The way you came when Doris Locke and I thought you were a gh——" For some reason Thorley did not seem to like the word "ghost." He stopped. He glanced over his shoulder, toward the windows. "Funny!" he said. "I thought I heard somebody out there just now. But it wasn't. Never mind."

He turned back, his hand on Holden's arm.

"Go away, Don. After all, the whole thing is your fault. Celia wouldn't thank you for upsetting her by turning up again. You had your chance; and, for whatever reason, you bungled it."

"It was because . . ."

"I know; it was because you were only making twopence-halfpenny a year; and I honor you for it. Still, you did rather hit her in the face. She's forgotten you now. Think of the disastrous consequences if . . ."

Again Thorley . stopped dead. His hand dropped from Holden's arm. He was staring past Holden's shoulder, staring at the door to the hall, with such an expression that his companion involuntarily swung around.

And the door to the hall opened, and Celia came in.

CHAPTER IV

THE door was in the upper right-hand corner of the room as you stood with your back to the windows. It opened inwards; Celia's hand was on the knob, and a dim light burned in the hall behind her. He afterward remembered that she had begun to speak, as though in explanation or warning to anybody who might be there, even while the door was opening.

"I think I left my handbag in here," the well-remembered voice said rapidly. "I'm going for a walk in the park, and . . ."

She saw Holden.

Then—silence.

All three of them stood as though paralyzed. In a sense this was true; Holden could not have spoken to save his life. He felt the light of the table lamp shining on his face, as though it were a physical heat; he felt himself caught there, unable to retreat even into darkness.

There was the flesh-and-blood Celia, after so many days and nights of the imagined one. And utterly unchanged. The broad forehead, the arched brows over gray dreaming eyes, the short straight nose, the lips a little quirked at one corner as though from looking wryly at the world, the smooth brown hair parted now on the left-hand side and drawn behind her ears to fall at the back of the neck, and—thank God!—the clear-glowing skin of health.

If memory plays tricks, we expect them to be poor tricks. In our hearts we, as cursers of hope, never expect a real meeting quite to live up to an imagined one. But for Holden it was the other way around. This was more; it was worse, as a dozen times more poignant. If only he hadn't wrecked it, hadn't hurt Celia, by this sudden . . .

Seconds passed. He would have said that minutes passed while Celia stood motionless, gripping the knob, slender in a white dress, without stockings and with red shoes, against the brown-painted door.

Then Celia spoke.

"They sent you on some kind of special military job," she said. Her voice went into a strange unnatural key; she had to clear her throat several times before she got the voice level. But she made this as a simple statement. "They sent you on some kind of special job. That was why you couldn't see me or write to me."

In an immense void he heard himself speaking.

"Who told you that?"

"Nobody told me," Celia answered simply. A hundred memories seemed to be passing behind her eyes. "As soon as I saw you, I just knew."

Her face seemed to crumple up; she was going to cry.

"Hello, Don," she said.

"Hello, Celia."

"I—I was going over into the park," said Celia; and suddenly looked away from him, out into the hall. He could see the line of her neck, the soft turn of the cheek, shining against the light there. "Would—would you like to go with me?"

"Of course. Then you didn't believe I was d . . ."

"I believed it," said Celia, as though trying carefully to define her terms. "I believed it. And yet at the same time I—" She broke off. "Oh, hurry, hurry! Please hurry!"

He went toward her, circling round the sofa and walking very carefully, because his knees were shaking. Also, in that unreal void, he had a wild idea that unless he walked carefully he might put his foot straight through the floor. Yet a certain memory whipped back at him.

"You said—into the park, Celia. You mean you weren't

out this evening? You've been in the house all the time?"

"Yes, of c-course. Why?"

"Thorley," observed Holden, "you or I are going to have one or two things to talk about. But that can wait. Until we all go down to Caswall tomorrow."

Thorley, too, was pale. Not once had Celia glanced in his direction.

"Until we go down to Caswall tomorrow?" Thorley repeated.

"Yes. You say you want to sell Caswall. Have you found a purchaser for it?"

"No. Not yet. But . . ."

"I'll buy the place," snarled Holden. He became aware that he was shouting. "In the excitement of the moment I forgot to tell you that the report about an inheritance wasn't a part of the joke. It was true."

And he followed Celia out of the room.

Without speaking, in the same void, emotionally blind and helpless, moving like sleepwalkers, these two went toward the front door. They did not speak because they had too much to say. There was no starting point. A light in a cut-glass globe, hanging from the lofty ceiling in the hall, shone on the tall full-length portrait of a Regency gentleman with wind-blown hair and a cutaway coat, under which was a little brass plate engraved EDWARD AGNEW DEVEREUX, ESQ., by SIR H. RAEBURN.

Vaguely he noticed that Celia, who was trembling, glanced at this portrait as though she were remembering something.

He wanted to tell her . . .

Yes! He wanted to tell her he had sent a telegram, but that Thorley hadn't opened it. Why hadn't Thorley opened it? Telegrams convey a sense of urgency. You open them, as a rule, the instant they are received. If you don't, it is because something of overpowering interest distracts your attention at the same time. The telegram had arrived at the same time as small but vigorously grown-up Doris Locke.

Stop! Instead of being the first of a million explanations, this was only leading thoughts into a blind alley.

They were outside the house now, in warm and kindly darkness. They slowly crossed the little curve of the drive, out to the pavement of the main road where the white, clear-glowing street lamps showed a deserted road and trees on the other side.

"We cross here," said Celia.

"Oh?"

"Yes," Celia explained very carefully. "To the other side. About fifty yards up there's a side entrance into the park. This is where we cross."

Celia's nerves, he was thinking, were magnificent. Flighty, eh? There probably wasn't another woman anywhere who could have received such unexpected news with no more than a change of color or a turn of the eyes. It hadn't affected her at all. He thought so, that is, until—without any warning, when they were partway across the road—Celia's knees gave way; she would have fallen if he had not caught her.

"Celia!" he cried.

But she only sobbed and clung to him, while he held her very tightly.

The lights of a motorcar, moving rapidly, sprang up from the direction of Regent's Park Crescent and hummed straight toward them: yellow-blazing eyes which swallowed up the road as the car bore down. It is a sober fact that Holden did not even notice this.

He never realized it until the car—with a *whush* of air at their elbows, and a scream of curses from the driver—swerved violently past them within a foot's clearance. Then he picked Celia up, carried her back to the curb, set her on her feet under a street lamp, and, while she held him just as tightly, he kissed her mouth for a very long time.

Presently Celia spoke.

"Do you know," she said, with her head against his shoulder, still crying, "that's the first time you ever kissed me?"

"In times gone by, Celia, I was twenty-eight years old and the biggest bloody fool in recorded history."

"No, you weren't! You were only . . ."

"I was about to point out, anyway, that we have a great deal of lost time to make up for. Shall we continue?"

"No!" said Celia. Her soft body tightened in his arms. She ran her hands over his shoulders, as though to make sure of his reality. She threw her head back and looked up at him: her lips smiling, the imaginative fine-drawn face tear stained, the shining wet gray eyes searching his face—searching it, and searching it again, with intensity—under the white pallor of the street lamp.

"I mean," she added, "not here! Not now! I want to think about you. I want to get used to you."

31

"I love you, Celia. I always have."

"Are we in love?"

Don Holden felt lightheaded with happiness.

"My dear Celia," he began oracularly, "consider indisputable proof in this matter. Did you hear what the driver of that car said when he roared past?"

She looked puzzled. "He—he swore at us."

"Yes. To be exact, he said 'god-damnedest thing I ever saw.' The remark, though inelegantly phrased, contains a deep philosophical truth. Shall we search the story of famous lovers . . . of Daphnis and Chloë, of Hero and Leander, of Pyramus and Thisbe, of (to be more prosaic about it) Victoria and Albert . . . for many instances of two persons standing locked in each other's arms in the middle of a main motor road?"

"I love you when you talk like that," Celia said seriously. "It's not exactly romantic; but it seems to make everything so much more fun. Where have you been, Don? It was rather awful. Where have you been?"

He tried to explain: a little of it, and somewhat incoherently.

"You—you got Scharführer von Steuben? That Dachau man who said he'd never be taken alive?"

"He had to be taken alive. They're hanging him this month."

"But—what happened?" (He felt her shudder.)

"Well, it took some time to run him down. Then there was a dust-up."

"Please, Don. What happened?"

"He'd got himself up disguised as a priest. We shot it out in a churchyard about three miles from Rome. I nicked him through the kneecap, and it was so painful he just rolled over and screeched. The funny thing was . . ."

"Yes, Don?" she pressed him more tightly.

"Do you remember that time we met, in Caswall churchyard, under the trees, after the wedding? And I made such a hash of things? Well! Once or twice when I saw Steuben's dial, under the broad-brimmed priest's hat, looking at me around a tombstone over the top of a Luger, I kept thinking that a number of important incidents in my life seemed to be happening in churchyards."

There was a pause, and a sudden odd change in her mood.

"Do you know," cried Celia, suddenly looking up and around as though she had just realized it, "we're standing under a street lamp? And there'll probably be a policeman along at any minute? Let's go across to the park, Don. Please!"

They crossed the road hurriedly. Some fifty yards up, as Celia had said, there was a side entrance. (They did not see the immense dark shadow, apparently too huge to be real, which, as soon as they were gone, seemed to materialize from behind the trees guarding the little crescent of Gloucester Gate, and stretch out after them. No; they did not see it.)

The night fragrance of the park enclosed them. A broad path, of fine-crushed brown gravel, stretched away into dimness through lines of thick-leaved dwarf chestnut trees like the alley of a formal garden. Once into the shadow of the trees, they became aware of moonlight: clear moonlight, of soap-bubble luminousness, making images even more unreal. Celia, in her white dress, might have seemed insubstantial if he had not held her tightly.

Celia spoke in a small, troubled voice.

"Don. I want to tell you something. I feel I'm partly— becoming myself again."

"How do you mean?"

"When I thought you were dead . . ."

"Don't! That's all over now!"

"No. Please let me finish." She stopped and faced him. "When I thought you were dead, I didn't seem to care about anything. Then, at Christmas, Margot died. Did Thorley tell you?"

"Yes."

There was nothing more he could say. A light breeze, the first stirring on that hot night, made a whispering among leaves.

"You know how it is when you're," she pressed her hand against her breast, "you're all mixed up inside. You get a thing, an idée fixe, about whatever seems most important. Not that this matter about Margot isn't important. It is. But it doesn't seem to matter so much now."

She paused for a moment.

"So," Celia went on, "you do things you'd never dream of doing, in the ordinary way. Just as I did after Christmas. When you look back on them," she laughed a little, "they seem grotesque. I'm frightened now at my own temerity. And yet I was right! I was right!"

He put his hands on her shoulders. "My dear, what are you talking about?"

"Listen, Don. We're not out taking a casual walk, really. We're—meeting somebody."

"Oh? Who is it?"

"Dr. Shepton. There's a secret that so far I haven't told to a soul outside the family, except Dr. Shepton."

"He was Margot's doctor, wasn't he?"

"Yes. I knew he was coming to town today to see a friend of his, in Devonshire Place: a psychiatrist. About me. But I couldn't ask Dr. Shepton to come to the house. I couldn't! They spy on me. They think I'm mad, you know."

Despite the slight jar of hearing that word from Celia's own lips, as though she had uttered a blasphemy, he almost laughed at her.

"Do they, now?" he said mockingly.

"Didn't Thorley tell you?"

"Yes," replied Holden. Wrath boiled up inside him, hurting and blinding: the memory of Thorley's glutinous voice, trying to spoil happiness and pull apart dreams that had become realities. "Yes, by God! He told me. And the more I see of Mr. Thorley Ruddy Marsh, the fellow I once thought was my best friend—!"

"Don. You don't believe I'm . . . ? No! Please! Don't kiss me for just a minute. I want you to understand something."

The deep earnestness of her voice held him back.

"If I go on with this," Celia whispered, "something dreadful will probably happen. And yet it's *right*. Besides, I don't see how I can back out now. That one man would have been safe enough, the old friend of Mammy Two. But now that I've actually written to the police . . ."

"You've written to the police? About what?"

"Come here," Celia requested. "Follow me."

On their right, where the row of trees was interrupted, he could discern a very tall privet hedge closed off by iron railings. In the fence there was a wide gate, left ajar. The gate creaked as he followed Celia's white dress through a deep arch in the hedge, round a corner, and into an open space.

It was a children's playground: surrounded on three sides by hedges, on the fourth by another iron fence which showed dim fields of the park beyond. It was not large. Moonlight lay eerily on the iron ribs of swings, on a children's roundabout swing with a circular platform, on a forlorn-looking seesaw, on a very large oblong sandbox set a little below ground. The ground, scuffed and trampled free of grass, exhaled a dry earthy smell on that hot night. No place, deserted, could have seemed more secret or more desolate; it might have been a playground for dead children.

Celia lifted her arms above her head, in a gesture of passionate emotion. He could not see her face. She stopped by the roundabout swing; on a sudden impulse she stretched out her hand and set the swing turning. It creaked a little, the platform rising and falling as it swept around.

"Don," she said, "Margot didn't die of cerebral hemorrhage. She died of poison. She committed suicide."

He had been expecting something like this, of course. Yet all the same it took him aback. He had been expecting . . . well, what had he been expecting?

"She killed herself, I tell you!" cried Celia.

"But why should Margot kill herself?"

"Because of the life Thorley'd been leading her." The swing had been slowing down; Celia gave it another fierce turn. Then her voice grew quiet. "Tell me, Don. You say Thorley is, or was, your best friend. How would you describe him?"

"I'm not sure. He's changed. I think this determination to get on in life has gone to his head. But at least: easy going, rather phlegmatic, and good-tempered."

"You really think that?"

"It's what I've always believed, anyway."

"I saw him hit her across the side of the face with a razor strap," said Celia. "And then throw her across a chair and start to strangle her. That had been happening, off and on, whenever he got really annoyed, for three or four years."

This was growing worse and worse. The creak of the roundabout jarred thinly, under a placid moon.

"And it wasn't as though," Celia's voice faltered, "she had ever done anything to deserve it. Margot was so—so inoffensive. That's the word. She never meant anybody the least harm. You know that, Don."

He did know it.

"She may not have been very intelligent or 'artistic' in Danvers Locke's sense of the term," Celia went on. "But she was so beautiful, Don! And such a good sport that . . ." Celia stopped. "On Thorley's side, I'll do him the justice to say that so far as I know there wasn't any other woman. It was simply meanness, and spitefulness. Thorley was too prudent to take out his ill-temper on anybody else. So it had to be Margot."

Holden tried to marshal his wits in this nightmare.

"And you say," he demanded, "this had been going on since—?"

"Since about a year after Mammy Two died. Margot was

35

frantic about it; she used to weep, when nobody saw her. But she would never tell me anything about it, when I tried to ask her. I was only the Little Sister, though I'm twenty-eight now."

"Was Margot still in love with him?"

Celia shivered. "She loathed him. And do you think Thorley was ever once, for one minute, in love with her? Oh, no. It was the money, and the social side of it. In your heart, Don, you must have guessed that."

"But, hang it, Celia, why was all this allowed to go on? Why didn't she leave him? Or divorce him?"

Celia gave another savage turn to the swing, whose shadows moved up and down on the scarred brown earth. Then Celia swung round to face him.

" 'Extreme physical cruelty.' " Her lips made a movement of distaste. "It sounds almost funny, doesn't it, when you read about it in the newspapers? 'My husband hit me about,' like a brawl in a cheap pub. It isn't funny; it's horrible. But some women are so dreadfully respectable, and have such a horror of what people will say, that they'll go on and on and put up with anything, rather than have a soul know it isn't a happy marriage.

"Margot had a horror of any kind of scandal. So has Thorley, of course; more so than Margot. But the—the source was different. Thorley's frightened of the social effect on his friends. He's standing for Parliament, you know, at the next Frinley by-election. But Margot's was a sort of . . . of . . ."

"Noblesse oblige?"

"Something like that. Something Mammy Two instilled into her." Celia's lips were wry in the moonlight, her face pallid, her eyes shining. "You see, Don: Margot was respectable. Whereas I'm not. No, don't smile; I'm not, really." Her voice rose. "But, oh, Don, what a relief it is to tell you all this! What a blessed relief!"

And once more, for the dozenth time, they were in each others arms: in a dangerous and exalted emotional state.

"Margot," Celia said, "would have died rather than say what was going on. And that's it, don't you see? She couldn't endure it any longer. So she took some kind of poison that the doctor wouldn't recognize as poison, and she—she did die. She died a 'natural' death."

Holden's heart was beating with a slow, heavy rhythm.

"Listen, Celia. Hadn't any other possibility occurred to you?"

"What do you mean?"

36

"I mean Margot wasn't what I, or anybody else, would have called a suicidal type. Can't you see any alternative?"

"What alternative?"

"Murder," said Holden.

The ugly word, which under any other circumstances it might have been impossible to utter, sounded louder than it really was. It seemed to ring out amid the looming shapes of the children's swings, and the seesaw, and the sandbox. It had a curious effect.

He felt Celia grow tense. Since her head was lowered, the fleecy brown hair brushing his cheek, he sensed rather than saw the sudden turn of her eyes, sideways, while she hardly seemed to breathe. When she spoke again, it was in a whisper.

"Why do you say that?"

"Just one or two things I noticed tonight. There may not be anything in it."

"Th-Thorley?"

"I didn't say Thorley." (But he had meant it). "I feel like a suspicious sort of hound," he burst out, "for thinking what I am thinking! All the same . . ."

"If it could be!" breathed Celia in a kind of ecstasy. "Oh, if only it could be! To see him hang, after all he made her suffer!" Celia shook her head violently. "I—I'd thought of that, Don. Of course I had. But it's not true, I'm afraid. It can't be true."

"For the sake of argument, why not?"

Celia hesitated.

"Because," she answered, "I don't see why he should want her out of the way. I don't see any motive. I suppose you could say Margot was—was useful to him. And then there are so many other reasons! Margot's changing her gown on the night she died, and the poison bottle openly on the shelf . . ."

"Wait a minute! What's all this about gowns and poison bottles?"

"You'll understand, dear, as soon as Dr. Shepton gets here. And finally, as a reason why I'm sure it wasn't Thorley, I—I'd better tell you Margot tried to kill herself once before."

(Black waters, swirling and rising! That metaphor of his, fancied this evening, had come from a true instinct.)

"Once before," Holden echoed dully. "When was that?"

"Over a year before she really did die."

"And on that occasion how did she try to kill herself?"

"She took strychnine."

"Strychnine!"

"Yes. I know it was strychnine, because I looked up the symptoms she had. Margot had tetanic convulsions: they end in lockjaw, the book said. But Dr. Shepton managed to save her. Afterward Margot admitted it to me, or as good as." Celia threw back her head. "Don, what's wrong?"

"There's something very much wrong. If I remember correctly, the only kind of book Margot ever opened was a detective story or a murder trial?"

"We-ell, no. For a long time she'd been terribly keen about palmistry and fortune telling. But she did read murder trials. I don't. I loathe them. And it's odd you should mention murder trials, because . . ."

"In fact," he was searching his memory, "I once recall talking to Margot about the trial of Jean Pierre Vaquier. That's a strychnine case."

"Is it? That's out of my line, I'm afraid. But what about it?"

"Strychnine, Celia, is the most agonizingly painful poison in the register. Nobody in his or her senses would think of using it for suicide. Margot would never have done that of her own free will!"

Celia stared at him.

"But—Margot as good as admitted it to me, though she didn't dare say too much! I thought Thorley'd been given a good scare over it. Because, only a few weeks after she was up and about, Margot began to grow like her old self again (only far happier) before she was married. Happy, and bright eyed. That lasted until . . . well, until almost before she died."

Celia paused. With another sharp change of mood, her eyes grew fixed.

"Listen!" she urged. "Don't speak! There's somebody coming in from the road now!"

CHAPTER V

QUICKLY Celia drew away from him. There was, in fact, a distant noise of somebody blundering about in the around-the-corner entrance to the hedge. But, when the newcomer emerged into the moonlight, Holden could not fail to recognize Dr. Eric Shepton.

Dr. Shepton was a tall, heavily built, stoop-shouldered man with a near-sighted air and a somewhat shambling gait. But he was still vigorous; the near-sighted eyes behind his pince-nez could at times be disconcertingly keen.

His bald head shone, indistinguishable in color from the clear-white hair above his ears. Winter and summer he wore the same heavy dark suit, with gold watch chain across the waistcoat; he was now carrying an old Panama hat. He stood blinking and peering, turning his head from side to side, until he caught sight of Celia.

Celia's inexplicable terror, which should have disappeared when she found the newcomer was only Dr. Shepton, was increasing. Holden, startled, saw a look of panic flash across her face: as though she wanted to wring her hands, as though she had just remembered something which in a welter of emotions had been forgotten.

"I should have warned you," she whispered.

And there was worse. As Celia called out to the doctor, Holden detected a new note in her voice—a note of sheer defensiveness.

"I'm over here, Dr. Shepton!" she said in a high, breathless voice. "Terribly sorry to drag you to such an odd place at a time like this."

There was a shambling noise of Dr. Shepton's big shoes on the sandy earth as he moved toward them.

"Er—not at all," he disclaimed, as though appointments in a playground at such a time were all in his routine. He had, as always, that half-apologetic air which was a relic of his Victorian boyhood: when the social status of medical men, for some reason, was not very high. But he kept his eyes fixed steadily on Celia. "After all," he added, "it's quite close to your house. Bit difficult to find, though. I'm a countryman. London upsets me."

Then his near-sighted eyes blinked round, discovering for the first time that Celia had a companion. Since the doctor had seen Holden not more than three or four times in past years, he knew nothing of the latter's history or supposed death; no explanations were necessary.

"Dr. Shepton," continued Celia in that same breathless voice, "this is Mr.—I beg your pardon! It's 'Sir Donald' now, isn't it? Dr. Shepton of course you remember Sir Donald Holden?"

"Yes, of course," murmured the doctor, who clearly didn't.

39

"Er—how do you do, sir?" And he made a slight gesture with the ancient Panama hat.

"He's—he's just come back from abroad," said Celia.

"Ah, indeed. Fascinating place, abroad. Pity one can't go there now." Dr. Shepton became brisk. "And now, my dear, if this gentleman will excuse us?"

"No!" cried Celia. "I want Don to stay!"

"But I understand, my dear, you wished to see me privately."

"I tell you, I want Don to stay!"

Dr. Shepton twisted round courteously. "Had you any special reason, sir, for wishing to . . . er . . . ?"

"Sir," returned Holden in the same formal way, "I have the very best reason in the world. Miss Devereux, I hope, will shortly become my wife."

Dr. Shepton, even though clothed in age and (an air of) absent-mindedness, could not repress a start, and a worried look which gave Holden a momentary qualm. The doctor put up a hand to his pince-nez.

"Ah, indeed," he smiled. "That's fine, of course. Many congratulations. At the same time, if you'll forgive me, we mustn't be too hasty about these things; must we?"

"Why not?" asked Holden.

The two words hung out, a whipcrack and a challenge, in that quiet place. Dr. Shepton gave the appearance of not having heard.

"And what, my dear," he asked Celia in his patient kindly voice, "did you want to see me about?"

"I," Celia glanced at Holden, and faltered, "I wanted to tell you about the night Margot died."

"Again?" inquired Dr. Shepton.

"I . . ."

"Listen, my dear." Putting his ancient Panama hat on the back of his head, Dr. Shepton took one of Celia's hands and enclosed it in both of his. "On Christmas day, shortly after your poor sister's death, you came to me and told me —er—what happened that night. Don't you remember?"

"Of course I remember!"

"Then come, my dear! Why distress yourself by going all over it again, six months after it's finished and done with?"

"Because there's new evidence! Or there will be, tomorrow night." Celia hesitated. "Besides, now Don's back with me, I want him to hear about it! I've been telling him . . ."

Dr. Shepton peered sideways. "Have you told this gentleman, Celia, about Mr. Marsh's brutal treatment of your sister?"

"Yes!"

"And about the—er—attempt at strychnine poisoning some considerable time before Mrs. Marsh died?"

"Yes!"

"And about your own experience in the Long Gallery, among the portraits, following Mrs. Marsh's death?"

"No!" said Celia. Even in the moonlight, Holden thought, her face was noticeably paler. "No. I haven't said anything about that. But . . . dear God," she breathed, in a real prayer which went to Holden's heart in a stab of sympathy as deep as his overwhelming love for her, "won't anybody listen to what really happened on the night Margot was poisoned?"

"Why not let her tell it?" said Holden, in a voice that meant a good deal more than the words.

"As you like." Dr. Shepton looked at him curiously. "Perhaps that would be best. Yes, on the whole that might be best. Er—is there any place to sit down?"

There was no obvious place to sit down: unless (the grotesque thought occurred to Holden) they occupied several swings. But Celia was already looking, with a strange fixity, at the immense oblong sandbox, set about a foot below the level of the ground.

Slowly she walked over to the sandbox. Celia sat down on the edge of it, swinging her legs inside. Putting one hand on the ground on each side of it, she leaned back—supple, graceful, not so tall as Margot—to stare up at the moon. Dr. Shepton, without any sense of incongruity, humped down big and stoop-shouldered on one side of her. Holden was at the other side.

Celia lowered her eyes. The sand seemed to fascinate her. It was dry sand, in the ten days' intense heat following a wet June. Celia scooped up a handful, letting the sand run between her fingers.

"The sand, the lock, and the sleeping sphinx!" she said, suddenly and unexpectedly. Her laugh, clear and ringing, echoed eerily under the trees. "I can't help it. It's awfully funny. The sand, the lock, and the sleeping sphinx!"

"Steady, my dear!" Dr. Shepton said rather sharply.

Celia brought herself up. "Yes. Of c-course!"

"You had something on your mind—eh?—about two days before Christmas?"

"Yes. Christmas," Celia repeated, and closed her eyes.

"I was telling Don," she went on, "that for a long time before then Margot had seemed so much happier, so much more like herself. She was so bright eyed, and danced and hummed round the house so much, that I once said to her (only as a joke, of course), 'You must have a lover.' Margot said no; she said she was going to a fortune teller, a Madame Somebody-or-other, in New Bond Street of all places, who told her tremendous things about the future.

"Then, about October, the trouble started again. There were dreadful scenes with Thorley; I could hear him shouting at her behind a closed door. Presently, at the beginning of December I think it was, things quieted down again. When we went down to Caswall for Christmas, we were at least all polite."

Celia kicked out at the sand.

"I love Caswall," she said simply. "When you go inside and close the door, you can imagine you're not in the present at all. The Blue Sitting Room! And the Lacquer Room! And the Long Gallery! The books and books and books! The old playroom, with the games and toy printing press with three different kinds of colored type!

"Anyway," she drew a deep breath, "it was only a small party. Maybe Thorley told you, Don? Margot and Thorley and myself; and, of course, Derek."

It was that "of course" which did it. Holden could keep quiet no longer.

"I imagine," he observed, in his turn scooping up a handful of sand and flinging it violently down, "I imagine that 'Derek' refers to Mr. Derek Hurst-Gore, M.P.?"

Celia looked at him with wide eyes.

"Yes! Do you know Derek?"

"No," answered Holden with cold and measured viciousness. "I—merely—hate—the—swine."

"But you don't know him!"

"That's just it, Celia. If I did know him, I probably shouldn't dislike him. It's just because I don't know him that I've been endowing him with all sorts of super and magnetic qualities. What's the ba—what's the fellow like?"

"He's rather nice, really. Tall, and with wavy hair"—she saw Holden's disgust—"good heavens, not effeminate! Just the opposite: rather jaw thrusting. He smiles a good deal, and shows his teeth. Don!" Consternation sprang into Celia's eyes, and she sat up. "You didn't think . . . ?"

"Well, you were his parliamentary secretary for some time, I understand. Weren't there rumors?"

"Derek tried to make love to me. Yes."

"I see."

Celia, her cheeks coloring darkly in the moonlight, avoided his eye. Scooping up more sand she slowly let it fall.

"Don, I—I'm not sure if you understand. If Margot had taken a lover, I shouldn't have blamed her. In fact, I should have thought it was an excellent thing. But it wouldn't do for *me*, don't you see? Because—whoever I had been with, if you know what I mean, I should always have been thinking about you; and it would just have seemed silly."

There was a silence.

"Celia," he said, "I'm humbled. I . . ."

Here he became aware of Dr. Shepton, immobile and sphinx-like—where had that word occurred to him?—sitting at the right angle of the sandbox, shoulders stooped, large-knuckled hands on knees, his hat off again and his big head inclined forward so that the chin almost touched the knuckles. Dr. Shepton was steadily watching him with a gaze in which appraisal mingled with something unreadable. The doctor's gaze shifted.

"You were saying, my dear," he addressed Celia, "that you arrived at Caswall on the afternoon of December twenty-third. The four of you, I believe, were going to a party that night?"

Celia nodded, biting at her underlip.

"Yes. We were going," she spoke to Holden again, passionately, "to Widestairs, to the Lockes' place. Formal evening dress had only just come back in again, and we were dressing for it. Please remember that; it's very important.

"I don't think you've been at Caswall, Don, since Margot and Thorley had a suite of rooms done over for themselves on the east side over the Long Gallery. Everything very modern. A bathroom with green tiles and a black marble tub that didn't clank like the other tubs at Caswall. Margot had a lovely sitting room in white satin, and a bedroom in old rose: the bedroom opening into the bathroom, with Thorley's rooms beyond. I want you to see all this; I tell you it's very important.

"It was a cold night, not quite freezing, with a little snow. It wasn't very chilly inside, because Thorley had got thirty tons of coal (yes, thirty tons). But the hot-water system wouldn't work; Obey had been carrying up little cans of hot

43

water for washing. I finished dressing first. So I went over and knocked at the door of Margot's bedroom.

"Margot wasn't nearly ready yet. She was standing in front of the big triple mirror around the dressing table, in her step-ins and stockings, with a wrap over her shoulders, and scrabbling about among things on the dressing table. She called out to me: 'Darling, do go and look in the medicine cabinet in the bathroom and see if my nail varnish has wandered in there.'

"I went and looked. The medicine cabinet is built into the wall, just over the wash basin, behind a mirror. There were about three dozen bottles there, all crammed together on the shelves. But I saw the nail varnish, right enough. I was just stretching out my hand for it when I saw the poison bottle. I tell you," Celia almost screamed, "I saw the poison bottle!"

Dr. Shepton glanced round quickly, and shushed her.

"Of course, my dear," he said. "Of course. So you told me. Now think very hard: what sort of poison was in the bottle?"

(A strange sort of chill was creeping into Don Holden's heart. He could not understand why, or would have said he could not understand.)

"What sort of poison," persisted the doctor in his bluff kindly voice, "was in the bottle?"

"But I don't know! How could I?"

"Can you describe this bottle?"

"It was round and brownish colored, maybe two or three ounces, with a label that said *Not to be taken*, and then in red letters, POISON."

"Was it a chemist's label? Anything else on it except those words?"

"N-no. At least, I don't remember. The main thing, Dr. Shepton, is that it was *new*—if you understand what I mean —among old dusty bottles with withered-looking labels. I swear it had just been put there!"

"Go on, my dear."

"The funny thing was," continued Celia, reaching out to grasp Holden's hand, "it didn't frighten me so much at first. I mean, it seemed so open. If you were going to poison yourself, after trying once with strychnine as Margot did, you'd think you would hide the poison; and not put it there only partly hidden between a bottle of Optrex and a tin of talcum powder.

"I came out and gave the nail varnish to Margot. I watched

44

her getting dressed. She was wearing a silver lamé gown—please remember that, Don—a silver lamé gown, and she looked stunning in it. At last I said: 'Margot, about that bottle in the medicine cabinet.' She turned round from the mirror and said: 'What bottle in the medicine cabinet?' But just then Thorley came in; and in a very cold voice he said we were half an hour late and would we please, please, please hurry?

"Thorley had been like that all evening: so white that Obey asked whether he was ill, and with furious dead-looking eyes. He was very polite, too. Margot was—excited. I don't know how else to describe it. Quick breathing, as though she'd made a decision and meant to keep to it.

"Neither of them spoke much, in the car on the way to the Lockes'. Derek Hurst-Gore kept laughing and telling jokes, but Thorley didn't say much even to him. At the Lockes', after dinner . . . Did Thorley tell you?"

"He said," Holden answered, "that you played games."

"Games!" echoed Celia, and moved her shoulders convulsively. "He didn't tell you about that ghastly one where we dressed up in masks? As executed murderers?"

"No."

. Despite himself Holden had to fight down a growing nervousness. This picture Celia painted, against a background of cold night and a few drifting snowflakes, was anything but a Christmas atmosphere. Dr. Shepton did not move or speak.

"You've seen Sir Danvers' collection of masks," Celia went on. "Hung all over the walls in so many rooms. Some impressionistic. Some modeled from real life. Some that even go over your head. Nearly all of them painted and lifelike. murderers' masks, as they looked after they'd been executed?"

"No." Holden cleared his throat. "No. I didn't know it."

"Neither did we," Celia confessed. "Until he took us upstairs, with only the light of a candle to make it more effective, and unlocked the door of a little box room and showed us. Everybody had been drinking pretty freely, or I expect he wouldn't have done it.

"Besides ourselves and Sir Danvers, there was Lady Locke, and Doris looking perfectly exquisite (she is a nice child), and young Ronnie Merrick who's so mad about Doris. I don't think I shall ever forget people's expressions when Sir Danvers unlocked the door, and held up the candle, and we saw all those lifelike horrors looking at us without eyes.

"Sir Danvers explained that most of them were impressionistic. But three of four (he wouldn't say which) had been taken direct—first in wet paper, then in papier-mâché—from real death masks preserved in the museums at Scotland Yard and Centre Street and the Sûreté in Paris. Afterward they'd been colored to the likeness of these people after death, after the pain of death; with real hair or beard attached; and, in some cases, with the mark of the rope still . . ."

"Celia! For God's sake stop upsetting yourself!"

Her hand, in Holden's, was cold and trembling. She drew it away as he cried out a protest. Dr. Shepton remained uncannily motionless and silent.

And Celia went on.

"The idea, Sir Danvers said, was that we were to play an old-fashioned game of Murder. Only, this time, we were each to wear the mask of a famous murderer in real life. Afterward, when the 'murder' had been committed, we were each to answer questions as much as possible in the manner of the original.

"So he began handing out the masks at random, saying who each one was.

"Everybody was delighted with the idea, or pretended to be. And I daresay it's all very well if you're well read in crime, and can tell all about these people and play your part.

"Thorley was Landru, the French Bluebeard, with a thin bald skull and a ginger beard; they guillotined him. Derek was George Joseph Smith, the brides-in-the-bath murderer. Those two I did know. Oh, and Margot. Margot said: 'I won't be Old Mother Dyer; she's too awful looking; let me be Edith Thompson!' Doris Locke was Mrs. Pearcey, with front teeth sticking out a little. And Lady Locke—who's terribly sophisticated, like her husband—was big Kate Webster, with red hair. They all seemed pleased.

"But Ronnie Merrick, who was dithering, whispered to me: 'My name's Dr. Buchanan, but I don't know who the hell I am or what I'm supposed to have done; can you help me?' And I said: 'I'm Maria Manning; but I can't tell you who I am either.'

"Just then Sir Danvers came up, very lean and elegant. He was to be the detective in the game; his mask was a relic, a metal one worn by a German executioner in the seventeenth century. It had a pointed chin, like a combination of a skull and a fox's mask; it was sort of greenish and rust colored. When he suddenly thrust it down into my face, I grabbed at Ronnie for support.

"Yes; I think everybody had taken too much to drink.

"Because afterward, during the game . . .

"You know how, at parties, a sort of devil gets into people? And the blood rushes to their heads, and they go too far?

"Downstairs, where we played the game, it was all dark except for a big bowl of lighted spirits set burning in the hall: burning and wavering with a bluish flame. With the masks and hair, and eyes looking out through the eyeholes, nobody was real. They kept wandering up and down, up and down, past that bowl of bluish flame. The bald head of Landru, the projecting teeth of Mrs. Pearcey, the scrubby moustache of Dr. Buchanan. But they kept—of course it was only a joke—but they kept moaning, you know; and suddenly darting at each other before fading back into the dark again.

"I . . . I dare say I looked worse than any of them. My Maria Manning mask was swollen, one eye open and the other partly shut, though it was the face of a woman who had been pretty. And all of a sudden I thought to myself: Suppose this thing against my face is one of the *real* masks, and I'm looking out through the eyes of a woman standing on the scaffold?

"Then someone 'screamed,' to show the crime had been committed."

Celia drew a deep breath.

"Oddly enough," she laughed nervously, "oddly enough, the person who turned out to be 'murdered' was Margot.

"It was better, of course, with the lights on. Sir Danvers started a tremendous cross-examination of everybody. Some of the parts, I admit, were very well played. Derek—Derek Hurst-Gore was awfully good as George Joseph Smith, who killed the brides in the bath."

"I'll bet he was," said Holden.

"Because he's a lawyer, you see, and well up in the case. But," and Celia clenched her hands, "there was something wrong in all that questioning. I didn't understand it; I can't explain it; I could only feel it. Perhaps it was only because we were warm and tired and a bit ashamed of ourselves. But Sir Danvers, standing under the mistletoe in the hall with our group of masked monstrosities around him, still couldn't find the murderer.

"It went on and on. Finally Lady Locke, who's usually the most self-possessed of mortals, cried out: 'Oh, let's end this! Who *is* guilty?' That's where (of all people, as a sort of anticlimax) young Doris Locke carefully lifted the mask off her hair. She said: 'I'm Mrs. Pearcey; once I killed my rival, and cut up her body and wheeled her in a pram; and this time I've got away with it.' And," added Celia, "everybody roared with laughter, and things were normal again."

CHAPTER VI

"NORMAL again," repeated Holden.

He tried to speak without irony. Momentarily he had forgotten that they were sitting round a children's sandbox, in a dark corner of Regent's Park at what must be close to midnight. Instead he saw himself at Widestairs, in the cold hall among the wry-mouthed masks, as Celia had wished him to do.

Celia's eyes and imagination were those of the dreamer, the poet. She was intensely conscious of, and moved by, all outward things: shapes and colors, the texture of a cloth or the inflection of a voice, which she could reproduce with extraordinary vividness. But of inner meanings, the human motives behind the look or gesture, she knew little and could guess less.

She was utterly unsuspicious. It never occurred to her . . .

It never occurred to her, Holden realized, that there might be a flaming and dangerous love affair between Thorley Marsh and Doris Locke.

This, his original idea, had earlier occurred to him only in a fleeting way. But it couldn't be escaped. When he remembered Thorley and Doris springing apart in the gloom as he appeared at the window, when he remembered the unopened telegram, when he remembered Thorley's whole disturbed conduct, it became a certainty.

Such an affair, of course, might have begun after Margot's death. After all, Thorley had been a widower for more than six months. And, if marriage were contemplated—well, Thorley was thirty-nine or forty and Doris only nineteen; but no insurmountable difficulty could be made over that, and there might be far worse matches from the money point of view. Only one black, crawling question remained.

Suppose the affair had begun before Margot's death?

Would Thorley, no matter how much he might have ill-treated Margot, have gone so far as to. . . ?

Holden's thoughts were drawn back to the present by the fact that Celia had been speaking to Dr. Shepton in a low, quick, blurred voice, and the doctor was answering in his quiet benevolent way.

"Of course, my dear! But you understand that the murderers' masks in that game made a very deep impression on you? A deep, deep impression."

"Naturally," Celia agreed in a tight-throated voice. "It made me partly responsible for Margot's death."

Two voices exclaimed, "Nonsense!" with Dr. Shepton's exclamation perhaps a trifle quicker than Holden's. But Celia would not be denied.

"I knew there was a bottle of poison in that medicine cabinet at Caswall," she insisted, with slow and restrained lucidity. "I knew that I'd seen Margot in that mood of hers: all flushed, as though she'd come to a decision. It shouldn't have required much intelligence to realize what decision.

"And yet, when we got back to Caswall that night, what did I do?

"Instead of going to Margot, instead of speaking to her, instead of emptying that wretched poison bottle down the drain, what did I do? I was so upset by the 'murder' game, which you'll admit was stupid of me, that I didn't do a thing.

"I had plenty of time, too. We'd got back early, at not much past eleven o'clock. But, oh, no! I must hurry off to my room and be by myself! The funny thing is that in spite of my nerves I felt as exhausted as if I'd been playing tennis since morning. I was dizzy; I could hardly get undressed. Maybe it was all that sherry.

"I dreamed, too. I dreamed I was standing on a platform, in an open space, over a huge crowd that was all shouting and jeering and singing my name to the tune of 'Oh, Susannah.' It was foul; it was beastly. People kept walking about the wooden platform. I couldn't see anybody, because there was a white bag over my face. Then I knew there was a greasy cord round my neck.

"That's all I do remember, when . . .

"Somebody took me by the shoulder and shook me. I saw it was Thorley. There was an orange light in the room, from the sun coming up, and a crackly kind of cold. Thorley was standing beside me, in a dressing gown, with his hair rumpled and stubble on his face. All he said was:

49

" 'You'd better get up, Celia. Your sister is dead.' "

And here, as she approached the climax of her story, Celia's whole bearing changed. In her voice there was no tremor, not a trace of nervousness. The voice rang cold and clear and hard, with a hardness and determination Holden had never suspected in her nature. Celia was sitting up very straight, her knees together, her red shoes dug into sand, the beautiful neck a little arched, her hands flat on the ground. He never remembered her better than at that moment.

So the cold metallic voice measured out its syllables.

"Thorley didn't say, 'Margot is dead.' He said, 'Your sister is dead,' like a solicitor or an undertaker. I just looked at him. Presently he started to gabble something like, 'She was taken with a fit in the night, before she'd gone to bed; I called Dr. Shepton, and we put her to bed and did what we could; but she died a little while ago.' And he told me how he'd found her on the chaise longue in her sitting room. And then: 'Dr. Shepton is downstairs now, writing out the death certificate!'

"That was all.

"I didn't say anything. I got up, and put on my dressing gown, and ran across to Margot's bedroom, and opened the door.

"The curtains weren't drawn; the orange light was streaming in. Margot was lying in bed, very peaceful, in a rucked-up nightgown. She would have been thirty-six years old in January; she was so fond of young people. I didn't touch her. She had that dead *look*, just as Mammy Two had. I looked at her for a minute; then I ran into the bathroom. My hands were perfectly steady then, and I searched all through that medicine cabinet.

"The poison bottle, which I had seen the night before, wasn't there."

Celia paused for an instant.

"I went back into the bedroom again, and looked at her. The whole house seemed as still and dead as Margot. Presently (in that way you're aware of things before you really see them) I noticed something else. I noticed her clothes, scattered all over the place just as Thorley and Dr. Shepton had thrown them down.

"Now I told you, I carefully impressed on you, that on the evening before Margot had been wearing a silver lamé gown. But the gown I saw now, thrown down across a chair, was *black*. It was a black velvet, cut low, with a diamond clasp at the left shoulder. I'd never seen her wear it.

"Scattered across the foot of the bed, and on the floor, were gray stockings, and black shoes with rhinestone buckles, and step-ins, and a suspender belt. That, I think, was where I understood everything.

"Margot was romantic and sentimental. That black dress had some sentimental association with the last time she wore it, or some time she wore it. So after the Lockes' party she came back here, and in the dead of night she changed her clothes and dressed again as though for a great dinner. (That's what I might do if I were going to commit suicide, though I should never have the courage and I admit it.) Margot swallowed the poison. She threw the bottle out of the bathroom window. And she walked into her sitting room, and stretched herself out on the chaise longue to die.

"She'd often said she might. And now she had.

"I turned around and flew into the sitting room. The electric lights were still blazing there—she'd have left them on, of course—and I saw the ashes of a big fire in the grate. I had one more chance to make sure.

"Margot always kept a diary. She wrote pages and pages and pages; I can't think how; I could never keep a diary myself. It was always there, in a big locked book, in a Chinese Chippendale desk in her sitting room. I found the book, unlocked; but the diary for all the year had been cut out. In the fireplace . . .

"I remember noticing, in a vague kind of way, that among the fire irons there were now two pokers: one of them brass handled, from among the fire irons in Margot's bedroom. But there wasn't anything left of the diary. It was all powdered ash, burnt page by page, on top of the other ashes.

"She was still being respectable, you see. She didn't want anybody to know. I looked around the room, white-satin and gold, with the dark-red carpet and the crimson curtains, and I saw that chaise longue. It was over there, you know, that Thorley tried to strangle her.

"A kind of craziness came over me then. I raced out of the sitting room, through the old-rose bedroom where Margot was lying dead, and into the bathroom again. I felt I must, I must, must be certain that poison bottle wasn't in the medicine cabinet. I started to go over the bottles again. But this time my hands were shaking. Down came one bottle, then another and another, crash bang clatter into the wash basin, with a noise that filled the place and deafened you.

"I looked up. And there was Thorley, standing in the doorway to *his* bedroom, with his left hand gripped around the sill of the door, looking at me.

"In the bathroom there's a high-built swing-together window of colored glass, that never would latch or fit together properly; I remember feeling an icy-cold current of air against the back of my neck.

"Thorley said, in a high voice: 'What the hell are you up to?'

"I said, 'You did this.' And then, as he just looked at me and took a step forward from the door, I said, 'You killed her with the way you treated her, just as surely as though you'd given her that poison yourself. And I'll pay you back for it, Thorley Marsh.'

"All of a sudden his left hand swung back, and he banged it against his razor strap hanging on the wall beside the wash basin.

"And I said, 'Go on. Hit me with that razor strap, just as you did Margot. But I won't take it meekly, like Margot. You'd better understand that.'

"For a second he didn't answer anything; he only breathed. Then—which was what made me sick—he smiled. He smiled under all that stubble on his face: a really gentle, affectionate, martyred kind of smile. You'd have sworn butter wouldn't melt in his mouth, and he'd fly straight up to heaven among the holy angels.

"He said: 'Celia, you're upset. Go and get dressed.' And he went back into his bedroom, and closed the door."

Again Celia paused. All this, even the account of her conversation with Thorley, had been delivered in the same cold, level, unemotional tone. In conclusion, as she kicked out at the sand, her voice was almost casual.

"Margot was buried in the new family vault in Caswall churchyard. Do you remember, Don, how Mammy Two always said she wanted to be buried in the new vault, because the old one was so crowded?"

"Yes. I remember."

"Mammy Two never did get her wish," said Celia. "The new tomb wasn't finished until after her death. But, a day or so before Margot's funeral—because, mind you, Thorley said it would add sanctity and solemnity and I believe he added 'swank' to the new vault—some coffins of the old, old Devereuxs were carried down to it and interred there. Even in death Margot isn't with Mammy Two, or our own parents. Oh, no! She's with . . ."

Here Celia's voice did change, in fury and anguish. She sprang to her feet, stepping back out of the sandbox, and stood breathing hard and fast.

"Dr. Shepton," she pleaded, "you were the one who attended Margot. Can't you say something?"

"Yes, Doctor," Holden agreed grimly. "I was about to ask you the same question."

Dr. Shepton, with a grunt and shamble, also got to his feet. Holden followed him. Automatically Dr. Shepton adjusted his pince-nez. His broad face, with the fringe of white hair fluffed out round the bald head, wore a benevolent air as he turned to Celia.

"Well, my dear?" he asked pleasantly.

"Well—what?"

"Don't you feel better?" inquired the doctor.

Celia stared at him. "Yes. Of c-course I feel better! But . . ."

"Exactly!" Dr. Shepton nodded. "That's where the Roman Catholic Church is so wise in the matter of confession; though, of course," his broad face wrinkled up in half-humorous apology, "nowadays we add frills and give it some scientific name. Now, Celia, as an old friend of your family for many years, I want you to do me a little favor. Will you do it?"

"Yes! Certainly! If I can."

"Good!" said Dr. Shepton. He reflected. "Tomorrow, as I understand it, you're going to Caswall for a few days. I—er—believe Mr. Marsh wants to look over the property with a view to selling it."

Holden saw Celia's start, though this was evidently not news to her. But Dr. Shepton's attention was occupied with other matters.

"We-ell!" said the doctor, waving his hand tolerantly. "That's all right! A few days in the country; country air; bit of a holiday; can't stand London myself. It's when you come back to town, Celia, that I want you to do this favor."

Her voice was rising. "What favor?"

Dr. Shepton carefully felt in his upper left-hand waistcoat pocket, then in his upper right-hand pocket, before producing a visiting card. He examined it closely, with a happy and gusty sigh, and handed it to Celia.

"When you get back to town, my dear, I want you to go and see the man whose address is on that card. Mind you! He's a fully qualified medical man, admirable in his own right, as well as being an analyst. I want you to tell him . . ."

This was the point at which Don Holden felt he had received a physical blow in the face. The effect on Celia must have been even worse.

"That's the psychiatrist," Celia said. "You came to London to see him about me. You—you still don't believe a word I've been saying!"

"We-ell, now!" mused Dr. Shepton, and pursed up his lips. "As a famous character said on a certain occasion, what is truth? The matter . . ."

"Doctor," said Holden, and tried hard to keep his voice from shaking with rage, "you might be good enough to answer one straight question. We've just been listening to a forthright and convincing narrative of facts. Do you, or don't you, believe what Celia says?"

Dr. Shepton considered this.

"Let me answer that question," he suggested, "by asking Celia another. Eh?" He addressed Celia persuasively. "Let's suppose (for the sake of argument, mind!) that Mrs. Marsh did kill herself. Let's suppose Mrs. Marsh was driven by her husband's brutal treatment to take her own life."

"Well?" asked Celia, with her eyes glistening under the long lashes.

"What could you gain, what could you possibly hope to gain, by creating an unpleasant scandal and even (heaven help us!) wanting a post-mortem? The law could take no action against Mr. Marsh. You must see that, my dear. Legally, you couldn't touch him."

"No," Celia answered calmly. "But I can ruin him. I can puncture his thick hide at last. I can ruin him. And I will."

Dr. Shepton was gently shocked. "My dear girl! Come, now!"

"What's so wrong with it?"

"My dear girl! That would be merely vindictive, don't you see? And in all the years I've known you, my dear, I've never once known you to be vindictive. You wouldn't like to start now, would you?"

"It isn't question," Holden cut in, "of being vindictive or anything else. It's a question of plain justice!"

"Ah, yes. No doubt. Do you believe Mrs. Marsh committed suicide, sir?"

"No," answered Holden.

"You don't believe it?"

"No. I think she was deliberately murdered."

The Panama hat dropped out of Dr. Shepton's big-knuckled fingers, and rolled over wabbling in the sandbox. Clearly the word "murder" had never occurred to him. He bent over, grunting, to retrieve the hat; and then straightened up again.

"You think it was murder, eh?" he ruminated. "Dear, dear,

54

dear!" The dryness of Dr. Shepton's tone, the hint of irony, at once infuriated Holden and shook his confidence.

"Doctor, listen! May even a layman ask how some perfectly healthy person can die of cerebral hemorrhage with no contributing cause?"

"I'll tell you what I'll do," offered Dr. Shepton, smiling man to man and extending his hat. "I had—er—intended to return to Wiltshire by the first train tomorrow morning. But I'll tell you what. I'm staying at a little hotel in . . . where is it? Ah, yes. Welbeck Street. Welbeck Street! Why not come round there and see me tomorrow morning? Say ten o'clock."

"No!" cried Celia. Her eyes appealed to Holden, with the whole strength of her nature in that appeal. "Don't go, Don! He—he wants to see you alone. He wants to tell you things about me, when I'm not there to defend myself!"

"Easy, Celia!"

"You won't go, will you?"

"Doctor," said Holden, "I thank you for your very kind offer. I'm afraid I can't accept. Only: could you answer, here and now, the question about Margot Marsh's death?"

"I could, sir," Dr. Shepton retorted. His eye strayed toward Celia. "But I don't propose to do so."

"Very well. Then we know where we stand. Celia, she tells me, has already written the police . . ."

Dr. Shepton's stooped shoulders quivered. "She's written to the police?"

"The day before yesterday," Celia told him.

"And in any case," Holden was desperately trying to make this interview friendly, when he could see it was reaching a dangerous pitch of tensity, "tomorrow morning I intend to go to Scotland Yard. I also have a friend at the War Office, Frank Warrender, who may be able to pull a few strings."

"Young man," quavered Dr. Shepton, with age and weariness breaking through that formality, "you don't understand what you're doing. You're in love. It's bad for the judgment. This is a tragic affair. A very tragic affair."

"I quite appreciate that, Doctor. I was very fond of Margot myself."

"Are you forcing me to tell you, in this young lady's presence, something that concerns her? Something that can only cause you pain? And that will distress her still more?"

Holden was taken aback. "Well! If you put it like that . . ."

"I force you," Celia interposed clearly.

From somewhere close at hand, yet muffled by trees and hedges, there rose up at that moment a calling and clamoring voice. It was so close, indeed, that they could also hear the noise of heavy footsteps clumping on gravel in the path outside the playground: footsteps starting, stopping uncertainly as though someone were peering around, and moving on. What the apprehensive voice kept crying was:

"Miss Celia! Miss Celia! Miss Celia!"

It was Obey's voice.

Holden would have known it anywhere. Obey, surname remotely rumored to be O'Brien, but long since lost to any trace of Irish speech; Christian name unknown, but never called anything except Obey since either of the Devereux children could speak. Obey, short of breath, her hair still done in the style of the First World War, who loved Celia and Margot as she had loved no other persons on earth.

"Yes," announced Celia, as the voice called out. "It's Obey. Thorley's got her to such a state, unfortunately, that she's alarmed if I even go for a walk. Don't answer her," and then, as Holden was about to protest, "don't answer her, I tell you! She may not think of the playground. Dr. Shepton!"

"Well, my dear?"

"Didn't you have something to tell Don?"

"If it will stop Scotland Yard and the other powers that be," returned Dr. Shepton, wiping his sleeve across his forehead, "very well. Celia has told you, young man, about Mr. Marsh's brutality toward his wife? How this went on and on? How, on one occasion, she saw Mr. Marsh attack his wife and try to strangle her?"

Holden flung the answer back at him.

"Celia's told me that, yes! What about it?"

"Only," said Dr. Shepton, "that there is not one word of truth in the whole story."

"Miss Celia! Miss Celia! Miss Celia!" Dinning against the stillness, as Dr. Shepton's words dinned into Holden's ears, the wailing cry still rose.

Dr. Shepton held up a hand, palm outward.

"Mr. Marsh," he stated, "never did any such thing. On the contrary. I am in a position to testify that his conduct throughout the whole distressing affair was that of," the old voice shook, "what my generation would have called a perfect gentleman. Toward his wife he was kindness itself."

"Miss Celia! Miss Celia! Miss Celia!"

"Next, young man, there was the so-called attempt of Mrs. Marsh to kill herself by means of 'strychnine poisoning.' It never occurred. Nobody had any strychnine; nobody took any strychnine. I tell you that simply."

"*Miss Celia! Miss Celia! Miss Celia!*"

"For God's sake," said Holden, suddenly whirling round in the direction of Obey's voice, "will somebody shut that woman up?" He inflated his lungs for a shout. "In here, Obey! In the playground!" He whirled back to Dr. Shepton, taking a step forward and almost pitching headlong into the sandbox.

"Mrs. Marsh's complaint, on the occasion referred to," continued Dr. Shepton, "was a simple illness. *I* attended the case. You will concede that I ought to know. The strychnine was a sheer delusion of Celia's.

"If," he added, "it had been only that!" Dr. Shepton fumbled at his watch chain; he sounded even more troubled. "If it had been only that, I mightn't have taken the romancing so seriously. For it's true that once or twice there may have been . . . well, certain unavoidable misunderstandings."

"Ah!" said Holden. "Misunderstandings! So we're hedging, are we? We now admit that there may have been something to misunderstand?"

"Sir, will you allow me to finish?"

"Go on."

"Celia's delusion that Mrs. Marsh actually died from some unnamed poison, out of a bottle which (I assure you) did not exist, grew out of the other fancies. It was caused by them. It's dangerous."

"To Thorley Marsh?"

"To herself. Nor, unfortunately, have you heard the worst. Has Celia told you about the night, immediately after her sister's death, when she saw ghosts walking in the Long Gallery?"

Again a silence, painful to the eardrums, stretched out into hollow night.

"Well!" said Dr. Shepton. "It was probably caused by those infernal murderers' masks, which made so deep an impression on her at the Lockes'. But—has she told you?"

"No," said Holden.

Celia, with a convulsive movement, turned her back.

"My dear girl!" Dr. Shepton exclaimed unhappily. "Nobody's blaming you. Don't think that. You can't help yourself. That's why we want to cure you. And I," his big face wrinkled up, "I'm only an old-fashioned country g.p. I'm certain this gentleman, when he gets the rage out of him, will agree with us. What do you say, Miss Obey?"

"Yes!" muttered Holden, and snapped his fingers. "Yes! Yes! Obey!"

A few steps behind him, her red face showing grayish in this light, her eyes popping, the wheezing of her breath rising from a vast bosom, hovered Obey.

"Look at me, Obey!" Holden said. "Do you recognize me?"

"Mr. Don!" She first gulped, and then was reproachful. "As if I wouldn't know you! Besides, Mr. Thorley told me you were here. He—oh, dear!" Obey clapped her hands to her mouth. "Mr. Thorley told me I was to be sure to call you 'Sir Donald,' because he was going to do a business deal with you and we'd got to play up to you. Oh, dear, that's worse than ever! If you'll excuse me, now, sir, I really must get Miss Celia home and . . ."

"Listen, Obey." His gaze stopped her, as though she had run into a wall. "I'm not sure how much you've heard of this poisonous nonsense Dr. Shepton has been talking. But I know how you feel about Celia. I know how you've always felt. I trust you. What Dr. Shepton says isn't true, is it?"

The trees whispered; one of the swings stirred with faint spectral creaking; and Obey whimpered like a hurt animal. But she could not, physically could not, turn away from his gaze.

"Yes, Mr. Don," she said brokenly. "It's true."

CHAPTER VII

HIGH grew the grass in the fields round Caswall Moat House, at Caswall in Wiltshire, on that following evening of the eleventh of July.

It was no longer necessary, after another day of fiery sun, to stand in the shade of one of the few beech trees in the field on the south side or front of the house. But Don Holden still stood there, his back propped against the tree, a twentieth cigarette between his lips, trying to think.

Rich land, watered by underground springs, stretched away

in thick grass exhaling summer drowsiness. Westward, where the trees of the carriage drive curved up from the south not quite to the main door, the sky was pale gold. Caswall, low and dun-colored, prepared for sleep.

It was not really a vast place, consisting only of narrow galleries built on two floors round and above an inner quadrangle where the cloisters lay. But its long twinkling-windowed court of what had once been stables, bakeries, and brew houses, westward, shut off and for many years disused, added length to make it seem vast. And around everything, placid as it had lain for seven hundred years, stretched the moat.

Seven hundred years.

No stone, no arrow of war, had fallen into that moat since the forceful Lady D'Estreville, in the thirteenth century, had turned an already-old building into an abbey. For who attacks a religious house? The nuns, shuffling to orisons through semiunderground cloisters, had kept carp in the moat for fast days. But the Reformation attacked religious houses; and down the immensity of time strode William Devereux, rattling a well-filled purse, to bedeck Caswall with furniture out of Italy and pictures out of Flanders.

If there were any ghosts here . . .

Holden, so utterly dispirited that he had let his thoughts stray into a murky past, started as though stung at that word "ghosts." He straightened up from leaning against the tree, and flung away his cigarette.

"Stop this!" he said to himself. "Stop thinking! It won't do any good. You've just got to believe."

"Ah," whispered the devil, "but believe what?"

For in whichever direction he wrenched them his thoughts always snapped back, an elastic released, to that scene of last night: of the playground, and Obey mumbling out, "It's true." Of Celia, though he tried to stop her, rushing out of the place and running for home without another word. Of Obey lumbering after her. Of Dr. Shepton, mortally offended, speaking only to wish him a freezing good night before marching away.

And how he himself (as somehow the villain of the piece) had tried to get a word with Celia, only to be met at the front door of Number 1 Gloucester Gate by an injured-looking Thorley who tactfully barred his way. Even so, Thorley's first words had been those of business.

"Look, Don," Thorley had said confidentially. "Are you seriously thinking of buying Caswall?"

"What's that?—Oh! Yes, of course."

"Then here's the point." Thorley, guarding his voice, peered into the hall behind him; the light shone on his sleek black hair. "Would you mind going down in the train like Obey and Cook? There's plenty of room in the car, of course; only Doris Locke to go with us. But it's better you don't see Celia for a little while. You've played Old Harry with her tonight."

"*I've* played Old Harry with her?"

"Yes. Speaking as a friend of yours . . ."

"A friend of mine, eh? After all those lies you rattled off tonight? 'Celia isn't at home.' 'Celia's forgotten all about you.'"

"One day, old man," said Thorley, looking at him very steadily, "you may realize it was for Celia's good and yours. However," he shrugged, "just as you like. It's your funeral."

His funeral.

Standing now under the beech tree, with evening coming on and Caswall reflected dingy yellow-brown in the waters of its moat, Holden faced an issue which was quite clear-cut. It might be maddening, it might be incomprehensible; but it was quite clear-cut.

Either Thorley Marsh, whom he had once considered his closest friend, was an unctuous hypocrite who had married Margot Devereux for her money, turned on her savagely, and then, for some motive as yet not established, had either killed her or driven her to suicide.

Or, on the other hand, Celia Devereux—whom he loved; whom he would continue to love—had dreamed all these accusations out of a diseased fancy, and was an unbalanced person who might become dangerously insane.

There was no alternative. You had to take your choice.

God!

Holden banged his fist against the rough, gnarled bark of the beech tree. He fished another cigarette out of his pocket, lit it rather unsteadily, and blew out smoke while he considered.

Of course, there could be no doubt on which side he stood. He loved Celia. But reason backed him up as well. He could tell himself, calmly and with no trace of wishful thinking, that he knew Celia to be in no way abnormal and that he believed everything she said . . .

"Are you sure?" whispered the devil.

Well, almost sure; but that was just the difficulty in this

matter. Last night, or during the thin morning hours when he had sat wide awake at the window of his hotel room, he had tried to find the factor in this affair which had kept him (normally an even-tempered person) always in a state of exasperation.

And it was this: that nobody would listen to evidence.

You said, "This case"; and they said, "What case?" If they began with the assumption of Celia's malady, then any word she spoke became suspect. Lucidly she had given a detailed account—of anger between Thorley and Margot, of a poison bottle in a cupboard, of Margot's changing a silver gown for a black velvet one in the middle of the night, of a burned diary, of the poison bottle's disappearance—and all this Dr. Shepton smiled away to nothingness.

Interpret that account, then! Explain it how you like, but try to explain it! Say it is moonshine, summer shadow, mandragora dream; but at least, in the name of decency, give it the fairness of an investigation! He himself had heard his friend Frederick Barlow, the eminent K.C., speak of a certain sharp-witted gentleman named Gideon Fell. If only . . .

At this point in his meditations, slumped back again against the tree, Holden heard someone call his name.

He looked up, and saw Miss Doris Locke.

She was standing almost to her knees in the thick grass, some distance away from him in the field, a vivid little figure against the massed trees of the carriage drive westward. Doris was smiling at him rather archly; but the smile faded.

For a moment they appraised each other. Doris, he remembered, had come down from London in the car with Celia and Thorley; she must have heard a good deal about last night's events.

Then Doris hurried toward him, swishing in the long grass. In her light blue frock, with the elaborately dressed hair golden in the gold evening light, she had the round chin of a girl but very much the round figure of a woman. She had assumed an air of brightness and alertness, a careless poise; but behind this he sensed (why was it there?) a strong nerve tensity.

"Hello, Don Dismallo," she said.

He returned her smile.

"Hello, Mrs. Pearcey," he answered.

Doris looked at him, startled, the blue eyes narrowing. Then her eyes opened wide, and she laughed.

"You mean," she exclaimed, "the night I played the part

of Mrs. Pearcey in the Murder game at home? Yes. They tell me I was rather good." She glanced down over herself, not without approval. "That was last Christmas. It was the night when—" Doris stopped.

"Yes," he agreed, without the appearance of much interest, "it was the night Margot Marsh died."

"So very sad, wasn't it," murmured Doris in a perfunctory voice. "When did you get here?"

Holden studied her.

Doris Locke unquestionably knew that Celia Devereux was supposed to be suffering from some sort of mental distress; probably many others knew this as well. But that the details of Celia's accusations were known to Doris (or Sir Danvers, or Lady Locke, or Derek Hurst-Gore, for that matter) Holden very much doubted. Celia hadn't told this to anybody except Dr. Shepton and "the family," meaning Thorley and Obey and Cook; and these people were interested only in hushing it up.

Remember the old service rule: Handle with gloves until you're sure of your evidence!

"When did I get here?" he repeated. "By the six o'clock train. Thorley met me with the car."

Doris looked at the ground. "Have you—have you seen Celia today?"

"No."

"Not at all?"

"No." His burnt-down cigarette had begun to scorch his fingers; he threw it away into the hot grass, where it sent up a straight line of smoke. "Celia is resting, by doctor's orders. Thorley and I have just finished dinner alone."

"I . . . I . . ." Despite her inner emotional preoccupation, quick sympathy made Doris's lip tremble. "By the way, what do I call you?"

"Call me Don Dismallo. It's as good a name as any. Lord knows I feel like it."

Doris's sympathy increased.

"About—Celia?" she asked.

"Yes, that. And things. Just things!"

"I know," Doris nodded wisely. She stepped softly into the cleared space under the big tree. It was as though, with those few words, a deep understanding had been established between them.

"There are other people who feel like that, Don Dismallo," Doris said.

"Incidentally, Doris: on that night of the Murder game,

you don't happen to remember what Margot was wearing?"

Doris stiffened. "Why do you want to know that?"

"Well, Celia"—he saw her sympathy return again—"Celia said Margot had never looked more beautiful than on that night, in what she was wearing."

"Oh?" murmured Doris.

"So I just wondered what she was wearing. But," he gestured, "that was over six months ago, so naturally you wouldn't remember. Since you had no special reason for remembering."

"I remember perfectly well," Doris told him coldly. "Mrs. Marsh was wearing some kind of silvery thing. It didn't suit her at all. I don't mean she wasn't very good looking; of course she was, for her age; I simply mean it didn't suit her."

"A silvery dress. You're sure it wasn't a black velvet one?"

"I'm positive it wasn't. Positive! But . . ."

A cloudy memory stirred at the back of Doris's blue eyes. Holden, with a flash of instinct, was after it.

"Margot's death must have been a great shock to Thorley," he said. "And to your family, since you were all such great friends. I suppose he rang up your parents, after it happened?"

"Oh, yes." Her eyes were far away. "Early in the morning!"

"And perhaps you all went over to Caswall?"

"Yes. Straightaway. Father and mother," the pretty face darkened, "didn't want me to go. Funnily enough, Don Dismallo," she laughed a little, "that's exactly what I was thinking about! While they were talking to—to Thorley . . ."

"Yes, Doris?"

"I ran up the back stairs and peeped into That Woman's room. Just for a second, you know. And there was a black velvet dress on a chair at the foot of the bed. And gray stockings. Nylons. I noticed them, you see; they were nylons."

Bang had gone the shot, straight to the center of the target.

Holden, trying to breathe freely and easily, glanced toward the yellowish-brown front of Caswall. The flap of a pigeon's wings, in a white flicker from the stable courtyard long disused except for one garage, rose distinctly across the field. There was a small splash and ripple from the moat.

Here was Celia's story—"unbalanced" Celia, damn them! —confirmed by a girl who doubtless had no idea she was confirming it, and who would be the one witness (for reasons of her own) to remember everything about Margot.

"Thorley . . ." he began.

"What about Thorley?" Doris asked quickly.

He smiled. "You're rather fond of Thorley, aren't you?"

"Ye-es. I dare say I am." She spoke offhandedly, with that nineteen-year-old reluctance, combined with the rush of blood to the face, which conceals sheer adoration. It disquieted Holden and rather frightened him.

"You—you say," Doris added, "Thorley's over there now. You've finished dinner?"

"Yes. And a very lavish dinner it was."

"Of course. It would be." Then Doris let herself go. "Thorley knows his way about, thanks. He tells me he's got the black market lined up just like *that*." She drew an invisible line in the air. "If there's something he wants, then nothing will stop him from getting it. And I don't think there's anything he can't do, either. Even to—walking on logs."

"Even to . . . what?"

"It's nothing, really. But it was on the day you were talking about, the afternoon before the Murder party. You remember the trout stream that runs through our grounds?"

"I think I've seen it."

"Well, Thorley and Ronnie and I were out after the big blue trout that hangs about in the deep pool under the sycamore." (Now it was the girl speaking, rather than the poised, arch, alert young lady.) "That blue trout, you can't catch him; he's too wily; but you can have some fun with him. There was a thin log over the pool. Ronnie tried nonchalantly to walk across it, and only fell in with a splash. Thorley said, 'Come, now!' And Thorley walked across the log, and then turned around and walked back with his eyes shut. Mind you, *with his eyes shut*."

Holden only nodded gravely.

"I mean," said Doris, pulling herself together, "that's how I like a man to be!" She surveyed Holden. "You know, Don Dismallo," she said abruptly, "you're sort of," she groped for a word, "sort of *sympathetic*."

"Am I, Doris? Thanks."

"And I never used to think you were."

"Well! You've grown up now."

"Of course I have." Though she still held one shoulder elaborately high, as though aloof, she came closer. The blue eyes were angry. "You—you said you were down in the dumps about Celia."

"Yes. But you've helped me."

"I've helped you?"

"By George, you have!"

"Anyway," Doris disregarded this, "I told you you weren't the only one. I mean, it was too utterly absurd of my father and mother to be absolutely livid just because I chose to go to London on my own for a few days!" Doris laughed. Her whole face and expression became genuinely, subtly mature. "The things I could teach my own mother!" she said.

"I see. But . . ."

"But," interrupted Doris, with a short gesture, "their getting into a flat spin about a few days in town was the last straw. It was, really. And, what's more, tonight I'm going to end it."

"End what?"

"You'll see," answered Doris, nodding her head in a meaning fashion. "There are certain secrets about certain people, and maybe dead people as well, that ought to have an airing. And they're going to get one. Tonight."

"Meaning what?"

"You'll see," Doris promised again. "I'm off now, Don Dismallo. You're nice."

"Here! Doris! Stop a bit!"

But she was already running lightly through the long grass toward the house, her short skirt swinging at her knees.

There was going to be trouble, an explosion of some kind. Under that assumption of casualness Doris was in a feverish state of mind. Holden's eyes strayed toward the left. Far over there westward, hidden now by the trees of the carriage drive, lay Caswell Church of so many memories, and the churchyard sloping up into a hill; and, a mile or more beyond that hill on the road to Chippenham, the large modern house called Widestairs.

Doris Locke had stamped over here, flaming. "It was too utterly absurd of my father and mother to be absolutely livid just because I chose to go to London on my own for a few days!" And then that look as she laughed and added: "The things I could teach my own mother!"

Trouble!

Dusk was settling softly in clear, warm air. Caswall's narrow windows had lost their reflected light. The floor of the stone bridge across the moat, built there when the south front had been remodeled in the eighteenth century, showed whitish against darkening water.

Farther down, where sparrows hopped, another and smaller bridge spanned the moat to the stable yard. Holden moved slowly forward toward the house. The dingy gilt hands of the stable-yard clock, facing eastward and only to be seen when you drew near, indicated twenty minutes to nine.

"There are certain secrets about certain people that ought to be given an airing."

Confound it, why worry about Doris? After all, hadn't she given good proof that Celia had been telling the truth?

Holden's footsteps crunched on the white gravel of the drive. Beyond the bridge across the moat, thirty feet broad and faintly rippling, a double flight of stone stairs led up to an arched front door. Those stairs were necessary. Caswall's inhabited floors lay above the semiunderground rooms and cloisters, bleached museum pieces now, where the first abbess had held office over her nuns.

And, as Holden crossed the bridge and ascended the steps, the whole breath and atmosphere of the past reached out and drew him in. When he had closed the front door (which worked on a ponderous mechanism of bars and bolts always locked at nightfall), the atmosphere rose about him like water. Caswall, despite its antiquity, was not dead. It breathed; it stirred in sleep; it inspired dreams.

Dreams. Celia's dreams . . .

The renovated great hall, all scrubbed white in carven stone, contained a few bits of more modern furniture to relieve its chill. But several carpets only patched it; a big wine-colored sofa looked lost in it; a brass candelabrum became a mere toy. Margot and Thorley, Holden reflected, had held their wedding reception here. So had other Devereux girls, amid stringed music plucked and twanging, years before the accession of Queen Elizabeth.

Nobody here now; nobody stirring.

He turned to his right, and walked down the echoing length into the high, echoing Painted Room: green paneled except for its murals, the colors of whose figures were almost lost in the fading light.

Nobody here, either. But over there across from him, in the north-east corner, a short flight of carpeted stairs in an embrasure led up to the Long Gallery.

"Has Celia"—Dr. Shepton's voice returned to him as clearly as though the stoop-shouldered doctor, no fool, were here in the flesh—"has Celia told you about the night, immediately after her sister's death, when she saw ghosts walking in the Long Gallery?"

Celia wasn't mad! She wasn't! Celia was here now, amid the spell and the dreams of Caswall: "resting," they said. If she had beheld anything (anything, say, that crept out of these walls between the lights), it had been no delusion. Suppose he, Donald Holden, were to go over there now; and slip up the carpeted stairs to the Long Gallery; and suppose *he* were to see . . . ?

He went, making hardly a sound on the steps.

The gallery, appearing narrow because of its great length, stretched from south to north. A single drugget of brownish carpet ran along the wooden floor to where, at the far end, another short flight of steps under an arch led up into the Blue Drawing Room. The Long Gallery was lighted, on the eastern side, by three very large oriel windows, deeply embrasured, with tall lights and diamond panes.

Modern upholstered chairs and smoking tables—as a rule in the window embrasures—were set out to give the effect of a lounging room. There were bookcases. But dominating the Long Gallery, vivid and powerful, loomed the line of portraits which stretched along the western wall. The light was still clear, though fading; nothing seemed to move or stir.

What Holden did hear, what stopped him dead in his tracks, was a real voice: a young voice, crying out in a tone of such utter and abject misery that Holden's nerves shrank from it. The owner of the voice imagined himself alone; he was not really speaking loudly, but the acoustics of the Long Gallery carried it.

"God, please help me!" the voice said, in the form of a prayer. "God, please help me! God, please help me!"

It was a little naïve, and utterly sincere. A lanky, leggy young man in sports clothes, who had been sitting in a chair just outside the embrasure of the middle window, bent forward and pressed his hands over his eyes.

CHAPTER VIII

Holden very softly crept back down the stairs again. When anybody feels as deeply as that, whatever the cause, you cannot let him know you have overheard him.

So Holden waited for long seconds, in the Painted Room,

before making loud shuffling noises, coughing, and going up the steps again with a heavy and obvious tread. He strolled slowly along the gallery: disturbingly, the eyes of the portraits seemed fixed steadily on him as he passed.

The lanky and leggy young man, who might have been between nineteen and twenty, was now sitting sprawled back in his armchair, one hand shading his eyes, staring out at the fields through the oriel window.

"Hello," said Holden, and stopped beside him.

"Oh!—Hello, sir."

Instinctively, as a schoolboy rises when a master enters the room, the young man had started to get to his feet; the newcomer grinned and waved him back.

"My name's Holden," he explained. "You're Ronald Merrick, aren't you?"

The young man stared at him. His face, ravaged by anguish only a few moments before, had smoothed itself out.

"That's right. How did you know . . . ?"

"Oh, I rather thought you were. Cigarette?"

"Th-thanks."

Holden saw instantly, as a light switch is clicked on, that he had made an ally. For this was the sort of young man who instinctively, out of a sixth sense, recognizes that congenial (and rare) type of schoolmaster whom he knows, whom he really respects, and in whom he sometimes confides as he will confide in no other person on this earth.

"Look, sir," pursued young Merrick, as he hastily scrabbled to light a match for their cigarettes. "Weren't you at Lupton before the war?"

"Yes."

"I thought I'd heard Tom Clavering speak about you! And: wait a minute! Didn't Celia tell Doris"—his eyes widened—"weren't you in MI5? Intelligence?"

"That's right."

Ronald Merrick's dark-haired, rather Byronic good looks were set in a kind of glaze. Holden studied him as the young man sat there, half raised up out of his chair, in an old sports coat patched with leather at the elbows. He had the artist's face, the artist's hands, the artist's discontent; but his jaw was strong, and Holden liked the set of his shoulders.

"You mean," young Merrick was so impressed as to be almost hypnotized, "you mess about in disguise? And get dropped out of planes in a parachute?"

"That sometimes had to be done, yes."

"Crikey!" breathed Ronald Merrick, and his figure grew tense. He was obviously contrasting, in his mind, the wretchedness of his own lot with what he conceived to be the bliss of messing about in disguise and foiling the Gestapo according to film versions of how this is done.

"Sir," he burst out hopelessly, and whacked his fist down on the arm of the chair, "why is life so ... so. ..."

"Bloody?" suggested Holden.

The other looked a trifle startled. "Well—yes."

"Because it often is, Ronnie. I've been thinking exactly the same thing."

"You?"

"Yes. It depends on the nature of the trouble."

"Look, sir." Ronnie stared very hard at the cigarette between his clasped fingers. He cleared his throat. "Do you know Doris Locke?"

"I've known her for a long time."

"And of course you know," his face darkened, "Mr. Marsh?"

"Yes."

"They're here now. In the Blue Drawing Room. I opened the door; I didn't mean to open the door, you understand; I just did. And they were ..."

He stopped. Grinding out his cigarette on the glass top of the table, he jumped up in a fever of anguish and began to pace outside the embrasure. It never occurred to him to wonder whether or not Holden might understand what he was talking about; he simply assumed, like a sixth former in front of a master, that the latter would naturally be acquainted with any subject he chose to mention.

"You see, sir, I can't understand it!"

"Understand what?"

"It wouldn't be so bad," declared Ronnie, running his hands through his hair, "if I could only understand what Doris sees in him. I mean, a man old enough to be her father! See what I mean?"

"You were referring to Doris and—and Mr. Marsh?"

"Yes, of course. Mind you," added Ronnie, suddenly assuming a very lofty and disdainful attitude with his hand on the back of a chair, "I think I'm tolerably sophisticated myself. Broadminded, and all that. These things happen. They're a part of nature, and we can't help 'em. If," he added anxiously, "you follow what I mean?"

"Yes. I think I follow you."

"But the point is, there ought to be decency in it!" Ronnie hesitated. "You take Mrs. Marsh; for instance. The one that died."

Holden's pulses gave a violent jump and throb, though he only continued to study the tip of his cigarette.

"What about Mrs. Marsh?"

"Well, she was all right. When she had an affair (mind; I'm not saying she did), then she chose somebody as old as herself: yes, and I should think a good deal older! But"—he dismissed Margot with a wave of the hand—"but Doris is different, don't you see?"

"Doris is on a different plane. Spiritually, and everything else, from all these other people. Naturally, I know there's never been anything of what you could call wrong between her and Marsh." This idea, to Ronnie, was quite plainly inconceivable. The mere thought of it so revolted him that he shied away from it.

"It's only," he argued, "a sort of adolescent fad. It always happens in books. The only trouble is," his voice rose, "what does Doris see in *him*? It isn't as if he were some dashing kind of bloke that women would fall for. I—I met Doris in London last night. Took her dancing. I asked her if I could come down to Widestairs today. She said yes; only I couldn't go with her, because she'd be in the car," his face wrinkled up, "with Mr. Marsh. Even when I got to Widestairs, she was hiding from me. I came over here, hoping to find her . . ."

And again he found her.

At that moment, as Ronnie Merrick's voice trailed away, three persons appeared in the Long Gallery.

From the south end, up the little flight of carpeted stairs from the Painted Room, appeared Sir Danvers Locke. From the north end, down the little flight of stairs from the Blue Drawing Room, came Doris Locke and Thorley Marsh.

All three stopped and stood motionless.

The Long Gallery, with those curiously portentous and somehow menacing figures at each end, gave back no sound of footfall. Through three great windows, diamond panes of clear glass, purplish-tinged dusk touched the line of portraits hanging against the opposite wall. It touched a glint of gilt or ebony in portrait frame, but it softened the richer, more somber colors of the portraits themselves.

Sir Danvers Locke moved first.

They heard his footsteps creak and crack, slowly, down that gallery with its long strip of brownish carpet. Doris and Thorley advanced to meet him. They met in the middle, just by the embrasure of the oriel window where Holden and Ronnie Merrick were standing. Yet Holden had the feeling that he and Ronnie were forgotten, unnoticed, in that meeting of eyes.

Locke, in his early fifties, remained lean and fastidious looking even when he wore country plus fours. He carried a cap in one hand and an ash stick in the other. The iron-gray hair, the high intellectual forehead, the thick dark eyebrows, the prominent cheekbones and rather beaked nose, even Locke's mouth which should have worn its usual serene smile: these features were without expression, polite and waiting.

It was Doris, flushed and bright eyed, who broke the silence.

"Tell him, Thorley!" she cried.

Thorley smiled, a little nervously.

"Tell him, Thorley!"

You could see Thorley, under the line of watching portraits, adjusting his face as clearly as a man adjusts a necktie.

"Locke old man," he said in a low, hearty, sincere voice, "I hope you're going to congratulate me. Doris and I have decided to get married."

And nothing happened, during a long silence. Locke did not even nod or move. Thorley, who had started forward with his hand outstretched, stopped uncertainly. Thorley's eye fell on Ronnie Merrick, and his expression grew as black as thunder; but Thorley spoke quite pleasantly.

"I think we can excuse you, young man," he said.

"Yes," said Ronnie, abruptly coming to life like a young man who has been hypnotized. "Of course. Sorry to have intruded. Congratulations."

And he marched out of the gallery: long-legged, utterly disdainful, but bumping into a little chair before he reached the stairs to the Painted Room.

"Ronnie!" Doris cried out uncertainly, with a ring of contrition in her voice. "Wait! I didn't mean to be so . . . !"

"He's all right," Thorley told her reassuringly, and patted her arm. "Let him go. But your father . . ."

Doris's father, at the moment, had caught sight of Holden. Locke's face lighted up with the old smile, of virile charm, which made him seem a dozen years younger. Putting down cap and walking stick on the table, he grasped the wanderer's hand.

"My dear Holden," he exclaimed, "I'm delighted to see you back again! We're all delighted to hear your 'death' was

71

only (what shall I say?) a *ruse de guerre*. No"—as Holden made a strong, embarrassed attempt to follow Ronnie—"no, don't go. I think you ought to remain. Tell me, my dear fellow: how was Italy? And did you get into Spain?"

"Father!" cried Doris.

"Yes, my dear?" Locke dropped Holden's hand and turned around.

"Aren't you," gasped Doris, with her high color making the blue eyes seem paler, and shivering all over, "aren't you at least going to pay at-at-*tention* to me? I've been in love with Thorley for months and months and months. We're going to get married just as soon as . . ."

"As soon as," remarked Locke, politely running his eye over Thorley's clothes, "as Mr. Marsh gets rid of that deep mourning he is now wearing?"

Silence.

It was a deadly thrust, however thin and lightly held seemed the rapier. Locke rolled an upholstered chair around so that its back was to the window, and sat down. Behind him lay the darkening moat, and the dim green fields dotted with a few beech trees. Thorley, deeply hurt and really shocked, stared back at him.

"I thought," Thorley burst out, "you were a friend of mine!"

"So I am," assented Locke, and inclined his head.

"I love her," said Thorley. It was impossible to doubt, apparently, his honesty or his deep feeling. Doris, still clutching at Thorley's sleeve, looked up at him with eyes of sheer adoration. Holden, in spite of himself, could not help feeling oddly touched.

"I love her," Thorley repeated, with real dignity. "Is there any reason, financial or—or social, why we shouldn't marry?"

"None whatever."

"Well, then!"

Locke crossed his knees comfortably.

"Let's put aside," he suggested, "certain considerations which (I suppose) don't matter. Young Merrick, who, with your exquisite courtesy, has just been kicked out of here . . ."

"I know. I'm sorry." Thorley passed a hand across his forehead. "But the damn little nuisance—!"

"The damn little nuisance, as you call him, is the son of my oldest friend, Lord Seagrave. He is also, I am inclined to believe, something of a genius."

Thorley, baffled, appealed to the ceiling.

"An artist!" he said.

"I beg your pardon," corrected Locke. "He is a painter. Whether or not he is an artist remains to be seen. There are very few good painters nowadays. They are afraid of color, and they are afraid of detail. Ronald is not. He is now studying under Dufrèsnes, the only teacher in Europe," Locke lifted long fingers and snapped them, "worth *that*; and we shall see. Still! This is not important."

"I know that," retorted Thorley. "And I'm glad (if you'll excuse my saying so, old man) you have the sense to see it too. Then what's the devil's so wrong if Doris and I get married?"

"You see no objection?"

"No!"

"Perhaps not," said Locke. "But before my daughter becomes your second wife, I should prefer to be sure how your first wife died."

Around the window-embrasure behind Locke's chair ran a window seat of padded red velvet. Holden, dropping his long-dead cigarette on the floor, had crept into it. All this time Holden had been experiencing the extraordinary sensation that one of the portraits—a Devereux lady of the seventeenth century, with wired ringlets—was looking at him fixedly. So strong was the illusion that he had to wrench his gaze away, even to look at Thorley, when Locke's quiet remark exploded.

Doris, who evidently had heard nothing of the undercurrents, dropped her hand from Thorley's arm and was staring at her father in bewilderment. Thorley's voice grew thick.

"You've been talking to Celia!" he said.

"I beg your pardon?" said Locke.

"You've been talking to Celia," Thorley almost shouted. "The little devil's as mad as a coot, and . . ."

"Easy, Thorley!" said Holden, and got to his feet.

"I assure you," interposed Locke, turning round his dark arched brows and prominent cheekbones for a brief glance at Holden, "I haven't been talking to Celia. I haven't even seen her. I understand the poor girl has been," he hesitated, "ill."

"Her illness," Holden said bitterly, "consisting in the statement that Thorley had treated Margot brutally, and probably driven her to suicide."

But Holden stopped there. He couldn't, literally and

73

physically couldn't, pour out the whole grisly story. He didn't quite know why. But he couldn't. He left it there, in the air, while Locke stared around and Doris uttered a gasp.

"Indeed!" was Locke's only comment.

"That's a lie!" said Thorley.

"Indeed?" Locke inquired politely.

"I tell you, it's a lie," Thorley repeated, with white earnestness. "I think I must be the most misunderstood man on earth. But," he moistened his lips, "about Margot's death. If you haven't been talking to Celia, who have you been talking to?"

"Nobody," answered Locke calmly.

"But nobody's *said* anything about it!"

"Of course not. Certainly, at least, not in your hearing. But—my dear Marsh!"

"Well?"

"Your wife, in perfect health, dines at my house and goes home with you, and in less than twelve hours she is dead. I say no more. But if you imagine that nobody hereabouts has wondered at it, or has even thought about it, you've been living in a fool's paradise."

"I see," muttered Thorley. And he turned his head away.

But it was different with Doris.

After that one gasp, there had flitted across Doris's face such a wild, contemptuous, half-pitying look that she became incoherent. Her blue eyes, half tearful with hero worship, turned toward Thorley as toward a martyred champion fighting in a ring of enemies. Thorley gave her a brave smile and a half-humorous shrug of the shoulders, to imply that they were fighting together.

And so they were. Tough little Doris, with a mutinous underlip, braced herself as she saw her father bend forward to speak.

"Doris?"

"Yes, father?"

"Understand me, my dear. I don't say there's anything at all in these rumors against our friend Marsh."

"No, father?" (Her frantic lips half-breathed the words, "How nice!")

"I daresay there isn't, and I hope there isn't. But it concerns your welfare. That's the only reason why I mention it at all."

"So now," Doris cried out suddenly, "you're *pleading* with me."

"I shouldn't exactly call it pleading, my dear."

"Shouldn't you? I should." Her voice rose to a small scream. "It's all very well for you to sit in the corner, like Voltaire or Anatole France or somebody: that is, when we're in public and not at home. But you see now I'm determined to marry Thorley (yes, and I can get married at nineteen; don't think I can't) and now you're *pleading* with me!"

"That was another matter, my dear, which I hadn't mentioned. After all, there *is* a considerable difference in your ages."

"Really?" said Doris, very pleased with herself. "Oh, I don't think that'll make much difference."

"How can you be sure of that?"

"Well!" She lifted her shoulders and laughed. "I suppose by such a long time of what the lawyers call 'intimacy.' "

"Doris!" exclaimed Thorley, genuinely shocked that this should be mentioned in public. Thorley made fussed gestures which implored the others to be calm.

Danvers Locke was as white as a ghost.

"Intimacy." He managed to swallow the word.

"That's right, father. I'll use a cruder term if you like."

Locke's arms were extended along the arms of the chair, his fingers gently tapping.

"And how long has this 'intimacy' been going on? Was it —was it before Mrs. Marsh's death?"

"Oh, father dear! Ages before."

"So that," Locke spoke with an effort, "if anyone got the notion that for your sake (your sake!) Mr. Thorley Marsh might have hastened his wife's departure . . . ?"

"Locke, for God's sake!" said Thorley.

"Oh, why not be frank about it?" Doris demanded. She turned to Thorley with her eyes brimming over. "Darling," she said, "are you ashamed of loving me? I'm not ashamed of it. I'm proud. But I want them to *understand* you. I want them to see how fine and brave and noble you are."

"Yes, Thorley," observed Holden, not without dryness. "You might begin telling us how fine and brave and noble you are."

"Just one moment, please," said Doris, darting in immediately to defend her now-groggy champion. "If there's going to be any ghastly rot talked about how people behaved, let me say something. I—I shouldn't have said it else."

Here Doris swallowed hard.

"You—you always want to attack Thorley," she went on.

75

"And, of course, he's too contemptuous to say anything, or you'd hear a lot. Thorley's been my lover. *But who was Margot Marsh's lover?*"

Locke started to get up from his chair, but sat down again. It was Holden who walked across to Doris.

"Margot," he asked, "had a lover?"

"Yes!" sniffed Doris.

"Who was he?"

"I don't know." Doris threw out her hands. "Thorley didn't know himself."

Doris's flares of rage were never of long duration. This one, under her father's cold and steady eye, began to flicker and falter. She caught at Thorley's arm for support. Yet she fought back.

"That Woman," she gave Margot the capital letters of sheer hatred, "That Woman was so intolerably prudish—oh, dear me, yes!—and she'd never done anything like that before —oh, dear, no!—that she was terribly, terribly secret about it. You'd have thought it was an awful sin or something. She was wild about him toward the end, though, whoever he was. Absolutely *wild.* You could see the signs. And . . ."

"Doris," interrupted her father. Still he did not speak loudly, but there was something in his voice which made her falter still more.

"Doris," continued Locke, "despite your vast experience in these matters, and your understanding of our poor human problems, has it ever once entered that scatterbrain of yours" —suddenly he whacked the arm of the chair—"that Mrs. Marsh was probably poisoned?"

"I . . ."

"Has it, my dear?"

"I don't know," flamed Doris, "and I don't care. All I mean is: you're not going to look so shocked at Thorley for doing what That Woman did too, after she'd already made his life so unhappy about other things. And you're not going to say Thorley was mean and brutal and 'hastened her departure.'"

"No, Doris," Holden said gently. "But then we're not going to say Celia is mad."

"Celia's nice, Don Dismallo," said Doris, lifting a flushed face. "But she's crazy. Thorley told me. Crazy, crazy, crazy!"

And they looked at each other.

"Gentlemen," Locke said formally, after a long pause, "it would be an understatement to say that we are in the middle of an abominable mess."

He rose to his feet.

It just then occurred to Holden that here in the Long Gallery they were directly underneath the suite of rooms where the crime (if you could call it that) had been committed. Up there, if you glanced southward, would be the white-and-gold sitting room where Margot had been taken ill, and the rose bedroom where she had died.

Perhaps the same thought occurred to Locke, for he lifted his eyes briefly before clasping his hands together with close, controlled emotion.

"Somehow," Locke continued, "we got into this. Somehow we must get out of it. The life of every single person connected with this affair has become involved in the web. It's no abstract problem. It's a violent personal issue. Yet it's a web we can't see; can't understand; can only feel. We're not even sure what the problem is. Until we solve that problem, we shall touch frantic states of mind and we shall not be able to sleep at night. But I can't solve the problem. Apparently you can't. In the name of heaven, who can solve it?"

It was Obey's voice which startled them then, Obey's voice calling the announcement of someone's arrival from the steps to the Painted Room. What Obey bawled was:

"Dr. Gideon Fell."

CHAPTER IX

"**A**HA!" said Dr. Fell.

How a figure of such vast dimensions managed even to squeeze through the arch, let alone navigate the steps, was something of a mystery. But Dr. Fell managed it.

Down he came rolling majestically, an enormous shape with a box-pleated cape round his shoulders, supporting himself on two canes. His shovel hat was clutched under a hand which held one of the canes. His shaggy mop of gray-streaked hair framed a beaming red face with three chins and a very small nose, on which was perched a pair of eyeglasses with a broad black ribbon. A bandit's moustache, uncombed for several days, curved round his mouth. And he beamed on them like a walking furnace.

Dr. Fell's dignity, it is true, was a little impaired by the fact that the ridges of his waistcoat were spattered with cigar ash, and in an upper waistcoat pocket was stuck a long folded envelope carefully inscribed with the words *Don't forget this*.

But the whole gallery shook to his tread. You might have imagined that the portraits, in which the last light picked out the red of an officer's uniform or the white of a wig, rattled in their frames as he advanced along the narrow strip of carpet.

Dr. Fell, after a vague glance at those portraits, seemed in danger of walking straight into them in order to examine them properly. But he remembered his purpose. Approaching the group by the middle window, he cleared his throat with a long challenging sound like a war cry.

"Mr. Thorley Marsh?"

Thorley, white-faced but stolidly himself again, nodded and stared.

"Sir Danvers Locke?"

Locke smiled and inclined his head.

"Er—Miss Doris Locke?"

Doris, who was furtively wiping her eyes, uttered a kind of squeak at this apparition towering over her.

"Aha!" said Dr. Fell, pleased to have got that straight. He wheeled round toward Holden. Whereupon, inexplicably, he began to laugh.

It started as a kind of chuckle deep in his stomach, and then spread upward like a minor earthquake. It made cigar ash rise in clouds from the ridges of his waistcoat, and blew wide the broad ribbon of his eyeglasses. It chortled and roared and thundered, turning Dr. Fell's face scarlet, bringing moisture to his eyes, and, with an outward whoop of the stomach, sending his eyeglasses flying. Its effect was rather like one of those laughing gramophone records: in which, if you are not careful, you will join without knowing why.

"Would you mind telling me," asked Holden, who like Doris and her father had been about to join in, "why I look as funny as all that?"

Dr. Fell stopped dead.

An expression of deep concern overspread his face as he got his breath back.

"Sir," he wheezed, in a voice of real distress, "I beg your pardon! I do really beg your pardon!"

It poured with a contrition out of all proportion to the offense. But he meant it. Everything about him was huger than life, including emotions. Putting down his shovel hat

78

and one walking stick on the table beside Locke's, he groped
down the ribbon of the eyeglasses and stuck them awry on
his nose.

"You will—er—accept my apologies?" he demanded anxiously. "It was only, sir, that you unconsciously allowed me
to accomplish something which (archons of Athens!) I had
never believed possible. You see . . ."

"Look here," said Thorley. "What is all this?"

Dr. Fell slowly wheeled round again on one cane.

"Oh, ah! Yes! Sir, you must allow me to explain this un-
warranted intrusion."

"No, no, glad to have you!" Thorley assured him, with a
shade of Thorley's old hearty smile.

"You see," explained Dr. Fell, with his vague wandering
round the gallery, "this is not the first time I have visited
Caswall. At one time I had the honor to be a friend of the
late Mrs. Andrew Devereux. The lady whom you called, I
believe, Mammy Two."

"Mammy Two, eh?" murmured Thorley.

Through Holden's mind flashed certain cryptic words of
Celia's on the night before. *I don't see how I can back out
now. That one man would have been safe enough, the old
friend of Mammy Two. But*—Could "that one man" refer to
Dr. Fell? He had no time to consider this. Dr. Fell was speaking to him.

Dr. Fell, after diving into the pocket of his coat under the
big box-pleated cape, had produced a sheet torn from a small
notebook and was holding it out to him.

"Before we—harrumph—continue," wheezed Dr. Fell, with
an odd flash out of those absent-looking eyes, "will you be
good enough to glance over this and tell me whether its con-
tents are correct?"

"I beg your pardon?"

"Sir," said Dr. Fell rather testily, and shook the paper in
the air, "will you please read this?"

Holden took the paper. It was now so dusky that little
of expression could be discerned, but there had been a defi-
nite warning in Dr. Fell's eyes. Kneeling sideways on the
window seat, Holden held the paper close to the glass to read
it. In the night stillness around Caswall he could hear the
ripple of the moat.

Then the penciled words leaped out at him.

*I cannot speak in front of anyone else. As soon as it is fully dark,
will you be a witness when I unlock the vault in the churchyard, to*

see whether ghosts have really walked there? Say yes or no, and return this paper to me.

Twice Holden read it without lifting his eyes. When he did look up, after a glimpse of the dun-colored side of Caswall and a terra-cotta drainpipe beside the window, no muscle in his face moved. He handed the paper back to Dr. Fell.

"Yes," he assented "That's perfectly correct."

Sir Danvers Locke spoke suavely: "You were saying, Dr. Fell?"

"I was saying," returned Dr. Fell, "that my previous visits to this house, except one, have been pleasant." He swayed back and forth a little, partly supporting his weight with both hands on the cane. "This visit, I regret to tell you, is official."

"Official," said Thorley. "Representing whom?"

"Representing Superintendent Madden of the Wiltshire County Constabulary. On instructions from the Metropolitan C. I. D. It refers, as you have probably guessed, to the death of Mrs. Marsh."

"I knew it!" Thorley whispered.

Quickly, with a cool and curt nod, Thorley strode to the north end of the gallery, where he touched three electric switches. It bathed the gallery with a soft glow of ceiling lamps, and of red-shaded table lamps in the window alcoves. Thorley returned to find Dr. Fell teetering back and forth on the crutch-handled stick, glowering down at his clasped hands.

Dr. Fell scowled still more.

"The matter was—harrumph—delicate," he said, without raising his head. "Hadley thought it might be less embarrassing if I, the old duffer, looked into it first. In case, you see, it proved to be a mare's nest."

"Ah!" said Thorley. "So you've found it's a mare's nest."

"No," answered Dr. Fell, with rounded and ominous distinctness.

"All right. Let's have it. What's the betting?"

"In my humble opinion, it was murder." Dr. Fell looked up. "Mrs. Marsh was poisoned with a toxic agent which I think I can name, and almost certainly by one of the other seven persons who were present at the Murder party on the night of December twenty-third.—One moment!"

He spoke sharply, though none of that rigid group had ventured to reply.

"Before you make any comment, will you listen to my proposition?"

"Proposition?" Thorley said quickly. "You mean: it might be hushed up?"

Dr. Fell did not appear to hear this.

Becoming aware that something was sticking him under the chin—it was the long folded envelope inscribed *Don't forget this* and thrust into his upper waistcoat pocket for just that purpose—he drew it out and weighed it in his hand.

"I have here," he went on "a very long letter, addressed vaguely to Scotland Yard, giving a full account of the affair. I am also in a position to know, through circumstances I needn't go into now, perhaps more about it than most of you know yourselves.

"When I entered this room, sir," Dr. Fell opened his eyes at Locke, "I heard you calling on heaven for a solution to your problem. It's really not as bad as that, you know. That's my proposition. Answer my questions truthfully, and *I'll* solve your problem."

There was a long pause.

"*Now?*" asked Sir Danvers Locke.

"Perhaps sooner than you think. I can at least settle the dispute between Miss Celia Devereux and Mr. Thorley Marsh."

Again Holden's heart began to beat heavily, a feeling probably shared by everyone else.

"Are you," Locke hesitated, "are you sure you can?"

"Am I sure?" suddenly thundered Dr. Fell, rolling back his head and firing up with a sizzling kind of noise as though water had been sprinkled on the furnace. "Archons of Athens, the man asks me if I'm sure!"

"I only meant ..."

"Is a judge ever sure? Is a jury ever sure? Is the recording angel himself, with the vast books of all eternity, ever sure? No; of course I'm not sure!" Dr. Fell ended this oratorical flourish, rather apologetically, by scratching his nose with the envelope. "But I have—harrumph—a certain Christian confidence."

And he wheeled round majestically, and lumbered over to sit down facing them on the window seat, beyond the glass-topped table with the red-shaded lamp.

"Who," asked Thorley, "wrote that letter?"

"This? Miss Celia Devereux."

A shudder went through Doris Locke at the mention of Celia's name, as though Doris had been touched by some well-meaning leper. "Thorley, I never *realized* the awfulness you've had to put up with!"

"Never mind, my dear," Thorley assured her, and smiled and patted her hand. "I'll get through."

"Thorley! As if I ever doubted that! But Celia! Even if she can't help herself!" Doris's voice altered. "Oughtn't Celia to be here?"

"I entirely agree she should," Holden said grimly. "If you'll excuse me, I'll just go up to her room and bring her down."

Thorley's glossy head swung round. "I wouldn't do that, old boy," he advised. "Celia's resting. I've given orders she's not to be disturbed."

"I'm a guest in this house, Thorley. But when you take it on yourself to give an 'order' like that . . ."

Thorley's eyebrows went up. "If you must hear the real reason, old boy—"

"Well?"

"Celia doesn't want to see you. Don't believe me! Ask Obey."

"That, sir," intoned Dr. Fell, looking at Holden, "is perfectly true. I have just come from a conversation with Miss Devereux. She absolutely refuses to see you. She has locked the door of her room."

A physical sickness touched Holden deep down inside him. When he thought of Celia at this time last night, under the street lamp, Celia in his arms, Celia speaking to him, all the scenes which returned in such vividness, it seemed impossible. All the eyes here were looking at him now: looking at him and (yes, worse!) pitying him.

Then, for a brief flash, he caught Dr. Fell's expression. That expression said: "You must trust me. You must trust me, by thunder!" as clearly as though Dr. Fell had spoken aloud.

And he remembered the penciled words: *I cannot speak in front of anyone else. As soon as it is fully dark, will you be a witness when I unlock the vault in the churchyard, to see whether ghosts have really walked there?* It brought back the nightmare. But it showed that he and Dr. Fell shared, or were about to share, a secret. That made them allies. That meant Dr. Fell must be on his side; and therefore on Celia's.

Meanwhile, Locke was speaking.

"Your question, Dr. Fell?"

"Oh, ah! As a person of extreme delicacy," said Dr. Fell, yanking the table closer to him and thereby spilling off all the hats and sticks; "as a person of extreme delicacy," he insisted, yanking the table still closer and nearly smashing the

82

table lamp as it fell off, "I wish to approach this matter with the greatest delicacy."

"Of course," agreed Locke, gravely picking up the lamp and putting it back on the table.

"Er—thank 'ee," said Dr. Fell. They had all taken chairs facing him around that table, Thorley sitting on the arm of Doris's chair.

A cold, still apprehension held the group. Dr. Fell dropped the long envelope on the table. With his elbows on the table, and his fingers at his temples, he shut up his eyes tightly.

"I want you," he continued, "to think back to the Murder game on the night of December twenty-third."

"Why particularly," asked Locke, "the game?"

"Sir, will you allow me to do the questioning?"

"Pardon me. Yes?"

"I want you especially, Sir Danvers, to picture that rather evil scene. Your guests and your family wearing the masks of famous murderers. Yourself in the green mask of an executioner. The bowl of lighted spirits burning blue. Those faces moving and dodging about in the dark."

For a moment, now, there was no sound except Dr. Fell's heavy wheezy breathing.

"You yourself, I believe, gave out the masks to the various people?"

"Naturally."

"It was the first time you had exhibited that particular collection?"

"Yes."

"When you gave out the masks," said Dr. Fell, without opening his eyes, "did you exercise any particular choice? Did you try to make the mask, however remotely, fit the character of the person to whom you gave it?"

As at a lightening of tension, a smile appeared under Locke's large nose. He sat up straighter in the chair. The light of the table lamps shone smoothly on his iron-gray hair and accentuated the hollows under his cheekbones.

"Great Scott, no!" he said in tones of amused outrage. "On the contrary! That's what I want to emphasize. Shall I give an example?"

"If you please."

"To Mrs. Thorley Marsh, for instance," Locke smiled, yet a cold little stir ran through that group as Margot's ghost entered it, "to Mrs. Marsh I gave the mask of old Mrs. Dyer, the Reading baby farmer of infamous memory. She wouldn't have it. She insisted on being Edith Thompson: because, I suppose, Mrs. Thompson was a remarkably good-looking woman."

"Oh, ah?" murmured Dr. Fell. He opened his eyes, for a curious look at the other, before closing them again.

"My wife," continued Locke, "played Kate Webster, a huge virago of an Irishwoman. As for little Doris . . ." Locke waved his hand. "You understand now?"

"I understand. But how were you sure these people could play their parts, if you made the choices at random?"

"It wasn't exactly at random. Having kept the collection of masks in reserve for a suitable occasion—"

"So!" grunted Dr. Fell.

"—and having a large crime library at Widestairs, I had already made privately certain that all our friends (except poor Celia, who loathes crime) were well read in their parts. There was, of course, a stranger. Mr. Hurst-Gore."

"Ah, yes," said Dr. Fell. "Mr. Derek Hurst-Gore."

"Fortunately, however, Mr. Hurst-Gore could enter into the spirit of it. He made an admirable Smith, of brides-in-the-bath fame."

Dr. Fell's eyes were wide open again, in a blank and rather creepy stare which to Doris Locke, who for some reason had stood in awe of this huge apparition ever since his entrance, seemed terrifying. Doris's own eyes were wide and innocent now, like a small girl's. Her hand crept up to find Thorley's as he sat on the arm of the chair.

"Now we come," said Dr. Fell, "to Mrs. Marsh's behavior on that night. Sir Danvers, how should you describe her behavior?"

Locke hesitated. "I—er—don't quite follow the question."

"Her state of mind, sir! Before she went home from the mock murder to the real murder. Eh?"

"In terms of the old-fashioned theater," answered Locke thoughtfully, "I should say Mrs. Marsh behaved like a tragedy queen."

"Aha! But did she look as though, in the words of one witness, she had 'come to a decision about something?'"

"Yes! Now you mention it: yes."

"Do you agree with that, Mr. Marsh?"

"Confound it!" complained Thorley. He had reached down to touch Doris's hair, but he drew back as though conscious of an impropriety. "Margot was always like that! I told Don Holden so last night. Overhearty!"

"Overexcited about that man," muttered Doris.

Dr. Fell's eyes flashed open. "I beg your pardon?"

"I didn't say anything!" breathed Doris, jumping violently. "Really and truly I didn't!"

"Harrumph. Well." (It was impossible, from that vast pink face with the lopsided eyeglasses, to tell whether Dr. Fell had heard.) "But can you confirm these versions of Mrs. Marsh's behavior, Miss Locke?"

"I'm afraid," said Doris, lifting one shoulder, "I can't help you there. I wasn't interested. I scarcely noticed the Woman all evening."

(Be careful, you little fool! thought Holden. Be careful!)

"Of course," added Doris instantly, before Dr. Fell could speak, "I did 'murder' her in that game. But it was simply because she was the person handiest. You couldn't help spotting that silver gown in the dark."

Holden intervened just as quickly.

"That's it, Doris!" he said. "It was a silver dress, wasn't it? You do remember that? Naturally! As a woman would!"

"Ye-es!" Doris seemed relieved. "Naturally!"

Dr. Fell looked at Thorley. "Do you agree about the dress, Mr. Marsh?'   ,

"I suppose so," Thorley said half-humorously. "I never notice what a woman is wearing. Dr. Fell; and I'll bet a fiver you don't either. You can tell whether it becomes 'em, or whether it doesn't; in either case you can't think why, so you let it go at that. But—"

"But?"

"Well! I do seem in a kind of a way to remember that silver thing without shoulders, because it was so conspicuous. Margot—Margot looked worse in that death mask of Mrs. Thompson than she looked after she was dead."

And a shiver went through his bulky body.

"I see," said Dr. Fell. "Now your own party, as I understand it—yourself, Mrs. Marsh, Miss Devereux, and Mr. Hurst-Gore—left Widestairs at about eleven o'clock?"

"Yes!"

"At that time your wife still seemed in excellent health?"

"Yes. Full of beans."

"Dr. Fell!" interposed Locke very softly.

"Hey? What's that?"

"At risk of being rebuked again," said Locke, with his finger tips together, "I am a little disturbed by those words 'still seemed.' Are you implying that this poison, whatever it was, might have been administered in my house?"

"That," admitted Dr. Fell, "is a possibility we must consider. And yet"—there was a faint roar under his voice, and he puffed out his cheeks and let his fists fall on the table— "no, no, no! In that case, the effect of the poison in question must have come on at a far earlier time."

"Ah!" said Locke serenely.

"But it suggests another point. Did Mrs. Marsh by any chance come over to your house that same afternoon? Before the Murder game?"

A faintly startled expression came into Locke's eyes; then it was gone.

"Yes! As a matter of fact, she did."

"Oh, ah? For what purpose?"

"Presumably," smiled Locke, "to say hello. They'd just driven down from London, you know. Ah, no! One moment. I remember now. She said she wanted to see her husband." He seemed puzzled; troubled. "Yes. Her husband."

"Did she see him?"

"No. Our friend Marsh was out at the trout stream with Doris, where I believe he performed prodigies by walking across a log with his eyes shut." Locke's beautifully modulated voice gave an (somewhat ironic?) account of the incident. "Mrs. Marsh, I remember, asked my wife and myself to send him home soon; she said she wished to speak to him urgently."

For a long moment Dr. Fell stared at Locke. Then his shaggy head swung round.

"And this (harrum!) this urgent message. What was it, Mr. Marsh?"

"It wasn't anything!" protested Thorley. "I keep telling you, over and over, Margot was like that! She—"

"Sir," interrupted Dr. Fell, "was it to ask you for a divorce?"

Long pause.

(Divorce? Holden was thinking. Divorce? Margot? Nonsense! But wait! If this suggestion of Margot Devereux having a lover were true—as Doris insisted and even Celia had suspected—that altered everything. Margot might have put up with any kind of unhappy home life rather than the alternative of divorce. But if she happened to fall violently in love, and wanted to marry: yes, that altered everything.)

"I regret the necessity for repeating the question," said Dr. Fell, who was genuinely distressed. "But was it to ask you for a divorce?"

"No," replied Thorley, with his eye on a corner of the window embrasure.

"In that case, sir, I must go into matters that will be painful and embarrassing. You are aware," Dr. Fell touched the envelope on the table, "of certain statements made by Celia Devereux?"

"Yes. God knows I am!"

"That on one occasion you were seen to slash your wife across the face with a razor strap?"

"Yes!" cried Thorley. "But that was only—"

"Only what?"

Statement and question were flung at each other with such quickness that they seemed to clash like physical forces.

Dr. Fell had partly surged up, the ridges of his waistcoat jarring out the table with a scratch of wood and a rattle of the red-shaded lamp. But he did not seem to be towering or threatening: only, in a curious way, imploring. Thorley had slid off the chair arm and stood up.

"Only what, Mr. Marsh?"

"Only a lie," said Thorley. "Only a lie."

Dr. Fell sank back, a mountain of dejection.

"And that on another occasion, because of your conduct, your wife attempted to kill herself by swallowing strychnine?"

"That's a lie too."

The grisly story was pouring out now. Locke and his daughter sat as though paralyzed.

"And that, on the night your wife died, there was a bottle labeled POISON in the medicine cabinet of your joint bathroom?"

"There never was any such bottle, so help me!"

"And that—"

"Stop," said Thorley. His hand went to his collar, running a finger around inside it; then he cleared his throat, and spoke in a perfectly normal voice. "I've had enough," he added. "I've had more than any man can take."

"Yes?" said Dr. Fell.

"Look here, sir." Thorley addressed Dr. Fell, though a little breathlessly, with his quiet and easy charm. "These charges against me are all guff. What's more, I can prove they're all guff at any time I like. I haven't done it up to now, I've put up with everything, because I wanted to be decent. That's finished."

And then, just when as a man cornered and down-and-out he had the utter sympathy of nearly everyone there, the illusion was shattered. Thorley's tone changed.

"By God," he said, "I've had enough of a family with one ice-cold daughter and one crazy daughter. As for this house, I hope it rots. Those pictures over there," he gestured toward the wall behind him, "let them do something about it; as Celia says they can. I've liked Celia. I've done my best for Celia. I've put up with it when she's told me these things in private. But, from now on, just let her dare say the same things in front of anyone else! Just let her dare do it!"

They had heard no sound in the Long Gallery, no creak of footstep. A little way behind Thorley, looking full at him, stood Celia.

CHAPTER X

CELIA, just as she had looked last night: even to being dressed in white. Celia, with the beauty of the imaginative fine-drawn face untouched by any emotion, even anger. Her gray eyes, with the black pin-point pupils perhaps dilating a little, were fixed on Thorley.

But just beyond Celia . . .

Looming up beyond her, his hand under her elbow in a proprietary way, was a tall man in some mysterious season between youth and middle age. A man with a confident bearing, a dental smile, wearing a gray suit of such admirable cut and newness as only influence can procure nowadays, and having hair the color of a lion's mane with a wave in it.

Thorley, as though warned by a telepathic instinct, had swung round toward them.

"Derek!" he exclaimed. "What the devil are you doing here?"

(At last, thought Holden, Mr. Derek Hurst-Gore! But he didn't need Thorley's words to guess it. The hair did that. Ugh, you swine!)

Now in this, as anyone could have told him, he was doing Mr. Hurst-Gore a complete injustice. Everyone knew that Mr. Hurst-Gore was a fine fellow, who meant well in everything he did.

"Doing here?" Mr. Hurst-Gore repeated, in a rich confident voice. "Oh, I'm everywhere." He smiled. "As a matter of fact, I came down with Dr. Fell. We're both staying at the Warrior's Arms."

Despite his smile, Mr. Hurst-Gore kept looking at Thorley in a fixed, meaningful, heavily significant way.

"Thorley!"

"Well?"

"There must be no scandal," said Mr. Hurst-Gore, very slowly and in the same significant tone.

"But, listen, Derek! They're now saying it was murder!"

"I know."

"But—!"

"Remember the Frinley by-election?"

Holden couldn't see Thorley's face. But he sensed a change in the broad back, and the movement as though Thorley would put up his hands to shield his eyes.

"There is one thing," said Mr. Hurst-Gore, still holding Celia's elbow in a proprietary way, "that a man in public life mustn't do. He mustn't show himself a fool."

Thorley stood for a moment motionless. Then, with affection and tenderness rushing out of his voice, he turned to Celia.

"My dear Celia!" he said reproachfully. "My dear girl! You shouldn't have come downstairs tonight! Here!"

Hurrying to one side, Thorley rolled forward an easy chair whose casters squeaked abominably on the wooden floor and strip of brown carpet. Though Celia shrank as though she had been burnt when he touched her, she was so amazed that she allowed him to push her down into the chair.

"If you do this sort of thing often," he added, with a sort of reproachful beam, "Old Uncle Thorley will have to speak severely to you. Did I tell you, by the way, that I brought down a special vintage of port for you? Never mind where I got it. Sh-h!" Thorley winked. "But you won't find a wine like it anywhere in London."

Celia looked up at him helplessly.

"Thorley," she said, " I don't understand you!"

"I'm the Inimitable, my dear. I'm the Sparkler. But why don't you understand me?"

"One minute you're shouting for my blood. And the next minute you're—you're pouring port over me."

"Live and let live," shrugged Thorley. "That's my motto. After all, Celia, we *did* live in the same house for six months with a flag of truce between us."

"Yes! But that was only because—" Celia stopped.

"Why *did* you come down tonight, Celia?"

89

"I have an appointment with Dr. Fell."

Thorley looked startled. "You know Dr. Fell?"

"Oh, yes. Very well." Now for the first time Celia's eye met Holden's; an intense awareness sprang between them across that gap, as Celia had seemed last night; but she colored and turned away.

"I think," Celia swallowed, "that everyone here knows everyone else. Except: Mr. Derek Hurst-Gore . . . Sir Donald Holden."

And up went the emotional temperature still higher.

The two men shook hands.

"A pleasure!" declared Mr. Hurst-Gore, flashing his dental smile. Seen at close range, the countenance under the wavy hair seemed older, and harder, and shrewder. "You mustn't mind me, you know; I'm everywhere. An old, old friend of Celia's. We've had some very good times together in the past."

(*You have, have you?*)

"She spoke to me about you just now," continued Mr. Hurst-Gore, cordially breezy, "when I went up to her room and had a talk with her."

"Indeed."

"I was thinking," pursued Mr. Hurst-Gore, "that meeting you was like meeting some character out of a play. With you playing the Mysterious Stranger."

"Oddly enough," said Holden, "I was just now thinking the same thing about you."

"Were you, my dear fellow? How?"

"With you," said Holden, "playing Mephistopheles to Thorley's Faust."

Mr. Hurst-Gore's eyes narrowed. "That's rather perceptive of you."

"We'll try to be perspective, won't we? In a murder case?"

"Oh, that!" Mr. Hurst-Gore dismissed it with a really friendly laugh. "We'll soon explode all that nonsense, about suicide and murder too, when Dr. Fell looks into it. The birds will sing again. You'll see. In fact, if I may say so in this assembled company . . ."

"Hey!" boomed a thundcrous voice.

It was that of Dr. Fell, who was also rapping the ferrule of his crutch-handled stick against the floor. He loomed above them, turning his head from side to side with a piratical air and vast sniffs above the bandit's moustache.

"Sir," he said, "I am deeply gratified to hear that the birds will sing again. It also gratifies me (by thunder, it does!) that outward amiability has been restored. We are sitting in a cosy little alcove of hatred, with all drafts blowing. Control it; or we shall get nowhere."

"You were," Celia said, "you were questioning witnesses!"

"There is only one witness I want to question."

"Oh?" demanded Thorley. "And who's that?"

"You, confound it!" said Dr. Fell.

All his piratical air dissolved. He leaned forward, his left elbow on the table.

"Up there," and Dr. Fell slightly raised the crutch-handled stick toward the ceiling, "a woman died. She died by means so well-contrived that under the circumstances (I repeat, under the circumstances!) any doctor would have been fooled into calling it a natural death. We are now immediately underneath the bathroom where a bottle of poison was, or was not, in the medicine cabinet."

"It was!" cried Celia.

"It was not," Thorley said smoothly.

Dr. Fell paid no attention to this.

"For nearly three mortal hours—between half-past eleven, when you all went to bed; and a quarter-past two, when Dr. Shepton arrived for the first time—Mr. Marsh was apparently the only person who saw his wife, touched her, went near her, or was even within calling distance of her.

"If he tells the truth, we can reconstruct what happened. But, if, as seems likely, the gifted Mr. Hurst-Gore has persuaded him to keep silent . . ."

While Mr. Hurst-Gore uttered an astounded protest, Thorley came quickly around from behind Celia's chair and stood in front of the table.

"I promised to tell you what happened that night," he declared. "And, so help me, I will!"

"Excellent! Admirable!" observed Dr. Fell. With one elbow on the table, he pointed a finger at Thorley. "Now picture the scene again. The four of you arrived back from the Lockes'. What happened then?"

"Well, we went up to bed . . ."

"No, no, no!" groaned Dr. Fell, making a hideous face and snapping his fingers. "Please be more detailed than that. Presumably you didn't just open the front door and rush frantically upstairs?"

"Celia did, anyway. I think the Murder game upset her. I didn't care for it much myself, to tell you the truth."

"But the rest of you?"

"Margot and Derek and I came through this gallery here,"

Thorley moved his neck, "and up those little steps to the Blue Drawing Room. There was a big fire there, and a decanter of whisky. The—the room was decorated with holly, but we weren't going to put up the Christmas tree until next day."

Very distinctly, beyond the lamp-lit table between Thorley and Dr. Fell, Holden could see the faces of the others.

Of Sir Danvers Locke, aloof yet intensely watchful. Of Doris, flushed as though she were choking, so upset by recent experience that she could not have spoken if she had wanted to. Of Derek Hurst-Gore, lounging against the window wall beside him. And, above all, of Celia.

What in Satan's name was wrong with Celia? Why had she refused to see him? Why, even now, did she refuse to look at him? Why did there breathe from her, with that radiation which in one we love we can almost feel with a physical sense, the message of, "Keep away! Please keep away!"

And yet . . .

Something was being woven, something being spun, as Dr. Fell held Thorley fascinated. The spectral image built itself up: of Caswall's galleries dark and gusty cold, of dead Margot in her silver gown, and her two companions in white ties and tails, going up to a bright fire in a blue-paneled room where there would be a decanter of whisky.

"Yes, Mr. Marsh? And then?"

"I turned on the radio. It was singing carols."

"A very important question; and oblige me by not laughing at it. Were you drunk?"

"No! All of us were only . . . oh, all right! Yes! I was pretty tight."

"How tight?"

"Not blind, or anything like that. But muzzy eyed, and uncertain, and hating everything. Liquor," said Thorley in a vague way, "always used to make me feel happy. It never does, now."

"What about your wife? That night, I mean?"

"Margot'd knocked back quite a lot; but it didn't seem to affect her much, as it usually does. I mean—as it usually did."

"And Mr. Hurst-Gore?"

"Old Derek was pretty nearly blind. He started reciting Hamlet, or something. I remember he said he hoped there wouldn't be a fire in the night, because nobody would be able to wake him."

"And then?"

"There wasn't anything. Margot banged down her glass

and said, 'You two don't seem very happy; but *I'm* happy. Shall we turn in?' So we did."

"The bedrooms occupied by Celia Devereux and Mr. Hurst-Gore, I understand, weren't near your own suite?"

"No. They were at the other side of the house."

"Do you remember anything else about this time?" Dr. Fell's big voice grew even softer and more hypnotic. "Think! Think! Think!"

"I remember hearing Obey locking up front and back. It makes a devil of a racket with those bolts."

"Nothing else? When you and your wife reached your rooms? What then?"

"Margot opened the door of her bedroom and went in. I opened the door of my bedroom and went in. That's all."

"Did you exchange any words at this time?"

"No, no, no! Not a word!"

Thorley was not merely telling this; he was reliving it. He was treading the misty steps of that night, his eyes fixed on it.

"And then?"

"I felt lousy," Thorley said. "It infuriates you, getting out of evening kit when you're tight. You have to tear the collar off; you have to tear the shirt off. You stumble against things. I got my pyjamas on and sort of stumbled into the bathroom to clean my teeth."

"Into the bathroom. Was the door to your wife's bedroom, on the other side of the bathroom, open or closed?"

"It was closed and locked on her side."

"How do you know it was locked?"

"It always was."

"You cleaned your teeth. And then?"

"I went back into my bedroom and slammed the door and went to bed. But that's the trouble. I wasn't tight enough."

"Go on!"

"It wasn't one of those nights where the bed swings around and you fly out into nowhere: dead asleep. I just dozed heavily, and partly woke up, and dozed again. All confused. But I must have fallen off pretty heavily, because there seemed to be an interval. Then something woke me."

"What woke you? Think! Was it noise?"

"I don't know." Thorley, in a dream, shook his head. "Then I thought I heard Margot's voice, sort of moaning and groaning and calling for help a long way off."

"Go on."

"I sat up and switched on the light. I felt sick and head-achy but a good deal more sober. It was two o'clock by the bedside clock. The voice moaning—it was awful. I climbed out of bed and went over and opened the bathroom door."

(Not a soul in that window embrasure moved, or even seemed to breathe.)

"Was the light on in the bathroom?"

"No, but I turned it on. The door to Margot's bedroom was wide open. Oh, yes! And while I'd been asleep, Margot'd taken a bath."

"She'd taken a *bath?*"

"Yes. There was a towel across the edge of the tub, and the floor was wet. God, how it annoyed me: that wet floor, and me in my bare feet! I went back and got my slippers, and came in again. Everything seemed quiet. I looked into Margot's bedroom."

Not a muscle or a fold of flesh moved in Dr. Fell's face or body. His propped elbow and pointing hand remained steady. Yet his eyes flashed round; moved with an unnerving furtive air, as though he were remembering and summing up. But the spell remained unbroken. Both their voices grew thicker, as Thorley walked back further and further into that night.

"I looked into her bedroom. The light wasn't on, but I could tell she wasn't there."

"Were the curtains drawn?"

"No; that's how I could tell she wasn't there. There was a little light from outside, stars or something. The bedspread was smooth and hadn't been touched. It was all quiet, and as cold as hell. Then the moaning and crying started again, so loud it nearly made me jump out of my skin. I saw the line of light under the door to her sitting room."

"Go on!"

Thorley spoke loudly and quickly.

"I opened the door. It was warm in there, with a fire still burning in the grate. All the wall lamps were burning too. A little way back from the middle of the room, with a table beside it, there's one of those chaise-longue things with cushions."

"Go on!"

"Margot was lying on it on her back, only a bit sideways. Her mouth sort of jabbered. I said, 'Margot!' but she just moaned and twisted; her eyes didn't open. I hoisted up her shoulders against the back of the chaise longue—she wasn't any lightweight—and her head fell forward. I shook her, but

94

that wasn't any good either. Then I was really scared. I rushed back into the bathroom."

"Was the poison bottle in the medicine cabinet at that time?"

"No, it was gone. Margot must have . . ."

Dead silence.

Thorley realized what he had said. His voice stopped in midflight, faltered, slowly repeated, "must—have," and then trailed away. He stood there, shocked awake but petrified, his dark eyes glazed.

Dr. Fell let his arm fall on the table.

"So we perceive," Dr. Fell remarked, without satisfaction or even without any inflection at all, "that there had been in that cabinet a small brown bottle labeled POISON. Just as Miss Devereux said."

Still nobody moved. On that group around the table, one of whom at least had been holding his breath until he felt suffocated, remained a strange and terrifying numbness. They seemed in a void, among the portraits of the Long Gallery.

"That was a trick," Thorley said. His voice rose. "A dirty, filthy trick!"

"No," returned Dr. Fell.

He laid down his crutch-handled stick across the glass top of the table.

"Sir," continued Dr. Fell, "I had reasons of my own for looking on you with an eye of extreme suspicion. If you had known of that brown bottle in the medicine cabinet, your first impulse at finding your wife in a dying condition would have been to rush back and look for the bottle. I—harrumph—merely led you to it. You follow me?"

Danvers Locke, elegant and aloof, rose to his feet.

"It's getting rather late," he observed. "I think, Doris, we had better go."

Celia was standing up, her eyes glistening with tears.

"I'm not going to crow over you, Thorley," she said. "But don't you ever, ever, ever, as long as you live, go about telling people I'm insane." Celia's whole manner changed. She looked at Holden, trying to keep her face straight against the tears, and held out her hands to him.

"Darling!" Celia said. Then he was beside her, gripping her hands tightly enough to hurt, looking down at her eyes as he had looked last night, under the trees beside the park.

"Listen, for God's sake," shouted Thorley.

There was so much pleading urgency in it that they swung round in spite of themselves.

"I want to answer that," gritted Thorley. "I've got a right to answer it." He swallowed. "It's true I did lie about that one little point, yes! But I thought it was for a good reason. I . . ."

" 'That one little point?' " echoed Holden. He could not even hate Thorley now; he could only regard the man with awe. "You know, Thorley, you're a beauty! You really are a beauty! You told the truth about everything else, I suppose?"

"Yes, I did!"

"It won't do, Thorley. You've been maintaining it was a delusion of Celia's that Margot changed her gown in the middle of the night, and put on a black velvet dress instead of the silver one. Whereas there's a witness to prove that's exactly what Margot did."

"Oh?" inquired Thorley coolly. "You think you're getting smart, like all the rest of them. And who's the perjurer who says that?"

"Your strongest supporter. Doris Locke."

Doris let out a cry. Her father immediately and blandly stepped in front of her chair, as though to shield Doris even from their sight.

"I think, Doris, we had really better be going."

Along the gallery had creaked the footsteps of Obey, Obey in a hurry, yet so deftly did she move, leaning over and whispering earnestly to Dr. Fell, that they were not conscious of her presence until Dr. Fell uttered an exclamation and surged to his feet, thrusting the long envelope into his pocket.

"O Lord! Oh Bacchus!" muttered Dr. Fell. "The appointment! I had completely forgotten. I sincerely trust the sexton is drunk. Er—my dear Holden!"

"Yes?"

Dr. Fell, completely scatterbrained now that he was not concentrating on anything, blinked round him in distress.

"My corporeal shape, while perhaps majestic," he said, "is not altogether suitable for bending and touching the floor. In some mysterious manner," he fumbled at his eyeglasses, "my hat and my other cane seem to have fallen off the table. If you wouldn't mind? . . . Ah! Thank 'ee. Yes. That's better! Let me remind you that we have an urgent appointment."

And he lumbered out of the embrasure, supporting himself on two canes. It was so unexpected, it left them so much in mid-air, that even Locke spoke in protest.

"Dr. Fell!"

"Hey?"

"May I ask," inquired Locke in a voice brittle with anger, "whether this inquiry is énded?"

"Ended. H'mf. Well. Not precisely *ended.*" Dr. Fell shook his head. "But I think, you know, the situation is fairly clear."

"Clear!" said Locke. "In some respects, yes. You said you could solve our problem, and to a great extent I think you have. What do you propose to do?"

"Do?"

"Our friend Marsh here," stated Locke, "has been caught in at least one flat lie of utterly damning quality. Must I repeat the rest of the tag about *falsus in uno?* What do you propose to do?"

"Do?" again repeated Dr. Fell, with sudden ferocity. "God bless the police, what can I do? The man's quite innocent."

Holden felt, not for the first time in this affair or yet the last, that his wits were turning upside down.

"Innocent?" said Locke. "Innocent of what?"

"Mr. Marsh," replied Dr. Fell, "never mistreated or abused his wife in any way. He didn't drive her to suicide. And he didn't kill her."

Celia's hands, in Holden's, had first tightened and then gone limp. She snatched her hands away, and pressed them over her face. Celia began to rock back and forth, soundlessly, while he gripped her shoulders and tried to steady her.

Then occurred something which was almost worse. Across the face of Mr. Dereck Hurst-Gore, who had been lounging there almost unnoticed, moved an airy and serene smile. He glanced at Thorley, and the glance said as plainly as print: You see? Didn't I tell you there'd be no trouble? *I* arranged this.

"Dr. Fell," said Holden, "are you trying to maintain, in spite of all the evidence, that Celia isn't—isn't in her right senses?"

"Great Scott, *No!*" thundered Dr. Fell. "Of course she's in her right senses!"

He rapped the ferrules of both canes against the floor. For the first time he looked fully at Celia. In that look, jumbled up, were affection and kindliness and yet disquiet.

"Though Thorley Marsh quite sincerely won't believe it," Dr. Fell said, "there isn't a psychopathic trait in that girl's nature. But I must make sure (curse it, if you could only see!) that she isn't . . ."

"Isn't what?" Locke asked sharply.

"Sir," said Dr. Fell, with an enormous wheeze of breath, "I have an appointment."

And he wheeled around, the great cloak billowing behind him, and lumbered at his ponderous pace toward the steps to the Painted Room.

CHAPTER XI

UNDER the brilliance of a full moon, in a sky without cloud, the south fields in front of Caswall still held a tinge of green-gray.

Donald Holden, hurrying out across the stone bridge, saw some distance ahead of him the figure of Dr. Fell stumping westward toward the tree-lined drive. Beyond that lay another immense meadow, and then the precincts of Caswall Church. Holden raced after him through the long grass.

But Dr. Fell did not hear.

He was completely absorbed, talking to himself aloud in a way which might have made his own sanity suspect, and occasionally flourishing one cane in the air by way of emphasis. Holden caught the end of this address.

"If only he hadn't worn his slippers!" groaned Dr. Fell. The cane flourished again. "Archons of Athens, if only the fellow hadn't worn his slippers!"

"Dr. Fell!"

The shout at last penetrated. Dr. Fell swept around, just under one of the chestnut trees lining the white gravel of the drive. He was now wearing his shovel hat.

"Oh, ah!" he said, peering to recognize Holden. "I—har-rumph—imagined you weren't coming."

"And I wouldn't have come," retorted Holden, "if Celia hadn't begged me to go after you. Seriously, Dr. Fell: you can't get away with it."

"Get away with what?"

Holden nodded toward the house. "There's merry blazes to pay back there!"

"I feared as much," admitted Dr. Fell, adjusting his features with an extremely guilty air. "Are they—er—at each other's throats?"

"No! They're just sitting and looking half-wittedly at each other. That's the point. You can't leave it at that. You've said either too little or too much."

"Bear witness," said Dr. Fell, pointing one cane, "that I tried to get out of there without answering questions. But you were all too upset. I couldn't put you off by spouting mystical hocus-pocus. I had to tell the truth."

"But what is the truth?"

"We-ell . . ."

"Let me see if I understand your position. Thorley Marsh tells a string of whoppers, especially about the two most important points in the case: the poison bottle and the changing of the gown. You then announce that Thorley is guiltless, sweet scented, innocent of everything from wife-beating to murder!"

"But hang it all!" protested Dr. Fell, and screwed up his face hideously. "It was just because he told lies, don't you see, that I knew he was telling the truth."

Holden stared at him.

"Paradox," he said politely, "is doubtless admirable . . ."

"It is not paradox, my dear sir. It is the literal truth."

"Well, take the next bit. You say it's nonsense to think Celia has ever been out of her senses, which is fine and grand. But you instantly qualify it by some—some half-suggestion . . ."

"Dash it all!" said Dr. Fell.

"Then the position is," asked Holden, "that both Celia and Thorley have been telling the truth? And that somehow they've just been misunderstanding each other, all through these bitter months. Is that it?"

Dr. Fell's shovel hat was stuck forward on his head, the eye-glasses faintly gleaming under it by moonlight. He struck at the grass with his right-hand cane.

"Apparently," he assented, "that is it."

"But that's impossible!"

"How so?"

"Those two long statements of Celia and Thorley, covering a period of years and concerning Margot, simply won't reconcile. They're oil and water. They won't mix. Either a person is telling the truth, or he isn't."

"Not necessarily," said Dr. Fell.

"But—!"

"Before too long a time, when I propose to tell you the whole story," said Dr. Fell, "you may have reason to change your mind. In the meantime, we have an errand."

"Yes! And, if you'll forgive my insistence, that's another thing."

"Oh?"

"Dr. Fell, how is it that you know so much more of this affair than you could possibly have learned from any letter of Celia's to Scotland Yard? What sort of game is being played between you and Celia? I'll swear there is one. Did she tell you the story of Margot's death?"

"No!" roared Dr. Fell, and viciously cut at the grass with his cane. "If only she had! Oh, my hat, if only she had!" He lowered his voice, wheezing less noisily. He looked very steadily at Holden. "You may have heard, perhaps, that Celia Devereux has been seeing ghosts?"

"Yes. But Celia doesn't suffer from delusions!"

"Exactly," agreed Dr. Fell. "It was just because she seemed to be seeing ghosts, you understand, that I knew she wasn't suffering from delusions."

Again Holden stared at him.

"Dr. Fell, I'm like Thorley. I'm afraid I can't take it. That's the second paradox in two minutes. But you don't want to hear someone talk like that, and play with words, when you're waiting for the hangman and yet hoping for a reprieve. I'm getting as desperate as Celia."

Dr. Fell pointed with the cane.

"I say to you," he declared, with extraordinary intensity, "that it is neither paradox nor playing with words. You should have realized it, from evidence placed squarely in front of you. And now," he hesitated, "we are going to open the tomb. And—"

"And?"

"It is the one part of this affair," said Dr. Fell, "which really frightens me. Come along."

In silence they walked across the drive, under trees again, and into the west meadow. A little distance away, rising up among oaks and beeches and a few cypresses, was the low square tower of Caswall Church.

In that gray church, ageless now, lay the stone effigy of Sir Walter D'Estreville, in stone chain mail, with his feet resting on a stone lion to show that he had been to the Crusades. When he died, in Palestine, under the Black Cross of the Templars, Lady D'Estreville took the veil to quit this world, and Caswall House became Caswall Abbey. His effigy lay there now, as Caswall did, in memory of the love that dieth not.

And there were other memories, too.

"I, Margot, take thee, Thorley," the husky contralto voice could barely be heard, "to my wedded husband." It rose again, ghostlike. "To have and to hold from this day forward. For better, for worse. For richer, for poorer. In sickness, and in health. Till . . ."

He could see the colors, and hear the organ music.

And, as they approached, there was the little iron fence close along the east side of the church: its gate now hanging open and a little rusty. Beyond was the low square tower, the church door being around at the other side. When you turned to the left past the tower, there was the path where he had met Celia.

On his left, now, the rough west wall with its pointed windows. On his right, arching over, the beech trees which guarded an ill-kept churchyard. The same breath of dry-baked mud and dew-wet grass, touching one's nostrils with even the scent of the past. Moonlight filtered down through the leaves, whose shadows were trembling where no wind seemed to stir.

And it was not only Celia's image. It was all the vastness of time. Dr. Fell, at his elbow, spoke softly.

"What are you thinking?"

" 'But, Mother of God, where are they, then? And where are the snows of yesteryear?' "

There was a silence. The old words seemed to ring softly, gently, in this gentle place.

Dr. Fell nodded without speaking. He led the way past the beeches into a little expanse of unkempt grass where many headstones, some at crooked angles and black-worn by time, stood amid a thickness of cypresses. Westward the churchyard stretched up into a hill; by some illusion of moonlight, there seemed to be fewer gravestones than there were trees.

Holden had a sudden recollection of an Italian churchyard, and of a face over a Luger pistol peering at him around a headstone. But this was swept away. In the flat ground ahead, facing them at the end of a crooked little lane of flat graves raised two or three feet above ground, loomed up a shape he had never noticed before.

It had been built between two cypresses; they did not shade

it, but they threw shadows straight ahead on either side. It was square, of heavy gray stone, squat, with a little pillar on each side of a paneled iron door.

"Is that"—Holden's voice seemed to burst out, against thick silence, before he lowered it to a mutter—"is that . . . ?"

"The new vault? Yes." Dr. Fell breathed ponderously; either from quick walking or from some emotion. "The old one," he added, "is up on that hill there."

"What exactly are we going to do?"

"As soon as my excellent friend Crawford gets here, we are going to unlock and unseal the door."

"Unseal it?"

"Yes. Merely to take one brief look inside. We shall do no more."

"But Mr. Reid! The old vicar! Will he like this?"

"The vicarage," returned Dr. Fell, "is on the other side of that hill. He will not know. As for one Mr. Windlesham, who is supposed to look after these premises, I have every reason to hope that he is now too full of beer to interfere."

"What do you expect to see in the vault?"

Dr. Fell did not answer this.

"Hear now," he said, "my story."

The crooked little alley leading up to the tomb, with its raised graves on either side, was paved with tiny pebbles. Dr. Fell's canes rattled among the pebbles as he sat down on the big flat stone of one of the raised graves. It was just inside the shadow thrown by the cypress on the right-hand side of the vault.

"I am the sport of fates and devilry," observed Dr. Fell, removing his shovel hat and putting it beside him. "At Christmas (yes, last Christmas) I was the guest of Professor Westbury at Chippenham. Two days after Christmas it occurred to me to go over and pay a call on Mrs. Andrew Devereux."

"On . . . ?"

"Yes. On Mammy Two, who had been dead for several years. That," said Dr. Fell bitterly, "is how we kept in touch with our friends during wartime. Unless they had been blitzed or otherwise hurt by some Satan's toy, we imagined them still as healthy as ever.

"With my customary careful presence of mind, I even neglected to send a telegram or any message. I merely hired a car and was driven the few miles to Caswall. In front of the house, among other motorcars, I saw a hearse."

Dr. Fell paused, putting up his hands to his eyes.

"My dear Holden, I didn't know *what* to do. My arrival on a social call seemed a little out of place. I was telling the driver of the car to turn round, when someone ran over the bridge and motioned to me. It was—"

"Celia?"

"Yes."

Again for a moment Dr. Fell pondered in silence.

"Now that girl was in a badly disturbed state of mind. One moment! I don't mean what you are thinking. I merely mean that she was not herself; and it worried me badly.

"She asked me if I would please come inside for a few minutes, on a matter of very vital importance. She further said we must on no account be seen. And we were not seen. She led me in through the back way. She led me through a maze of those short little staircases that connect the galleries, up to an old playroom, or nursery, or something of the sort, on the top floor."

A light wind, sweeping up from the south, set rippling the grass in the churchyard and made a dry scratching sound among cypresses. There was a brief rain of shadows until the wind died. What alarmed Holden most was the evident disquiet of Dr. Fell, who kept glancing round at the door of the new vault as though he half-expected to see something come out.

The devil of it was, perhaps something would.

"That playroom, yes," Holden muttered. "Celia mentioned it last night. Anyway, did she tell you anything about . . . ?"

"The circumstances of her sister's death?"

"Yes!"

"She told me very little," grunted Dr. Fell. "And we can see now why she didn't. On Christmas Day she had gone to Dr. Shepton and poured out her whole story. And Shepton, a trusted old friend, dismissed her very kindly and gently as a psychopathic case." Dr. Fell added, very quietly: "Curse him."

All Holden's nerves throbbed in agreement with this.

"Dr. Fell, have you seen Shepton?"

"Yes."

"Do you think he's crooked? Or a fool?"

Dr. Fell shook his head.

"The man," he answered, "is neither crooked nor a fool. He is merely very obstinate and very closemouthed; so infernally closemouthed, in fact, that . . ."

"Yes? Go on!"

"That," said Dr. Fell, with subdued violence, "he has nearly wrecked half a dozen lives."

"But you were saying? About Celia?"

"She told me," replied Dr. Fell, lowering his head, "that her sister's funeral was that afternoon. She begged me, implored me, pleaded with me to help her with something. I—er—hardly needed to tell the young lady," said Dr. Fell with a guilty air, "that if it would help her in any way she could have the shirt off my back.

"She pointed out that we should not be doing anything against the law. That we should not be hurting anybody, or interfering with anything. She even added, with a kind of naïveté which troubled me much as it touched me, that it wouldn't even be dark and we needn't be afraid. In short . . ."

"Please let me tell him, Dr. Fell," interposed Celia's voice.

Again the wind came rustling and seething across the churchyard. Celia had not come up the path from the church. She had taken a shorter cut, from the north side. They saw her stumbling among gravestones, catching at them to steady herself, among flying shadows.

Celia reached Dr. Fell's side. She looked at Holden, looked at the vault, and faltered.

"Dr. Fell," Celia said, "couldn't we call it off?"

For a long time Dr. Fell stared at the ground.

"Why should you want to call it off, my dear?"

"I was frightfully nervous." Again Celia looked at Holden, and smiled uncertainly. "I—I may have been dreaming."

"My dear," began Dr. Fell, and started to fire up again. "We could have forgotten all about it, yes, if only you hadn't written that letter to the police. In it you stressed evidence, direct evidence, which would be found if you and I opened the vault tonight."

(Exactly, Holden thought, what Celia had told Dr. Shepton last night in that playground. But there had been no mention of a vault.)

Celia, drawing a deep breath, went up to him. Her eyes searched his face, intently and questioningly.

"I couldn't tell you, Don," she said. "I couldn't! That's what's been worrying me all day; that's why I couldn't see you. But I want you to listen now. And don't laugh at me. Call me mad, if you like. Only: please don't laugh at me."

"Of course I won't laugh at you."

"Two days after Christmas, when Margot was—put in that place," she swung her head round, the soft brown hair flying, to look at the vault, and turned back again, "Dr. Fell and I attended to certain things.

"After the funeral was over, and everybody had left the churchyard, we came here just about dusk. I had the key of the vault; it was supposed to be Thorley's key, but I knew where he kept it. Call me a beast if you like, but don't laugh at me.

"Dr. Fell and I unlocked the vault. After we'd—we'd attended to something inside, we shut it up again and locked it. Then Dr. Fell was to do what I'd asked him. He was to seal up the lock, with modeling clay pressed through the keyhole until it was filled. He was to stamp that clay with some private seal or mark of his own, so he'd know it. Then . . ."

"Go on, Celia."

"Then," answered Celia, "he was to go away, with both the key and the seal, and not speak about it until I wrote to him. And that's what he did."

Abruptly Celia turned away, stamping her foot on the ground.

"I can't think now what made me do it," she said. "I must have been distracted. Anyway, that's what we did."

"But why did you do it?"

"Because of what happened in the Long Gallery," said Celia, "on the night after Margot died."

Still she would not look at him.

But, as though needing someone near her, she sat down beside Dr. Fell. Surprisingly, Celia did not seem at all frightened. She looked merely resolute, her chin up and a fixity of conviction in her eyes. She was just inside the shadow of the right-hand cypress: sideways to the vault, in the little crooked path of pebbles, and perhaps twenty feet from its door.

"It started as a dream," Celia said. "I knew that, as you always do, and I admit it.

"It was Christmas Eve, remember, though not exactly the sort of Christmas we had planned. Margot was dead, and she had committed suicide, and before our generation that was thought to be a fearful sin. And I was in bed, asleep, on Christmas Eve.

"I dreamed I was in the Long Gallery, standing on the lowest step down from the Blue Drawing Room, looking straight along the gallery from the north end. It was all dark, except for bright starlight. Then I realized, in my dream, that there was not a stick or shred of furniture in the gallery. On my right ran the bare wall where the portraits ought to have been. On my left was the wall with the three oriel windows, and the stars outside.

"I wondered, with that sense of being in both the present and the past at once, whether the gallery had been cleared for the old Christmas dances and games. And then, far away from me, by the third oriel window, I saw half of a white face.

"It was the side half, with the eye wide open. I saw a curve of hair out to the cheekbone, and a high uniform collar, and part of a red coat. And I thought: Why, that's the portrait of Lieutenant General Devereux, who died at Waterloo!

"And then . . .

"Something gave me a shock and a start, with a gasp in it, and a sensation of cold all over. Then I realized I was awake. Dazed and frightened, but awake.

"I was in the Long Gallery. I was standing on that lowest step, in blackness and starlight, after all. It was bitterly cold, because I had nothing on but my nightgown. I could feel the rough carpet of the step under my feet, and my heart beating to suffocation. I reached out and touched the side of the arch around the stairs. It was real.

"Then I looked down the gallery again.

"And the real house, all quiet and shadowy, it was looking at me. Something seemed to close up my throat, like fingers, when I saw that. I looked again, and it wasn't alone. There were others standing near it. They were the faces and figures that should have been in the portraits, but with one difference.

"The first horror was that they were all hatefully angry. I could feel that anger flowing toward me: dumb, dull, passive, yet still an anger. It filled the gallery with hatred. That was when, very slowly, they began moving toward me. The next horror was that, as they approached, I could see how each one of them had died.

"Those who died peaceful deaths had their eyes closed, like great dumb images. Those who died violent deaths had their eyes wide open, with a ring of white round the iris. I saw Madame Rambouillet with her wired ringlets, all bloated from dropsy; and Justin Devereux, in a starched ruff, with the dagger wound in his side.

"They were real. They had bodies. They could touch you. Past one window they came, and then another window, throwing shadows. But still I couldn't move. It was when the wave of them seemed to get higher and higher, and I could catch the gleam of a silver shoe buckle, I knew that their anger was not directed toward me at all. It was directed toward someone, a woman, crouching and cowering behind me, trying to shield herself.

"And all the time these dead things were speaking together, or whispering. First dry and rustling, then hatefully muffled like voices through cloth; but louder and louder, over and over, dinning and repeating, the same whispery three words. General Devereux, with the two bullet holes in his face, reached out and took my wrist to push me aside.

"And all the time those voices, paying no attention to me, went on with their refrain:

" 'Cast her out! Cast her out! Cast her out!' "

CHAPTER XII

CELIA's voice rose up wildly on those last words, and then trailed away. She sat there, just inside shadow, so that Holden could not read her expression. Her laughter, clear and ringing, rose up in the grass-scented churchyard.

"Stop that!" Holden said sharply.

"Stop what?"

"Stop laughing!"

"I'm s-sorry. But aren't you glad, Don, I didn't tell you this story last night?"

"What—happened after that? In the gallery?"

"I don't know. Obey found me lying there at daybreak on Christmas morning. She swore I'd die of pneumonia, and raved, and tried to pack me into bed with three or four hot-water bottles. But it didn't trouble me. I'm not sensitive to cold, as poor Margot was."

(At her side Dr. Fell made a short, slight movement.)

"Celia." Holden cleared his throat.

"Yes, Don?"

"You know, of course, that you dreamed all this?"

"Did I?" asked Celia. She edged sideways into the moonlight. The extraordinary glitter of her eyes, the set of her mouth, contrasted with the soft face. "They were real. They had bodies. I saw them."

"Do you remember last night, Celia? Dr. Shepton? I'd hate to agree with one single word Shepton said . . ."

"I don't blame you for agreeing, Don." Celia turned her face away. "It's only natural. I'm ma—"

"No. It was a quite ordinary nightmare. I've had some myself that were as bad or worse." (Lord, he prayed, let me handle this properly!) "But it was inspired, as Shepton suggested, by that thrice-damnable Murder game in masks."

"Don! Please!"

"You're intelligent, Celia. Use your wits on this. The very faces in your nightmare suggest masks. Now think of the voices, 'muffled like voices through cloth.' My darling, listen! That's exactly how voices sound when they speak inside masks, as you heard them all through the questioning of the Murder game."

"Don, I . . ."

"Let me appeal to Dr. Fell. What do you say, Dr. Fell?"

"I say," replied Dr. Fell, in a slow and ponderous voice, "that we had better settle this."

"Settle it?"

"By opening the vault now," said Dr. Fell. One of his canes fell to the ground with a clatter as he hoisted himself up on the other.

"But what in Satan's name do you expect to . . . ?"

"I was supposed," Dr. Fell swept this aside, "to wait for Inspector Crawford. He phoned that he was on his way, which was the message conveyed to me by Miss Obey. But (hurrum!) he is very late. I think we shall proceed without him."

A new voice interposed:

"*Just a minute, sir.*" They all jumped, and it seemed to Holden that Dr. Fell muttered something under his breath.

Up the pebbled path came tramping, rather out of breath, a hardy middle-aged man in old tweeds and a soft hat. The only feature of him now distinguishable was a remarkable moustache, which by daylight might have been anything from sandy to red. But he did not like this churchyard. He did not like it at all.

The newcomer gave Dr. Fell something between a touch of the hat and a formal salute.

"Had a puncture on my bike," he said. "Delayed. Sorry." Then he drew himself up. "What I want to know, sir, is this. Am I here officially, or unofficially?"

"At the moment," said Dr. Fell, "unofficially."

"Ah!" A breath of relief was expelled under the formidable

moustache. "Mind, not that we're doing anything exactly *illegal*. But I thought I'd better wear plain clothes."

Dr. Fell introduced his companions to Inspector Crawford of the Wiltshire County Constabulary.

"Have you," asked Dr. Fell, "got the necessaries?"

"Torch, knife, and magnifying glass," returned Inspector Crawford, slapping two pockets briskly. "All present and correct, sir." But definitely he did not like his surroundings. They saw his eyes move.

"In that case," said Dr. Fell, "will you please examine what I have here?"

Fumbling inside his cloak, fiercely concentrating to remember the right pockets, Dr. Fell produced first an electric torch and then a small wash-leather bag tied at the mouth with a cord. He handed the bag to Inspector Crawford.

By the light of Dr. Fell's torch, a small dazzle under cypress shadow and the loom of the vault behind them, Crawford opened the bag and turned out in his palm a heavy gold ring whose seal Holden could not see; it was turned the other way.

"Well, Inspector?" demanded Dr. Fell.

"Well, sir, it's a ring." The other peered at it more closely. "Bit of an odd seal. More intricate, like, than I ever saw. And this thing on the lower part, like a woman asleep . . ."

"Intricate!" roared Dr. Fell. "Saints and devils!" They all shied back.

"Easy, sir!" muttered Inspector Crawford. His moustache, in the light, was fiery red.

"I beg your pardon," also muttered Dr. Fell, guiltily hunching his chins down into his cloak. "But I *would*, at Christmas, be visiting a noted collector. I *would*, with graceful presence of mind, drop that infernal ring into my pocket and forget it completely. I would have it in my pocket when— never mind!"

Again he pointed with the light from the torch.

"The ring, Inspector, was cut for Prince Metternich of Austria. You may take my word for it, or Professor Westbury's, that there isn't another like it in existence."

"Ah!" said Inspector Crawford.

"It was designed, during the days of Metternich's Black Cabinet, so that the impression of the seal couldn't be copied or forged or replaced once it had been stamped on a soft surface. For reasons I needn't go into now, you may take replacement as out of the question."

Dr. Fell now sent the beam of the torch wheeling round to the vault between the cypresses.

"On December twenty-seventh, Inspector, I locked that door. I filled the lock with plasticine, the sort you buy at Woolworth's. I sealed it with the ring. This afternoon I convinced myself that the seal hadn't been touched or tampered with since. Will you go and convince yourself too?"

Inspector Crawford squared his shoulders.

"I'm a fingerprint man," he said. "This is my meat."

And, a little uncertainly, they all moved toward the tomb.

They could now see that the little pillars on each side of the door, instead of being stone like the rest of the vault, were of mottled marble. Against the heavy inner door, painted gray, the gray seal of the lock would have gone unnoticed by any visitor to the cemetery. While Dr. Fell held the light, Inspector Crawford stooped down, put the ring beside the seal with his left hand, and with his right hand held a magnifying glass over both.

Holden darted a glance at Celia.

Celia, her head slightly lowered, was breathing in short and quick gasps. Instinctively she reached out and found his arm; but she hardly seemed conscious she was doing so.

Silence.

For ten mortal minutes Inspector Crawford hunched there while he compared those seals, moving only to ease cramped muscles and never moving his head. A small pattern of night noises crept out: the scuttling of an animal in the grass. Once Celia broke the silence.

"Can't you . . . ?"

"Easy, miss! Mustn't rush this!"

Momentarily Dr. Fell's light swept around as the Inspector spoke. That expression in Celia's eyes, Holden thought: where had he seen it? It reminded him of something. Where *had* he seen it before? The light swung back again.

"Right you are, sir," declared Crawford, straightening up and abruptly moving back from the door as though he loathed it. "That's the original seal. Take my oath!"

"Would you also take your oath," asked Dr. Fell, "that this vault is solidly built?"

"Not much doubt that, sir," retorted Crawford, handing him back the ring and the wash-leather bag.

"You're quite sure?"

"I was up here once or twice," said Crawford, "when Bert

Farmer was building it. Walls eighteen inch thick. Stone floor. No vents or windows."

"Then if anything has happened," said Dr. Fell, "it must have been caused by persons or things inside?"

"Happened?" repeated Inspector Crawford.

"Yes."

"Come off it, sir!" said Crawford, with sudden loudness. "What *could* happen, among a lot of deaders?"

"Possibly nothing. Perhaps much. Cut the clay out of that lock and we'll see."

"Can't you *hurry?*" cried Celia.

"Easy, miss!"

The beams of two torches were now fixed on that door as Crawford went to work with a sharp knife.

Holden had to admit to himself, in honesty, that he was now more nervous than at any time in fifteen months. No, far longer than that! At the end of the war, theoretically, you could forget your impulse to dodge into the nearest doorway at sight of any policeman. With him the feeling had lasted much longer.

If only he could remember (his thoughts ran on while Crawford's knife scraped and scraped) where he had seen that expression on Celia's face, and what it meant! It was associated with some risky business. It was associated with . . .

"I only hope the key will work," Crawford kept muttering. "I only hope the key will work, that's all *I* hope. This clay stuff sets hard. But it's a very big keyhole; ought to be a simple lock. Got the key, sir? Ah! Thanks. Steady."

There was the heavy, clean click of a new lock as the key turned.

"All right," grunted Dr. Fell. "The door swings inward. Shove her open!"

"Sir. Listen." Crawford's red moustache turned slightly. "Do you honest-to-God think something's going to come out of there?"

"No! no! Certainly not! Shove her open!"

"Right you are, sir."

The door creaked and squealed. Celia deliberately turned her back.

Now the beams of two electric torches were directed inside. They remained steady for perhaps two seconds, which seemed two minutes. Slowly they began to move. Down, up, across . . .

Inspector Crawford uttered a ringing expletive which burst

out in that quiet place. The hand which held his torch was quite steady. But he had his left shoulder pressed to the side of the doorway as though he were trying to push the wall in. The red moustache bristled as he turned his head toward Dr. Fell.

"Those coffins have been moved," he said. "They've been moved."

" 'Flung,' " said Dr. Fell, "would be a more descriptive word. Flung as though by hands of such abnormal power that . . . Inspector!"

"Yes, sir?"

"When I locked and sealed that door, there were four coffins in the tomb. One was that of Mrs. Thorley Marsh. The other three had been brought down from the old vault to," Dr. Fell cleared his throat, "to keep her company. They were resting on the floor, in two piles, one on top of the other, in the middle of the vault. Now look at them!"

Celia, shivering, an utter stranger, still kept her back turned. Holden came forward and looked past the others' shoulders.

The vault was not large. It was as bare as a stone jug except for an empty little niche in each side wall. Set perhaps four steps below ground level, it gaped at the lights with an evil sight.

One coffin, of nineteenth century design, stood grotesquely and coquettishly half upright, propped there, against the rear wall. Another—of very new gleaming wood over its lead casing and its inner shell of wood, which could only be Margot's—lay pressed lengthways close against the left-hand wall. The third, an old one, had been flung around so that it lay sideways to the door. Only the fourth, the oldest and most malignant looking of all, rested quiet.

"And now," said Dr. Fell, "look at the floor."

"It's . . ."

"It is sand," said Dr. Fell, rounding his syllables hollowly. "A layer of fine white sand, spread on a stone floor and smoothed out, in my presence, just before the tomb was sealed. Look man! Use your light!"

"I'm doing it, sir."

"The coffins," said Dr. Fell, "have been lifted and thrown about. The sand has been disturbed. But there is not a single footprint in that sand."

Their voices, speaking through the doorway, reverberated and were thrown back at them. Warm moist air breathed out of the vault. It had a sickening effect. The propped, drunken-looking coffin against the back wall, Holden could have sworn, trembled as though precariously balanced.

"This ain't," declared Crawford, and corrected himself instantly, "this isn't possible!" He said it simply, as a reasonable man.

"Apparently not. But there it is."

"You and the young lady," Crawford's eyes flashed round quickly, "did this locking up and sealing up?"

"Yes."

"Why did you do it, sir?"

"To see whether there might be any disturbance like this."

"You mean," Crawford hesitated, "things that aren't alive?"

"Yes."

"Somebody," declared Crawford, "has been up to jiggery-pokery in there!"

"How?"

That one word, like a knockout blow, sufficed. Yet Crawford, after a long pause, recovered doggedly. His keen eyes, over the bristling moustache, grew almost pleading.

"Dr. Fell, you're not fooling me?"

"On my word of honor, I have told you the literal truth."

"But, sir, do you know anything about how modern coffins are built? Do you know how much they *weigh?*"

"I have never," said Dr. Fell, "actually occupied one."

"There's something funny about you." Crawford studied him, the eyes moving. "You look . . . by George," he pounced on it, "you look actually *relieved!* Why, sir? Did you expect something worse than this to happen?"

"Perhaps I did."

Crawford shook his head violently, like a man coming up from under water.

"Besides," he argued, "what's it got to do with you-know-what?" His glance was significant. "It's no concern of ours, I mean the police's, if coffins start dancing about in their tombs. That's God Almighty's concern. Or the devil's. But it's not ours."

"True."

"The superintendent," persisted Crawford, "tells me I'm to take orders from you. He tells me a little about this murdering swine who's been——" Here the Inspector's professional caution stopped him. "Anyway, he tells me something about what you've got up your sleeve. We're after evidence. But look there!"

Straightening up, Crawford thrust his arm deep through the doorway. He sent the beam of the torch slowly playing over the grotesquely sprawled coffins and the sand.

"They're deaders," he went on. "Deaders are no good to us, unless it's for a post-mortem. And that chap," the light fastened on the most malignant-looking coffin, a sixteenth-century one of decaying scrollwork, "that chap looks as though he'd be a good bit past any post-mortem."

"He was Justin Devereux," said Dr. Fell. "He died, in a sword-and-dagger duel at Barne Elms, more than three hundred years before you were born."

A physical chill, like the damp breath out of that tomb, seemed to touch their hearts again.

"Did he?" asked Inspector Crawford. "He won't fight any more duels: that's certain. And that's what I mean. What am I doing here? Why did the super want me to come here? There's no—"

Suddenly Crawford stopped, drawing in his breath. His whole voice and manner changed.

"Look there, sir!"

"What is it?" Dr. Fell spoke sharply.

"I didn't see it before, because I was concentrating on the floor. But look over there! In that left-hand niche in the wall!"

Lying in the niche, dusty and dirty but sending back gleams under the Inspector's torch, was a small brown bottle. It was rounded in shape; it would contain about two ounces. They could just see the edge of a label inscribed in colors. And it was still corked.

"I may not have heard much about this case," Inspector Crawford said grimly, "but I know what *that* is."

CHAPTER XIII

HOLDEN turned round to find Celia.

She was now facing the tomb, but well back and to one side; she would not look into it. All that sense of strangeness had gone.

"Celia dear . . ."

"Can you call me that?" asked Celia in a husky voice. "Can you even care anything at all about me? After tonight?"

"What in the world are you talking about?"

"I'm a beast," muttered Celia. "Oh, I am a beast!"

"Don't talk nonsense!" He took her shoulders and, in the dense shadow of the cypress, he kissed her. It was the same, the same as last night; nothing had changed. "But don't stay here!" he said. "Don't watch this. Go back to the house. It'll only be bad for you if you stay."

"No!" urged Celia. "No. Please. Don't send me away. I have a reason. I—want to look in there now. I have a reason."

Both of them, then, became aware of an ominous silence.

Inspector Crawford and Dr. Fell still stood motionless on either side of the tomb door. Dr. Fell had stepped back, switching off his torch. The Inspector, though he still held the light steadily inside, stared at Dr. Fell with hard intensity. It was as though, curiously, they were duelists.

"Orders, sir?"

"Oh, ah!" Dr. Fell woke up with a snort and gurgle, returning the other's hard stare. "Yes. You'd better go in and fetch the bottle. Or," Dr. Fell added with sudden inexplicable ferocity, "are you afraid of the man who'll never fight another duel?"

"No, sir," returned Crawford with dignity.

"Please go and get it, then."

Celia and Holden watched him.

It was far from a pleasant job for Crawford. Once he had gone gingerly down those few steps, he seemed to feel he was outside the protected circle. He was exposed. He was in an arena, among fanged monsters.

Yet, as his own shoes made clear sharp-printed tracks in the thin layer of sand, he conscientiously stopped to note the fact. His light bobbed and flashed eerily. The beam of Dr. Fell's torch followed him. Searching for other tracks, finding none, Crawford moved toward the left-hand wall. There, in a niche some five feet above the new-gleaming coffin lying flat against the wall, was the brown bottle.

"Keep your light on me, sir." Crawford's voice boomed out of the vault. "I've got to shove my own torch into my pocket when I pick the thing up. Might be fingerprints. Better use two hands, or I may mess it up."

"All right. Steady!"

With his own light out, and only that yellow eye watching him from the door, Crawford nearly lost his nerve. Stretching up his hands, he pressed one hand over the top of the cork and his right forefinger to the underside of the bottle. His foot banged against the new-gleaming coffin, and he lost his balance.

"God!" he said. "This is her own . . ."

"Steady!"

"Right, sir. Got it fast now. Keep the light on the floor ahead of me."

A few seconds more, and he was beside them.

"There she is, sir," said Crawford, a little short of breath and with a trickle of sweat running down his cheekbone. He smiled nonchalantly under the red moustache. "Didn't know the cork was pressed in so tight, or it'd have been easy. Cork won't take prints. See?"

And he wagged the bottle with one hand. Its grimy label was inscribed at the top with the blue letters, Not to be taken, and below with the large red letters, POISON.

Dr. Fell looked very steadily down at Celia.

"Do you understand now, young 'un," he inquired, "why Dr. Shepton didn't believe your story about the bottle?"

"I'm afraid," Celia said helplessly, "I don't understand anything."

"In reply to Shepton's questions, you kept insisting it had a printed label with nothing on it except what we see here. Any genuine printed label, of course, would have had the chemist's name, or the drug-manufacturer's name, and some reference to the nature of the drug. In this case, somebody has merely . . ."

Suddenly Dr. Fell broke off.

"Inspector!"

"Sir?"

"Let me get a closer look at that bottle! Hold it up where I can see it!"

Past the light of Dr. Fell's torch, fixed on the label, appeared a disembodied pink face and one hand feverishly adjusting his eyeglasses.

"But this," he said after a moment, "really is a printed label."

"Ah!" nodded Inspector Crawford. "I was wondering about that, sir."

"It's not drawn or painted. It's printed. Oh, ah. Badly printed, yes. Letters out of alignment. Amateurish. Ama . . ."

The wheezy voice trailed away. Dr. Fell lowered the torch. His eyes retreated into vacancy as his twisted face retreated into gloom.

"I say," he remarked. "Has anybody mentioned (anywhere?) that in the playroom at Caswall there's a toy printing press with three different kinds of colored type?"

"There certainly is," answered Celia. "Though how you knew that is more than I can think. But, Dr. Fell! Please listen! What I wanted to ask you . . ."

"Does Thorley Marsh know about this printing press?"

"Yes! But . . ."

"Might I (harrumph) perhaps see it?"

"At any time you like. But, Dr. Fell! Please! You don't mean," Celia reached out and would have touched the bottle if Crawford had not stopped her, "you don't mean that's *really* it? The—real thing?"

The sheer bewilderment in her voice, the amazement which had been growing for some time, made the others stare.

"Lord, miss," exclaimed Crawford, "what did you expect?"

Celia was taken aback. "I . . ."

"As I understand it, miss, you're the one who's been chasing this bottle. Then, when we find it, you sound as flabbergasted as though it had never existed. What did you expect?"

"I don't know. I spoke stupidly. Please forgive me."

"Inspector," gabbled Dr. Fell with fiery intensity, "the bit of luck here is that the cork is still in the bottle. Even if the stuff was in solution, it's possible traces will remain. Have you got access to a pathologist?"

"In Chippenham?" Crawford's tone rebuked him. "Best in England."

Calling on heaven for a notebook and a pencil, which he possessed himself but couldn't find, Dr. Fell was supplied by Holden with these articles. While Crawford held a light, Dr. Fell wrote two words on a sheet, tore it out, and handed it to the Inspector.

"Now!" he went on excitedly, stuffing Holden's notebook into his own pocket. "Get your pathologist to test for those two ingredients. The first in large quantity, the second in small. If . . ."

Crawford was frowning at the paper.

"But these, sir, are two very well-known poisons! Taken together, would they produce that effect on the poor lady?"

"Yes."

"Dr. Fell," interposed Holden, who could stand it no longer, "what are these infernal poisons? We've heard a lot about them, but nobody's said a word as to the name. I'm fairly well up in such matters myself. What did Margot die of?"

"My dear boy," answered Dr. Fell, rubbing his forehead blankly, "there's nothing mysterious about it. It's quite simple. It's not a new dodge. The poison . . ."

"Listen!" interrupted Crawford. "Out with that light!"

Darkness and moonlight descended.

"There's somebody talking down by the church," whispered Crawford.

"Attend to me!" muttered Dr. Fell. His hand descended heavily on Holden's shoulder. "We must not be interrupted now. And they've got as much right here as we have. Go down and shoo 'em away. Spin any yarn you like; but get rid of 'em. Don't argue! Go!"

Holden went.

Just when he seemed closer to Celia than ever before, just when a glimmer of understanding was about to appear in this business, he was torn away.

But was it a glimmer of understanding?

Moving quickly and softly on the grass margin beside the pebbled path, through the maze of graves and trees, he faced what had to be faced. Inside a stone box, with no entrance except a door whose seal had not been tampered with, someone had executed a *danse macabre* among the coffins yet had left not a footprint in the sand.

The effect not merely puzzled; it stunned. It seemed to leave no loophole. That this was supernatural, supposing such forces to exist, Holden could not believe even when the spell of it was on his wits. Supernatural forces, presumably, do not concern themselves with poison bottles.

Yet how? It was . . .

Recognizing the two voices which were talking beside the church, he stopped softly at the line of beech trees.

In the path beside the church—just as he and Celia had stood in that unforgotten time; just as unhappy as he and Celia had been—stood Doris Locke and Ronnie Merrick.

They stood wide apart, as he and Celia had done. Moonlight filtered down on them through the leaves. Behind them loomed the church wall with its painted windows drained of color. Both had a tendency to stare at the ground and scuffle shoes.

". . . and that," Doris was just concluding a rapid recital, "is everything that's happened tonight. I had to tell somebody or burst."

"Thanks very much for telling me," said Ronnie with powerful Byronic gloom. He kicked at a pebble in the path. Doris stiffened.

"Oh, not at all," she assured him airily. "Anyone would have suited just as well. What have you been doing?"

"Sitting on the roof of the church."

"What's that?"

"Sitting on the roof of the church."

"How very silly of you," said Doris. "Whatever were you doing that for?"

"Perspective. There's always a proper angle to see a thing from. You wouldn't understand professional matters."

"Oh, wouldn't I?" asked Doris in a shivering kind of voice. "How we do give ourselves airs, don't we?" She checked herself. "Ronnie! Which side of the roof were you sitting on? This or the other?"

"The other. Towards Caswall. I thought," said the young man, looking up at the sky with a white face and dark hair falling back from his forehead, "of throwing myself off and killing myself. Only it's not high enough. I've jumped off the damn church too many times.—Why do you want to know?"

"Ronnie, there's something funny going on here tonight!"

"How do you mean, funny?"

"That big fat man, with the stomach and the eyes, said something about an appointment and the sexton. Ronnie, don't you see?" Doris edged closer. "They're going to do a post-mortem on That Woman! Hadn't we better . . . ?"

Holden, who had been about to creep thankfully away in the belief that from these two there would be no interference, stopped dead. That did it! That unquestionably did it. Clearing his throat, he stepped out into the path between them.

"Sir!" exclaimed the young man.

"Don Dismallo!" cried Doris.

The rush of welcome in both their voices, the quickness with which they hurried toward him, touched his heart. To them he was right. He fitted. He could be confided in. At any other time he would have welcomed them. But now, with the clock ticking relentlessly on and something happening up there at the tomb . . .

"Doris," he said, "where's your father?"

"Father," returned Doris, "has gone on home. We took a short cut through here, and met Ronnie. Father said he thought I'd much prefer to walk home with Ronnie, and hurried on." Her voice shivered with disgust. "I thought it was so crude of him."

"Crude!" said Ronnie. "Your father! 'Crude.' Oh, save us!"

But for once Doris would not be diverted.

"Don Dismallo, there is something funny going on, isn't there?"

"Look here," said Holden, "I won't lie to you and say there isn't. But I want you both to go on home." (Mutiny impending!) "I'll walk part of the way with you, if you like. I have something very serious to say to you both."

He hadn't. All his thoughts were concentrated on Celia, and on coffins in the sand. But what he did was the only thing to do.

"Oh," murmured Doris. "We-ell! In that case!"

In sudden and rather furtive silence, with Holden between the two like an itinerant wall, they walked down the path. Southward the drive which led to the church curved back to the main road. By crossing the meadows to the main road again, they could cut off much of the distance to Widestairs.

Still in silence they tramped, through dew-wet meadow grass. It seemed to Holden that he could hear their hearts beating.

"Doris," he began, "you intimated early this evening that you were going to make the fur fly. And I must say you kept your promise."

"I did, didn't I?" asked Doris, between fear and complacence. "Thorley and I had been meaning to get married, sooner or later, ever since we'd been . . . you know."

(Holden gave her a warning look.)

"But tonight," Doris gulped, "I sort of forced the issue."

"Tell me, Doris. What do you think of Thorley Marsh now?"

"I think he's wonderful."

"Ha, ha, ha," said Ronnie, and uttered a long peal of laughter like somebody imitating a ghoul in a radio play. He stopped and appealed to Holden.

"I ask you, sir," he demanded, "if that's not a good one? From what Doris has been telling me, her fat boy friend first walloped his wife and then poisoned her. And she thinks he's wonderful."

"Don Dismallo," said Doris, "will you please tell that offensive person on your left to shut his mouth until I finish speaking?—And, anyway, he *didn't!*"

"Ha, ha, ha," said Ronnie.

"Oi! Easy! Both of you! Come on, now."

The swishing tramp of feet resumed. What was happening now, back at the vault?

"I—I love him," declared Doris. "All the same, I was a bit disappointed with him tonight."

"Why, Doris? (Quiet, Ronnie!) Why?"

"Oh, not over the walloping business! Which he didn't do anyway." Doris's eyes gleamed. "I'd rather have admired him for that."

"Well," said Holden, "of course that's one way of looking at it."

"I shouldn't really mind being knocked about myself now and then. You," said Doris, sticking her head past Holden's shoulder to look at Ronnie, "you wouldn't have the nerve to wallop me, would you?"

"Don't you be too sure of that," said Ronnie, sticking his head over Holden's shoulder to look at Doris.

"Oi! Wait a minute!"

For this wasn't funny. Certainly not to either of them. In the voice of the youth in the sports coat, his face white and twitching, there was a new, dangerous note. Holden had heard it in men's voices before; it meant business.

"You were saying, Doris," he prompted, "that Thorley disappointed you tonight."

"Well! When everybody started questioning him, I expected him to wipe the floor with them. And he didn't. I expected him to be like that man in the film, the Wall Street broker who . . ."

"Film!" echoed Ronnie tragically. "I ask you, sir!"

"Easy, now!"

"You take her to a film," said Ronnie. "And in comes some basket who acts like the Wild Man of Borneo. And she sighs and says, 'How lovely.' In real life," added Ronnie, with contempt, "you'd just tell the servants to sling the basket out of the house."

"Listen to Lord Seagrave's son talking!" sneered Doris.

Now they were over the fence, into the main road. Farther and farther, close to Widestairs, while these two wrangled. The minutes were ticking by; anything might be happening at the vault. Then, just as Holden thought he could decently get away, something Doris said rang a vivid warning bell in his mind.

"What infuriates me so much, you know, is that it's all That Woman's fault. Ronnie!"

"Uh?"

"You remember what I told you a long time ago? About the man that Margot Marsh was so mad about?"

"Distinguished-looking middle-aged bloke? The one Jane Paulton caught her with in that New Bond Street place?"

(*What the devil was this?*)

"Jane didn't see the man face to face," Doris said impatiently. "That's why we don't know who he is. And yet," she pondered, "though I denied it like fury tonight for Thorley's sake, I could sometimes swear Thorley knows who the man was, and for some reason just won't say."

"Well, what about the old geezer?"

"You find that man," Doris announced darkly, "and you'll find who poisoned her."

"Rubbish!"

"Is it?"

"If he was having an affair with her," Ronnie pointed out, "why should he want to bump her off? He'd be enjoying himself, wouldn't he?"

"She got on his nerves," said Doris, "so he killed her. Or maybe it was a married man, and *she* wanted to marry him and he didn't. So he poisoned her."

"Or maybe," retorted Ronnie with heavy sarcasm, "it was somebody in politics, who couldn't afford the scandal. Maybe it was Mr. Attlee."

"I tell you—!"

"Doris!" Holden interrupted softly, but in a tone that could not be mistaken. All three of them stopped in the road.

They had passed the vicarage, and passed the beginning of a tall yew hedge on the right. Ahead loomed the lights of Widestairs, shining against mellow red brick, with the sweep of semi-circular steps which gave the house its name.

"What's all this," asked Holden, "about Margot and 'the New Bond Street place?'" He had long ago begun to formulate a theory about Margot's death. "Don't you understand, Doris, that this may be important evidence? Don't you understand you may be quite right?"

"Oh, dear!" said Doris, appalled. Her reaction was instinctive. "You won't tell on me?"

"Naturally," answered Holden, recognizing the only point that worried her, "I won't say where the information came from."

"Don Dismallo!" She regarded him with a kind of pity. "Celia—Celia never notices anything. She doesn't even guess about Thorley and me. But hasn't *she* told you that a long time ago That Woman started going to a fortune teller in New Bond Street? And that's where she started getting worked up?"

(Yes, Celia had. Visits to a fortune teller, followed by angry rows with Thorley.)

"A fortune teller," he said aloud. "A Madame Somebody-or-other."

"Madame Vanya, 56b New Bond Street. Only there wasn't any Madame Vanya, you see. It was all a gag."

"I beg your pardon?"

"A gag, Don Dismallo! A hoobus-goobus!" Doris stamped her foot. "That's where they met, to avoid scandal, in two rooms dressed up as a fortune-telling place. Nobody would suspect a kind of office. That's how, nowadays, you can—"

Here she glanced quickly at Ronnie, and stopped.

"I mean," Doris gulped, "that's what I'm *told*. I don't *know*. From my own personal experience, that is."

"One last question, Doris." Seeing Ronnie's emotional state, Holden clamped a hand down firmly on the young man's shoulder. "You say you and Thorley—easy, Ronnie!—have always intended to get married?"

"Well . . . I thought so." Sudden misery flooded Doris's eyes.

"And there's good reason to believe, from the evidence, that Margot was in love with this mysterious gentleman. Then why couldn't a compromise have been arranged? After all, divorce is hardly a scandal nowadays."

Doris was back in her fighting mood.

"Thorley felt," she said, "that he—he owed a duty to That Woman. I thought it was too chivalrous. I thought it was *silly*. But there it was. Anyway, she's dead now and it doesn't matter."

"Listen, Doris!"

"Y-yes?"

"I won't presume to advise you. But you might do worse," he shook Ronnie's shoulder, "than what your father wants you to do. In any case, you might think it over."

"Thanks, Don Dismallo. All I know," Doris said violently, "is that if the fortune-telling place in New Bond Street hasn't been taken over by somebody else—which it probably has—you'll find out who poisoned her!"

"How so?"

"That Woman," said Doris, "was the most awful and incessant diary writer I ever did know. She couldn't see a piece of paper without wanting to write soul confessions on it. Or else," added a wildly romancing Doris, "you'll find a chest full of poisons or something. And I hope you do!"

"If you'll excuse me now, Doris . . ."

"Don Dismallo!" She was taken aback. "You can't leave now!"

"I'm sorry, Doris. I can't explain, but it's vitally important."

"I tell you, silly," cried Doris, "you can't rush away like that! This is our *house!*"

"I know; but—"

"You've got to come in and have a drink or something. Look! There's father coming out of the front gate now. He's seen you. You're caught."

And he was.

At Widestairs they gave him a hearty if rather preoccupied welcome. (A grandfather clock in the main hall, where the Murder game had been played, pointed to twenty-five minutes past eleven.) They pressed on him sandwiches and a whisky and soda. (Twenty minutes to twelve.) Lady Locke, a slender handsome woman looking older than Holden remembered, chatted pleasantly under a wall of painted masks. (Two minutes to midnight.) Sir Danvers, explaining in a preoccupied way that he must be off to London tomorrow, displayed some new items in his collection of pictures. (Eighteen minutes past midnight.)

"Good night!" they called at a quarter to one. And Holden, once away from the front door, ran like hell.

All the time he had been mechanically speaking, smiling, accepting, admiring, he had been fitting together the pieces of the puzzle. And he knew now how Margot had been poisoned.

He didn't know who killed her. But he knew how. It fitted together all the inconsistencies. It explained exactly how a murder plot had been devised to look at best like natural death, and at worst like suicide.

"Therefore—!" he said to himself.

He found the churchyard deserted, as he had expected. The iron door of the tomb (it gave him a momentary but bad fit of the creeps, as he thought of what lay inside) the iron door was again locked. He groped his way out of the churchyard, feeling that certain shapes were following him.

Even Caswall Moat House, as he saw when he raced across the fields, showed no light except a dim yellow glimmer through the tall windows of the great hall. He pushed open the front door. He found Obey, sitting by the fireplace in that big white-stone cavern, patiently waiting to lock up. Obey rose at him.

"Mr. Don!"

He steadied himself, panting, to get his breath.

"They've all gone, I suppose?" he asked through gasps.

"Yes, Mr. Don. And Miss Celia and Mr. Thorley have gone to bed."

"But some other damned thing has happened, hasn't it? I can see by your face! What is it?"

"Sir, it's Miss Celia."

"What about her?"

"Miss Celia and that big stout gentleman, Dr. Fell, came back here about an hour ago . . ."

"Was there a police inspector with them?"

"Police inspector?" exclaimed Obey, pressing her ample bosom. "Oh, *no!*"

"Yes? What happened?"

"First they went up to the old playroom. I knew I shouldn't 'a' followed 'em, Mr. Don, but I couldn't help it."

"Of course you couldn't, Obey. Go on."

"Well, then they went to what used to be Miss Margot's and Mr. Thorley's rooms. Mr. Thorley won't sleep in his old room now; not that I blame him. Anyway," Obey swallowed, "they started rummaging about in the rooms, mostly Miss Margot's old sitting room. I couldn't hear what they were saying, because both doors was closed. But it seemed all quiet.

"And then," her voice rose, "just before the stout gentleman goes back to the Warrior's Arms in the village, he starts talking to her low and soft. And *gentle*, you'd have said. In the sitting room.

"All of a sudden the door to the passage opens. Miss Celia comes out as white as a sheet—I'm telling you!—with the stout gentleman looking not much less upset than she was. Miss Celia didn't even see me when I was standing there. She could hardly walk when she went to her room."

Again Obey swallowed hard, composing herself.

"But don't worry, Mr. Don," she added consolingly. "You just sleep well."

CHAPTER XIV

Aɴᴅ it was Obey, too, whom he first saw when he opened his eyes on the morning of Friday, July twelfth.

They had put him in his old room, which he used to occupy at Caswall, at the southwest corner upstairs. Its giant Tudor bed, of carved oak with legs supporting a carved wooden canopy, would have suited Dr. Fell himself. First Holden became conscious of warmth, even though the strong sun was on the other side of the house; then a rattle, against his door, of dishes on a tray.

"I thought I'd better bring your breakfast up, Mr. Don," Obey panted apologetically. "It's past eleven. I didn't like to disturb you with tea."

Holden, irritated, sat up wild-eyed.

"No! Hang it! Look here!"

"Is anything wrong, Mr. Don?"

"You and Cook the only people to work the whole house, and you bring up breakfast! Why can't Thorley——?" He checked himself.

Obey carefully handed him the tray, which included two boiled eggs.

"If you only knew, Mr. Don," Obey said, "what a pleasure it is."

"Anyway, thanks. Is," he shook his head to clear it, "is Miss Celia up and about yet?"

"No." Obey eyed the floor. "But the big stout gentleman is. He's——he's in that playroom. He says, please, would you go there and see him as soon as you have your breakfast and get dressed?"

Holden, though uneasy, had no real premonition of disaster. But in the playroom some half an hour afterward, with a bath and shave to cool his head, he encountered something more than that.

The playroom, which he had some difficulty in finding, was on the same side of the house. It was hot and yet dusky, a long room with two tall but narrow windows in the long side facing west, and a fireplace between the windows. An old wire fire screen still guarded the rusty grate. The baseboards and lower parts of the walls were still scuffed and kicked except where two large wardrobes had once stood, filled with dolls and games, and the coconut matting was blackly worn.

Two large doll houses, with one or two of their occupants hanging in an intoxicated condition out of the windows, had been pushed away into one corner. In another corner stood a dappled rocking horse which still retained its tail. Yet over everything lay a film of dust, disturbed dust, which added to the dimness of the room.

Dr. Fell, who had discarded his hat and cloak, sat by the fireplace in an armchair once sacred to Obey. From one corner of the doctor's mouth hung a curved meerschaum pipe, long ago gone out. He had got hold of a large rubber ball, once colored red, which with grave absorption he was bouncing on the floor.

He stopped bouncing the ball as Holden entered.

"Sir," said Dr. Fell, taking the pipe out of his mouth as well, "good morning."

"Good morning. I'm up a bit late, I'm afraid. And last night I was . . ."

"Delayed? So I understand."

Dr. Fell scowled very intently at the rubber ball.

"I, on the other hand," he went on, "performed the incredible feat of getting up at eight o'clock. I have gone to Widestairs. I have had interviews with several persons there." He looked up. "I have also had a report from the police."

That glance should have conveyed a warning across the hot, dusky room. But it didn't. Holden was too absolutely, and properly, convinced of his own theory.

"Yes?" he inquired.

"You (harrumph) wish to lend all assistance in this unpleasant business?"

"Naturally!"

"Then would you be prepared," asked Dr. Fell, "to take a train for London leaving in about an hour? To go on another errand to an address I propose to give you?"

Another errand, eh?

For a moment his companion merely stared at him. Then rebellion, black and full of bile, rose in Donald Holden's soul.

"No, sir," he replied. "I am *not* prepared to do that."

"Oh, ah," assented Dr. Fell, contemplating the rubber ball with a somewhat guilty air.

"But before I tell you why I won't, Dr. Fell, I wonder whether I can guess the address where you want to send me? Is it 'Madame Vanya, 56b New Bond Street?' "

Dr. Fell, who had been about to bounce the ball again, stopped short. He grew intent. He raised his eyes, adjusting the lopsided eyeglasses.

"That's good," he said. "In the speech of Somerset, it is clever-good. Have you anything else to tell me?"

"Well, sir," Holden's throat felt dry, "if you wouldn't mind returning the notebook you borrowed last night—?"

"Was that yours? My dear boy!" said Dr. Fell, in a huge burst of contrition which blew wide a film of ash from his pipe and sent an alarming crack through the framework of the chair. "How extraordinary! I was wondering where and when I could have bought it. One moment! Here you are. And somebody's pencil."

"Thank you."

"But what—er—are you going to do?"

A pulse in Holden's temples thumped heavily. The heat and dust of the room pressed down. This was the test.

"Dr. Fell, I may be entirely wrong. But I'm going to adopt your own trick."

"Trick?"

"I'm going to write down, in two words, what I believe to be the key to the solution of Margot's murder." Holden scribbled the words, tore out the sheet, and handed it to Dr. Fell. "Will you tell me whether that's right?"

There was a little space of silence while, he looked down at Dr. Fell in the old black-alpaca suit, and around at the wardrobes and the doll houses and the rocking horse. Dr. Fell, who had put down pipe and ball to take the paper, sat with his eyes closed.

"Sir," announced Dr. Fell, "I am an old fool." He lifted his hand, as though forestalling comment.

"You will say," he went on, "that this leaps to the eye and needs no emphasis. Yet in spite of hearing it for so many years, especially from my wife and Superintendent Hadley, I never quite believed it, until now. Archons of Athens! I should have trusted your intelligence!"

Fiery certainty came to Holden.

"Then that's right, sir? What I wrote down?"

"So nearly right," said Dr. Fell, "as makes no difference. With one slight variation, which of course you will have deduced for yourself, a ringing bull's-eye."

Crumpling up the piece of paper, he flung it over the fire screen into the empty grate.

"I was an utter ass," groaned Dr. Fell, "to worry about it at all! I should have known you wouldn't misunderstand—er —well! certain things that are open to misunderstanding. My boy, how you relieve my mind!"

Holden smiled.

"Then you do appreciate my position, Dr. Fell? About not wanting to rush off to London?"

Dr. Fell looked at him blankly.

"Hey?"

"My only concern in this affair," said Holden, "is Celia."

"Exactly, exactly! But . . ."

"After a long time," said Holden, "I find her again. But no sooner do I try to see Celia, speak to her, have five minutes alone with her, than somebody tells me I can't possibly see her by doctor's orders. Or sends me haring off somewhere away from her, as you now want to send me to London.

"Well, I won't do it. I'm damned if I will. I'm sick and tired of obeying orders, Service or otherwise. What I want to do is to sit down with Celia, and keep her near me where I can touch her, for hours and days and weeks and months on end. That's what I propose to do, and—"

He paused. Dr. Fell, mouth open, was regarding him with a face of dismay.

"God alive!" whispered Dr. Fell. "Then you don't understand!"

"Understand what?"

"You have the wit," said Dr. Fell, pointing toward the crumpled paper in the grate, "to work that out. The difficult point doesn't escape you. Yet looming up, overshadowing everything, you don't see . . ."

"See what? What is all this?"

"My dear sir," Dr. Fell said gently. "Don't you see that in a few days the police will probably arrest Celia for murder?"

Dead silence.

There is a phrase about the room seeming to swim around in front of someone's eyes, which is often derided. Yet, perhaps from the physical effect of the heat, the closeness, the nerve strain of the past two days, something like that happened to Donald Holden now.

As though through blurred transparency, he saw the scuffed walls, the blackened matting, the fireplace with its biblical tiles, the wardrobes and doll houses, move out or up from their places, waveringly dissolve in line, and settle back again. The glass eye of the rocking horse seemed alive. Yet the effect of Dr. Fell's statement was such as to keep Holden outwardly calm.

"That," he said, "is too nonsensical to be talked about."

"Is it, my dear sir? Think! Try to think!"

"I am thinking." (He lied.)

"Don't you see the strength of the case that can be built up against Celia?"

"There is no case against her."

"Sit down," said Dr. Fell in a heavily wheezing voice.

Beside the nearer of the doll houses there was an old chair. Putting away notebook and pencil—that brave notebook and pencil!—Holden brought back the chair and planted it across the hearth from Dr. Fell.

He found and lit a cigarette, with a steady hand, before sitting down.

"Just a moment!" he interposed, as Dr. Fell started to speak. "You don't believe—?"

"In Celia's guilt? No, no, no!" said Dr. Fell. "My belief is the same as yours. And I think, if you use your wits, you will see the face of the real murderer."

Here Dr. Fell hitched his chair forward, earnestly.

"But it's not a question," he went on, "of what I believe. It's a question of what Hadley and Madden believe. That long letter of hers, her conversation with you in the playground on Wednesday night (which was overheard), and above all the events of last night, have played the very devil."

Holden took a deep draw at the cigarette.

"These gentlemen," he said calmly, "believe that Celia poisoned Margot?"

"They're inclined to. Yes."

"Then the charge is absurd on the face of it. Celia loved Margot."

"Exactly! Yes! Granted!"

"Well, then? Where's your motive?"

Dr. Fell spoke quietly, his eyes never leaving the stony face across from him.

"Celia," he said, "really believed her sister was being led, by Thorley Marsh, a life which no humane person could call fit enough for a dog. Celia believed this, and still believes it. You grant that?"

"Yes."

"Celia believed her sister to be the unhappiest mortal on earth. She believed Mrs. Marsh would never get a divorce, never get a separation, never go away. She believed that Mrs. Marsh sincerely and even passionately wished for death, as Mrs. Marsh told her. And so . . ."

The cigarette shook slightly in Holden's fingers.

"Are you telling me," he said, "that these police supermen think Celia poisoned Margot out of a kind of 'mercy?' "

"I fear so."

"But an act like that would be sheer insanity!"

"Yes," assented Dr. Fell quietly. "That is what they think it is."

Pause.

"Now one moment!" Dr. Fell's big voice rang out with authority, an authority which kept his companion still. His eyes never left Holden's face. "I see precisely what is going on in that brain and heart of yours. Oh, ah! And I sympathize. But, if you lose your head now, we are done for.

"I tell you," added Dr. Fell, "that of legal evidence I have nothing, I have not *that*, to rebut the strong evidence of the other side. Unless you and I can get Celia Devereux out of this, there will be nobody to do it. We are (I trust?) rational men, sitting quietly in an old nursery among toys, and discussing rational evidence. Shall we consider that evidence?"

"Dr. Fell," Holden said huskily, "I beg your pardon. It won't happen again."

"Good! Excellent!" said Dr. Fell.

Yet the doctor, though he tried to seem cheerful, got out a red bandana handkerchief and mopped his forehead.

"First I ask you," he proceeded, "to look at this."

"What is it?"

"It is a list," answered Dr. Fell, fishing up a folded paper from beside him in the chair, "of the real-life murderers who were impersonated in the famous Murder game at Widestairs on the night of December twenty-third. I have jotted them down chronologically, with dates and place of trial. Please glance at it."

Holden, trying to be very judicial, did so. Dr. Fell watched him steadily. The list of names read:

Maria Manning, housewife. (London, 1849.) Executed, with her husband, for the murder of Patrick O'Connor.

Kate Webster, maidservant. (London, 1879.) Executed for the murder of her employer, Mrs. Thomas.

Mary Pearcey, kept woman. (London, 1890.) Executed for the murder of a rival, Phoebe Hogg.

Robert Buchanan, physician. (New York, 1893.) Executed for the murder of his wife, Annie Buchanan.

G.J. Smith, professional bigamist. (London, 1915.) Executed for the murder of three wives.

Henri Desiré Landru, same as Smith. (Versailles, 1921.) Executed for the murder of ten women and one child.

Edith Thompson, cashier. (London, 1922.) Executed, with her lover Frederick Bywaters, for the murder of her husband, Percy Thompson.

"I say nothing of the list," continued Dr. Fell, "beyond expressing my belief that Mrs. Thompson was innocent and Mrs. Pearcey should have been sent to Broadmoor. But I call your attention to the first name on the list."

"Maria Manning," said Holden, drawing deeply at the cigarette. "That's the part Celia played in the game."

"Yes. And Celia," continued Dr. Fell, "loathes crime! Hates crime! Won't read a word about it! In fact, because of this well-known tendency she was amusedly tolerated by Sir Danvers Locke for her ignorance in the part of Maria Manning."

"Very well. What about it?"

"Yet, on going home that same night, she had a singularly vivid and horrible dream. You remember: she told you about it?"

"I remember something, yes."

"She dreamed she was standing on a platform in an open space, with a rope round her neck and a white bag over her head, high above a shouting jeering crowd of people who were singing her name to the tune of 'Oh, Susannah.'"

A jab of dread struck at Holden. He was looking round at the scuffed walls where Celia and Margot had played as children. But he said nothing.

"The dream," said Dr. Fell, "described sober truth. In 1849, you see, that tune was a popular song hit. And the mob sang it, with the substitution of the words, 'Oh, Mrs. Manning,' all night long before the woman's execution on the roof of Horsemonger Lane Gaol."

Again Dr. Fell mopped his forehead.

"Now this detail," he went on, "is far from being well known. Charles Dickens mentioned it in a letter to the *Times*, protesting against the foulness and indignity of public executions. But it is an obscure detail. Anyone who knows it . . ."

"Is well read in crime?"

"Yes. And is at least fascinated—morbidly so, the police think—by the whole subject."

Holden tried to laugh.

"Tuppenny-ha'penny evidence," he said. "Celia might have learned that detail anywhere! From one of the other people at the game! And quite naturally dreamed about it!"

"That," agreed Dr. Fell, "is quite true. But it is the sort of thing, don't you see, that rouses suspicion? What really interested Hadley was her insistence, in the letter, that important evidence would be discovered when she and I unsealed the vault on the night of the eleventh of July.

"Now mark the dates involved! Just after Christmas, at Celia Devereux's impassioned plea, she and I went through that ritual of spreading sand on the floor, locking the door, and sealing it. I went away entrusted with the key and the seal.

"Afterward, for more than six months, nothing! Not a word from her! Then, out of the blue, she writes to me and asks if I will redeem my promise to unseal the tomb. At the same time she writes to the police. What's up? Why has she waited as long as that? What does she expect to happen? Archons of Athens! Can you wonder, at least, that some curiosity was roused?"

"No. I don't wonder."

"And now," said Dr. Fell, "I'm afraid I have some rather bad news for you."

"All right. Let's have it."

Replacing the bandana handkerchief in his pocket, Dr. Fell took out a little wash-leather bag which was only too familiar. He opened it, and spilled out on his palm the big gold ring with the seal.

"The sleeping sphinx!" he said.

"What's that?"

"The lower part of this design," Dr. Fell scowled at it, "which Crawford described as being 'like a woman asleep.' In occult lore, it has—er—a meaning which is strongly applicable to this case. It is—harrumph—interesting. Yes. I could lecture on it: *dignus*, I hope, *vindice nodus*. I . . ."

"Dr. Fell, you're evading the point. You're floundering like an old woman! What is this bad news? Let's have it!"

His companion looked up.

"I told you," Dr. Fell said, "that I had been in touch with the police this morning?"

"Yes?"

"Dregs contained in that bottle we found in the vault,"

said Dr. Fell, "have been analyzed. Madden has applied to the Home Office for authority to exhume Mrs. Marsh's body and hold a post-mortem."

"All right! What about it? How does it affect Celia? If our theory is correct—"

Dr. Fell lifted his hand.

"Celia's fingerprints, and Celia's alone," he said, "have been found on that poison bottle."

After a pause he added;

"There is no doubt, even in my own mind, that she deliberately put it there for us to find."

CHAPTER XV

"As you say," observed Holden, depositing his cigarette in the grate with a steady hand, "we are rational men discussing rational evidence. But this has gone beyond the rational. Celia put that poison bottle in the tomb?"

"Yes."

Both of them kept their voices studiously level.

"Celia also, I suppose, managed to get in and out of a sealed vault? And hurled coffins about the place as though they were tennis balls?"

"No," returned Dr. Fell, rounding the syllable. "She had nothing to do with that. It is what I wish to emphasize. She had nothing to do with that. Yet she was expecting it."

"Expecting it?"

"I will go further, sir. She was gambling on it."

Dr. Fell threw up the big gold ring, and caught it against his palm. And Holden remembered. He remembered the elusive memory he had been trying to place last night, of the expression on Celia's face as the tomb was being opened, and of what it reminded him.

Mainz am Rhein! Early in '44!

He and a certain Swiss woman had been standing by a dark window, in an ill-smelling city, just as the siren squalled an alert against British bombers. The woman was opening a little packet; it would contain, she thought, certain information which would gain her a reward from the British and get her smuggled out of Germany to safety forever. She wasn't sure, but she thought so. She couldn't swear to it, but she was gambling on it.

As the air-raid siren squalled, a distant ack-ack battery cut loose prematurely. Pale-white light lifting in the sky, followed in a few seconds by the hollow shock of the guns, touched the Swiss woman's face. Her whole expression—the shallow breathing, the distended nostrils, the fixed and half-closed eyes—had been Celia's expression as Celia waited for the opening of the tomb.

Holden drew his thoughts back to the present, to Dr. Fell throwing up and catching the big gold ring.

"If Celia put the bottle in the tomb," Holden asked, "when did she put it there?"

"Before the tomb was sealed."

"Oh?"

"Before the tomb was sealed," insisted Dr. Fell, "at a time when Celia and I, and only Celia and I, were present. That niche was empty when we went in; I can swear to it. I didn't see her do it. I wasn't expecting anything of the sort. But there were a dozen opportunities, in a semidark place, while the sand was being put down. She was the only one who could have done it."

Holden swallowed. "And afterward . . ." he began.

"Go on!" said Dr. Fell.

"Afterward," said Holden, "after the vault had been sealed, Celia expected somebody or something to get in there and do what was done?"

"Yes."

"Are you plumping for a supernatural explanation?"

"Oh, no," said Dr. Fell.

"But look here! The utter impossibility of explaining how anybody got in and out of a sealed vault . . ."

"Oh, *that?*" exclaimed Dr. Fell in astonishment. He sat up. He made a gesture of distressed contempt. "My dear sir, that's the simplest part of the whole problem. I was expecting it before I got here."

Holden stared at him. Dr. Fell, with vast snortings and head shakings and a movement that made the whole chair creak and crack, was genuinely puzzled and concerned that this little point should have worried anyone.

"Fortunately for us, however," Dr. Fell added, "what we will call the Poltergeist Horror in the tomb has got Madden, Crawford, and Company completely floored. They think the poison bottle was put there at the same time as the coffins were disrupted, apparently by malignant ghosts. And they can't see how it happened.

"The trouble is, they won't stay floored. It's too simple. In a day or two at most, they'll see through it. Then the fat will be in the fire. And their case against Celia Devereux will be as follows:

"Celia poisoned her sister, using a drug whose principal ingredient was morphine—"

"Morphine, eh?" said Holden.

"Yes. Which is virtually painless. Celia arranged the crime to look like suicide. For, mark you! Another strong reason for the suicide, which she believed Margot wished for, was to expose Thorley Marsh to the world as a sadistic villain. To show him up! To give him what he deserved!

"And that didn't happen.

"The family doctor said this was a natural death. Celia, crying out that it was suicide and that Mr. Marsh had driven his wife to it, was hastily shushed. Having disposed of the poison bottle, Celia couldn't produce it in any place it should have been: that is, within reach of Margot Marsh.

"So (we are still stating the police case) she determined to go further. Out of a half-crazed imagination she invented this tale of ghosts walking in the Long Gallery, crying against Margot Marsh as a suicide. 'Cast her out!' was what they cried. Cast her out, from sleep among the just or honest dead!

"Nobody would believe that. But she would force them to believe it. So Celia, with my unconscious connivance, slipped the poison bottle into the niche. She gambled—for certain reasons of her own—that there would be poltergeist disturbances there. Then the tomb would be opened. And it would seem, among flung coffins and the poison bottle, that the very dead had cried out against Margot and Thorley Marsh."

Dr. Fell paused, wheezing.

His color had been coming up in spite of himself. He put the seal ring on his own finger and scowled at it.

"But—oh, Bacchus!" he added. "You see what follows?"

"I'm afraid I do."

"The police, once they've tumbled to the explanation of the intruder who throws coffins without leaving a footprint, will hardly view the matter as a supernatural occurrence. No, by thunder! Because . . ."

"Because?"

Dr. Fell checked off the points.

"Who could have killed Mrs. Marsh, except the sister who

had the poison bottle? Its very label was printed on a toy press," he pointed, "which you'll find in the wardrobe over there. Celia's fingerprints are on the bottle. She alone could have put it in the niche where it was found.

"And, heaven help me," added Dr. Fell, "I shall have to testify as much."

There was a long silence.

Holden pushed back his chair and got up. His legs felt light and shaky; heat pressed as oppressively as a cap on the brain. He began to walk about the room: blindly, not seeing it. It was all very well for Dr. Fell to talk about keeping your head, but this was bad. This was about as bad as it could be. It fitted in too well with so many things Celia had said and done.

"I do not ask," Dr. Fell observed politely, "what you think of the case against Celia. But you at least perceive we have got a case to answer?"

"My God, yes!—Can you answer it?"

Dr. Fell clenched his fist and scowled at the seal ring on his finger.

"I can answer it," he retorted. "Oh, ah! I can answer it in the sense of replying, 'Sir, thus and thus I believe to be true.' Especially since I put the cards on the table with Celia last night."

"That was what upset her so much?"

"It did, rather. But after you had left us, and Inspector Crawford so very obviously got a set of her fingerprints by handing her a silver cigarette case, it seemed better to warn her of the danger."

"What did Celia say?"

"Very little, confound it! Enough to make me sure I was right. All the same . . ." Dr. Fell hammered his fist on the chair arm. "No!" he added. "No, no, no! We are not going to mess about by trying to prove a negative. We establish a positive or die in the attempt."

"If we had any idea of who the murderer actually is—!"

"I know who it is," Dr. Fell said simply. "I've been certain ever since I questioned Thorley Marsh in the Long Gallery last night."

Holden, who had been looking blankly out of the nearer window toward the distant churchyard, whipped round.

"And now," inquired Dr. Fell, "will you go on that errand for me?"

"To the address in New Bond Street?"

"Yes. I can't send a police officer. My views (hurrum!)

differ from those of authority. I must withdraw my evil skirts from the case. Will you go?"

"Certainly. But what do you expect to find there? And, as Doris Locke said . . ."

Dr. Fell spoke sharply.

"Doris Locke? What has Doris Locke got to do with it?"

"She was the person who gave me the address." Holden narrated the incident, while Dr. Fell's eyes grew rounder and rounder behind the lopsided glasses.

"How very interesting!" he said in a hollow voice, and puffed out his cheeks. "How very interesting that it should be the woman's intuition of Doris Locke to light on so much. Harrumph, yes."

"All the same, Margot has been dead for more than six months. By this time those fortune-telling premises have been taken over by somebody else!"

"On the contrary." Dr. Fell shook his head. "I have reason to think the place is still intact. And that vital evidence may be there. I would go myself. But I must remain here, I tell you I must remain here, to find out whether anyone has discovered the real secret of the tomb."

"Yes," Holden cried out bitterly, "and that's just it!"

"What is?"

"That infernal vault! Look at it!"

And he pointed out of the window, though Dr. Fell was not in a position to see.

Just ahead of and beneath him, as he looked out from the northwestern side, Holden could look out over the quadrangle of stables and bakehouses and brewhouses: the diamond-paned windows that were dusty yet fiery, the cobblestoned court where pigeons fluttered, the gilt hands of the stable clock. Beyond yellow-green meadows, in Caswall churchyard, he could even pick out the tomb between the cypresses. Aside from the old vault on the hill, it was the only one there.

Holden clenched his fists.

"It's got into my head," he declared. "It may be simple to you. But it's got into my head. It muddles up every attempt to think. Something got through a sealed door, and threw the coffins about without leaving a footprint in sand. In Satan's name, what was it? Will you tell me?"

For a long time Dr. Fell regarded him somberly.

"No," answered Dr. Fell, "I will not. And there are two reasons why I will not."

"Oh?"

"The first reason," said Dr. Fell, "is that you must start your wits working again, or you will be of no use to us. I propose (by thunder, I do!) that you shall start them working by solving that little problem for yourself. And, if you like, I will give you one very broad hint."

Here Dr. Fell closed his eyes briefly.

"Do you remember," he asked, "the moment when the tomb door was opened?"

"Very vividly."

"The lower hinge, if you recall, squeaked and rasped as it opened?"

"I seem to remember the noise, yes."

"Yet the lock, when Crawford turned that key, opened with a sharp, clean click?"

"Then there *was* some crooked work about that lock! Crawford was right! There was some . . . I don't know! The seal had been tampered with."

"Oh, no," said Dr. Fell. "It was the original, untouched seal."

And he blinked at the seal ring on his finger.

"That," he went on in the same heavy tone, "is my hint. Now for my second reason for not telling you. You are not really thinking about that tomb at all."

"What the devil do you mean? I'm—"

"Only with the surface of your mind!" said Dr. Fell. "Only as an excuse! Only to avoid thinking about something else! Shall I read your mind?"

The sun, past its meridian now, was striking into these windows. Holden did not reply.

"You were thinking about Celia Devereux."

Holden made a fierce gesture as the other went on.

"You were thinking: 'I know she's not guilty of murder; I know she didn't poison Margot; but *is* she mad?'"

"God help me. I . . ."

"'How to reconcile,' you were thinking, 'how to reconcile with the facts Celia's insistence that Margot desired death, that Margot once swallowed strychnine, that Thorley Marsh's brutality drove her to it? How to reconcile with the facts Celia's behavior now, and her story about the ghosts in the Long Gallery?' Have I read your mind correctly?"

Holden, who had lifted his fists, dropped them at his sides.

"Look here," he said. "I'm going in now and have it out with Celia."

Dr. Fell did not try to prevent him.

"Yes," Dr. Fell assented. "That would probably be best. And I tell you again: that girl is no more mad than you are. But I warn you . . ."

The other, who had started for the door, stopped short.

"A part of the police's case against her," returned Dr. Fell, "is damning because it is perfectly true. On one point, and one point alone, that girl has been telling lies. That has caused a good deal of the trouble. She loathes telling lies in front of you."

"I'll see her! I'll . . ."

"Very well. But—what time is it now?"

Holden craned his neck to see the stable clock.

"A few minutes past twelve. Why?"

"You have just ten minutes," said Dr. Fell, "before you need leave here to catch that train."

The door to the passage opened. It was not flung open, since Mr. Derek Hurst-Gore caught it before it could strike the wall. Mr. Hurst-Gore, in his fine gray suit, his tawny hair agitated like his affable countenance, stood in the doorway looking from one to the other of them.

"Er—forgive this intrusion," he began. "But I heard voices. I could find nobody in the house." He took a few steps into the room, trying to smile and failing. "Dr. Fell! Have you heard this report that the police have applied for an order to exhume Margot's body?"

"I have."

"But why didn't you prevent it?"

Dr. Fell reared back; even in the chair he towered demonically. "Prevent it, sir?"

"You're a great husher-up," said Mr. Hurst-Gore, spreading out his hands. "I've heard how you hushed up everything in the case where the high-court judge was involved, and that business in Scotland at the beginning of the war. I —I was counting on you as a husher-up! Besides," he complained, "it's *nonsense!*"

"What is nonsense?"

"This! All this. *I* know the facts." Mr. Hurst-Gore's small, shrewd eyes grew hard and steady. "Dr. Fell, where's Thorley Marsh?"

"Hey?"

"Where's Thorley Marsh?"

"When I last saw him, sir, he was at Widestairs deep in conversation with Doris Locke. Isn't he still there?"

"Oh, no," replied Mr. Hurst-Gore, shaking his head. "He's

140

gone tearing off to London in his car. Where's he gone, exactly?"

If Derek Hurst-Gore had expected to produce an effect on Dr. Fell, he must have succeeded far beyond his hopes. Dr. Fell's mouth hung open. His eyes became fixed and glazed. It is not possible for a man of his complexion to become pale, yet he showed an approach to it now.

"Oh, Lord!" whispered Dr. Fell. "I heard it. With my own ears I heard it." He looked at Holden. "You told me. Yet with my scatterbrain on other matters, I never thought of the possibility that—" His bandit's moustache puffed in agitation. "My dear Holden! Listen! You have no time to lose. You must be sure of catching that train. Holden! Wait!"

But Holden was not listening. He was off in search of Celia.

The inner walls of those long galleries had windows which looked out over the center quadrangle, weedy and overgrown, of the cloisters where once nuns had walked. The bedroom doors, in this gallery, had outer doors of stuffed leather, edged with brass nailheads, to deaden sound. Holden threw open the leather door of Celia's room, knocked at the inner door, and opened it.

In a small bedroom with an oriel window, Celia sat before the mirror of a Queen Anne dressing table in the window embrasure. She had just finished dressing, and she was brushing her hair. Their eyes met in the mirror.

Holden took the two steps down into the room, amid a beauty of furniture whose polished age and grace showed brown-dark against white walls. There were little woven rugs on the floor.

"Celia," he said, "have you been telling lies?"

"Yes," answered Celia quietly.

She put down the brush. She got up, turned round, and stood facing him with her back to the dressing table.

"I invented that whole story," not a syllable was blurred in the clear voice, "about what happened in the Long Gallery on Christmas Eve. Not a scrap of it is true, and I don't believe in ghosts myself. Please wait, before you say anything!"

Though the gray eyes remained steady, utter self-loathing colored Celia's cheeks. Her fingers touched the edges of the dressing table behind her, and gripped the edges. So intense was the silence that he could hear a ring on her finger scrape against the dressing table.

"I wanted to tell you," she went on, "in the playground on Wednesday night. But I kept away from it, because I was so ashamed. Then—Dr. Shepton got there, before I could tell you the truth. And you heard things from him.

"That's been between us, Don. I kept away from you on Thursday because I was ashamed. Then, when Dr. Fell broke down Thorley's story in front of the Lockes and absolutely smashed him to bits, I thought it didn't matter any longer and I could tell you. But immediately Dr. Fell said Thorley was all innocent and holy; things turned upside down again. So I said to myself: All right; I *will* go through with the business of opening the tomb."

He could see the rigidity of her shoulders, under a thin gray silk dress.

"When I told you people that ghost story, Don, I was acting. Every bit of it. Now hate me. Go on: hate me! I deserve it!"

Still, all about him, the silence seemed to make an island.

"Why don't you speak, Don? Why do you just stand there and look at me? Don't you understand. I've been telling *lies*."

"Thank God," said Holden.

He spoke so softly, in such a deep and heart-felt relief, that it hardly whispered across the dazzling sunlit space between them.

"What's . . . that?" Celia whispered back.

"I said, thank God."

Celia's knees shook. Her fingers relaxed on the edge of the dressing table. She sank down abruptly on the brocade-covered seat in front of the table, staring at him.

"You mean," she cried, "you don't care?"

"Care?" shouted Holden. "I never was so delighted with any news in all my born days." In a dizziness of relief, he addressed the ceiling oratorically.

"The Cimmerian night," he said, "o'ershadows us. Howling monsters in outer darkness rage. But Celia has been telling lies; the sun shines again; and all is gas and gaiters."

"Are you j-joking?"

"Yes! No! I don't know!"

In four strides he covered the distance between them.

"I knew," he told her, "that what you said wasn't true. I knew it in my heart. But I was afraid you believed it yourself. So I was afraid it might be—something else. And now, glory be, I hear it's only . . ."

"Don! For heaven's sake! Don't hold me back over the dressing table! Mind the mirror! Mind the powder bowl! I mean—I don't care; hit 'em all over the place if you like. But . . ."

"But," he demanded, lifting her to her feet again, "Dr. Fell's told you what the police think of this?"

"Oh, the police?" said Celia, with weary indifference. "*That* doesn't matter. What *does* matter, don't you see, is that I can't ever look you in the face again?"

"Celia. Look at me now."

"I won't! I can't!"

"Celia!"

Presently, after a considerable interval, he added:

"Now listen. Whether you like it or not, we have got to get you out of this. You did put that bottle there, before the vault was sealed? Just as Dr. Fell suggested?"

"Yes."

"Why did you do it. Celia?"

"To prove," replied Celia, writhing in self-disgust, "that g-ghosts were denouncing Thorley for driving Margot to suicide. Because that's what Thorley did, Don! That's true!" She broke off. "I know it was silly. I told you Wednesday night it was silly. But I was desperate. It was all I could think of."

"Where did you get the bottle?"

"Don, I had no idea it was the *real* bottle!"

"The strongest part of the case against you, Celia, and so far the unanswerable part, is that you alone could have been in possession of the poison bottle after Margot's death."

"But I wasn't in possession of it. I found it."

"You found it?"

"All those bottles look alike, don't they?, Or, at least, I thought they did. I thought if I got hold of a fake bottle, that just *looked* like the original bottle, it would do just as well. You remember how dusty and dirty it was, so that you could hardly read the label?"

"Yes?"

"It was in the cellar," Celia told him, "among dozens and dozens of other discarded bottles. All dirty. I never thought . . ."

"The cellar here at Caswall, you mean?"

"Don! No! There's no cellar here, except the nun's rooms, and they're not really cellars. I mean at Widestairs. That was why I never dreamed of associating it with the real bottle, because I thought Margot'd thrown the real bottle into the moat."

"You found it in the cellar at Widestairs?"

143

"Yes."

Holden stepped back, away from the blaze of sun at the oriel window and the loom of a stableyard clock whose hands now pointed to fifteen minutes past twelve.

It was, he thought, exactly the sort of bitter and ironical situation he might have expected. Celia, in frantic search of an imitation bottle, finds the original and doesn't know it. Back comes boomeranging the evidence against this wily mistress of crime, who hasn't even the detective-story knowledge to remove her fingerprints from the bottle.

Celia finds the bottle (significantly?) at Widestairs. But could they prove that? Would the police believe it?

(It seemed to him that, somewhere in the galleries beyond the padded door, Dr. Fell was bellowing his name.)

"And, Don!" Celia put her hand on his arm. "I—I didn't know it until last night. It was only a guess or a joke before then. But Margot really did have a lover."

"How did you learn that?"

"In Margot's sitting room last night," Celia shivered, "in that Chinese Chippendale writing desk, we found the receipted bill."

"What receipted bill?"

"For a year's rent (yes, a year's! It must have been rather a grand passion) of flat something-or-other at number 56b New Bond Street. The fortune-telling place! Dr. Fell seemed awfully excited about it. The bill was dated early in last August. Dr. Fell even put through a call to the London Exchange, and found there's a phone still listed in Madame Vanya's name. I'm not sure what Dr. Fell is after . . ."

(Now the distant bellowing voice was plainer.)

"I'm sure what he's after," said Holden, suddenly waking up. "He wants to send me there, because the place is still intact. And he says something devilish will happen unless I catch that train! And the time now . . . Celia!"

"Yes?"

"You said once, if I remember correctly, that you'd have been glad if Margot had become somebody's mistress?"

"I did say it," Celia's eyes blazed, "and I do say it."

"You're wrong, my dear. It was the worst move she ever made."

"Why?"

"Because one thing," said Holden, "now seems fairly certain. When we find Margot's lover, we are going to find the murderer."

CHAPTER XVI

Margot's lover . . .

Or, after all, was he on the wrong track?

New Bond Street, when Holden's taxi set him down at the end of Oxford Street, had a gray-and-white solidity in mid-afternoon sunshine. Once the thoroughfare of fashion, it is now at least the thoroughfare of expense. Though less narrow than Old Bond Street, and with shop numbers less designed to confuse the enemy, it seemed a backwater after the Oxford Street tumult where a terrific walking race seems always in progress by half the population of London.

Nevertheless, even here, traffic plunged. Large if sedate banners, floating from second-floor flagstaffs, waved allurements in colored letters.

CONTEMPORARY PAINTINGS! said one. MODERN MASTERS! said another. EVERYTHING PHOTOGRAPHIC! rather sweepingly proclaimed a third. MR. DOG, a fourth said curtly in French, ARTIST-HAIRDRESSER! Brave but a little dingy, like shop fronts chary of exposing too much glass.

Plate and jewels behind wire netting. Furs. Gowns. Porcelain. Art galleries that showed dim recesses of green walls and gilt frames. Long windows displaying antique furniture, of heavy leopardlike magnificence. Holden saw it flow past beyond a dodging screen of pedestrians. 56b, now . . .

56b should be on the left-hand side of the street, unless the London County Council's usual sense of humor suddenly set the numbers running the other way.

56b! Got it!

Holden, walking rapidly on the right-hand side, dodged into a doorway to reconnoiter the address opposite. He was a little surprised to see, on the wall beside him, a brass plate announcing that upstairs was a Marriage Bureau, personal and confidential introductions performed. At another time he would have been intrigued with wondering what happened if you just walked upstairs and went in.

But he had too much on his mind now.

All the way up in the train, from Chippenham to Paddington, he had wildly mulled over those last instructions of Dr. Fell.

"I have not time," said Dr. Fell, who would have had plenty of time if only he had ceased his roundabout style of speech, "to explain fully. But I call your attention to the problem of the black velvet gown."

"If you want to catch that train," said Mr. Derek Hurst-Gore, who had generously offered to drive him there, "you'd better hurry."

"We agree," thundered Dr. Fell, so upset he could think of only one thing at a time, "we agree that Mrs. Marsh herself put on the black velvet gown in which she was found dying. She did it because of some sentimental association. Ah! But what association?"

"It *is* getting late," Celia urged.

"I have questioned," Dr. Fell pointed at Celia and Mr. Hurst-Gore, "these two here. Early this morning I questioned Sir Danvers Locke, Lady Locke, Doris Locke, Ronald Merrick, Miss Obey, and Miss Cook. Nobody has ever seen Mrs. Marsh wearing the black velvet, though it has been seen in her dress cupboard."

"That's perfectly true," agreed Celia. "It's now twenty-five minutes past noon."

"I have not," Dr. Fell looked at Holden, "a key to the premises at 56b New Bond Street. You (harrumph) are familiar with the technique of breaking and entering?"

"I've been known to employ it," Holden said dryly.

"And you can make a thorough search?"

"Yes! But that's just it! What am I supposed to be searching for?"

"Dash it all!" said Dr. Fell, drawing a hand across his forehead. "Didn't I explain?"

"No, you didn't. How the hell can I find any evidence against a murderer if you don't tell me what I'm looking for?"

"But, my dear sir! I don't want any evidence against the murderer!"

"You . . . ?" Holden regarded him in stupefaction.

"Not as such. No, no, no!" Dr. Fell assured him. "Just get me proof as to who was the man in the case, the *amant du coeur*, and I will apply it to explain what evidence is now in my possession.

"It also seems to me," added Dr. Fell, mopping his forehead, "that you are being extremely dilatory, my dear sir, and wasting an unconscionable amount of time in talking, when there is the greatest need for haste. This is really serious. There may only be a theft. Or there may be—"

"Well?"

"A tragedy," said Dr. Fell.

In New Bond Street, as Holden instinctively dodged into a doorway and mocked at himself for doing it, a string of heavy lorries rumbled past. Odd, how old instincts stayed with you! Even the sight of a British policeman, directing traffic at the intersection of Grosvenor Street, gave him a slight jump.

He looked across at the premises of 56b.

It was a narrow stone front, built perhaps fifty years ago; it had three floors above the ground floor, which was a bookshop agleam with rich bindings. On its left was an art gallery, on its right a stationer's displaying fans of blue note paper and envelopes. Just to the left of the bookshop he saw a big door wide open on a passage, presumably leading to stairs at the back.

Holden's eyes went up to the dead-looking, shadowed windows of the floors above the bookshop. Each floor showed two windows between stone pillars. The first set bore large gilt handwriting which said, ARCHER; FURS; that was no good. The two upper pairs of windows might have been curtained or merely shadowed, occupied or unoccupied; they remained blank.

It was one of the two upper floors, then.

Holden crossed the street.

At the left of the open door, under a brass plate of *Sedwick & Co. Ltd.*, he was surprised to see a smaller plate reading, *Madame Vanya*.

This was carrying realism rather far: Had Margot, as a sort of huge secret joke, really been practicing a fortune-telling trade here and bamboozling genuine clients? Such things were not unknown. Though Doris Locke had professed to find it so very modern, it was an old trick of the seventeenth century. And fortune telling was not against the law, unless you professed to psychic powers. But Margot? Of all people, Margot?

A low-ceilinged passage, dimly lighted by a concealed electric bulb on each landing, ran to a flight of stairs at the back. The place smelled of fresh brown paint; the brass bindings on the stair treads were new.

As he went up the stairs, he had to remind himself again that he was not in a foreign country; he was in England, in

147

peacetime, at half-past three of a drowsy July afternoon. Yet the palms of his hands were tingling and old memories returned.

ARCHER; FURS.

A long strip of a landing, the wall unbroken except for one door, of yellow-varnished oak with a Yale lock, at the side and toward the front. On the landing, by the stairs, a window giving on a dingy two-foot air space between this and the next house.

He moved on to the floor above. Exactly the same, except that there was no sign on the door. Oak door and Yale lock; that was bad.

This might be Sedgwick & Co. Ltd., or it might be Madame Vanya. If it were the first, whatever their business might be, the thing to do was to open the door and stroll in with some casual question. He turned the knob, easing it over gently, with the same instinct. It was not locked. He opened it.

It was Sedgwick & Co., and they were theatrical costumiers.

One comprehensive glance showed him a long dusky room, apparently empty, with two windows overlooking the street on the narrow side. Wigs, of extraordinary life-likeness, loomed up on the narrow stems of their wooden blocks. In one corner stood a female lay figure, in a fur-trimmed costume of the nineties. High rows of shelves, with costumes pressed flat, stretched along the opposite wall.

Then, as Holden was about to close the door, a voice spoke out of the empty air. That voice said, very distinctly:

"The secret of the vault."

Holden stood motionless, the door halfway open. It was as though he had caught that disembodied voice at the end of a sentence. For it continued, in the same agreeable way:

"Shall I tell you, between ourselves, how those coffins were really moved?"

A light flashed on somewhere at the rear of the room. And Holden, peering through the long crack between the hinges of the door, now understood.

The premises of Sedgwick & Co. comprised two rooms set in a line from front to back. In the rear room beyond an open door, someone was seated in front of a triple mirror, his back to the communicating door; and a light had just been switched on above him.

The front room was heavily carpeted. Holden slipped in without noise, and looked.

Facing him in the mirror, past the shoulder of the person who sat in the rear room, was a countenance of fat repulsiveness: high colored, yet pock marked and heavy jowled, sagging of eye, leering like a satyr under the white court wig.

The face admired itself. It tilted up its chin, turning from side to side, pleased with the puffy cheeks. It cocked its head like a bird's. Repeated in the triple mirrors, its moppings and mowings flashed, slyly, from every angle. Then it elongated itself when hands appeared on either side; the eyes were punched out into black holes.

It was a mask. Out of it emerged the thoughtful face of Sir Danvers Locke.

"Not bad," Locke commented. "But the price is too high."

"The price!" murmured another voice, in tones faintly shocked and reproachful. "The price!"

It was a woman's voice, pleasant, between youth and middle-age, and unmistakably French.

"These masks," the woman said, "are the work of Joyet."

"Yes. Quite."

"They are his best work. They are the last work he has done before he *die*." Her voice grew more reproachful. "I have sent you a special telegram to come quickly and see them."

"I know. And I'm grateful." Locke drummed his fingers on the table of the mirrors. He glanced up, past the light shining on his gray hair, at the invisible woman. His tone changed. "May I say, Mademoiselle Frey, that it is a great relief to come here and talk to you sometimes?"

"But it is a compliment!"

"You know nothing of me or my affairs. Beyond making sure my check is good, you don't want to know anything."

In the mirror above his head there was the shadow of a shrug. Abruptly, as though this made matters easier, Locke spoke in French.

"I am not," he said, "a man who speaks easily at home or even among his friends. And I am much troubled."

"Yes," Mademoiselle Frey agreed quietly, also in French. "One comprehends that. But monsieur was not serious about these . . . coffins?"

"Yes. Very serious."

"I myself," cried the woman, "have interred my brother. It was an interment of the first class. The coffin—"

"The coffin of the lady in question," said Locke, with his eye on a corner of the mirror, "was an inner coffin of wood, an outer casing of lead, then an outer wooden shell. Massive, airtight, good for years against corruption. So also was the coffin of one John Devereux, a cabinet minister under Lord Palmerston, the coffin made in mid-nineteenth century. Each of them: eight hundred pounds."

The woman's voice went up shrilly.

"You speak of the price?"

"No. I speak of the weight."

"*Mais c'est incroyable!* No, no, no! You are mocking me!"

"I assure you I am not."

"Such a formidable weight is moved about in this tomb; it would require six men; yet no footprint is in the sand? It is impossible!"

"On the contrary. It would not require six men. And this joke is very simple, when you learn the secret of it."

The old, aching riddle!

Holden, who knew he could not be seen beyond that down-shining light over the mirrors, stood rigid and motionless.

"I claim no credit, you comprehend," Locke went on, "for knowing this. It has happened before, twice in England, and once perhaps at a place called Oesel in the Baltic. In the library at Cas—at a certain place; forgive me if I do not mention names—there is a book giving all details.

"For myself," he declared in his smooth finely enunciated French, "I hear nothing of this at an interview early this morning with a certain Dr. Fe—a certain doctor of philosophy. No! I hear it only when I am entering the train, with a friend of mine, from a certain police inspector. I told him how the trick was done. He shook hands with me, this Crawford, and said it would enable them to arrest somebody."

Arrest "somebody"?

Arrest Celia! Holden, feeling that some fragile shield hitherto guarding Celia had been broken to bits, started to back toward the door over the soft thick carpet. Yet Locke's face in the mirror still kept him there, because its expression was so strained and more thoroughly human than he had ever seen it.

"And yet," Locke said, "this is not what troubles me."

"Indeed?" his companion murmured coldly. "Will it please you to see some more of Joyet's masks?"

"You think I am mocking you over this matter of the coffins?"

"Monsieur buys here. It is his privilege, within limits, to say what he likes."

"Mademoiselle, for God's sake!"

Locke struck the table. His urbane countenance was pitted with wrinkles. His pale eyes, over the high cheekbones, were turned up pleadingly.

"I was not a young man," he said, "when I married. I have a daughter, now age nineteen."

His companion's voice softened immediately. This was something understandable.

"And you are concerned about her?"

"Yes!"

"Without doubt she is a young girl of good character?"

"Good character? What is that? I don't know. As good, I suppose, as that of most girls who run the streets nowadays.— Give me another of the masks."

"Come, monsieur!" Mademoiselle Frey's voice was laughing and chiding at once; all asparkle. "Come, now! You must not speak like that!"

"No?"

"It is cynical. It is not nice."

"Young people," said Locke, "are utterly callous. You agree?"

"Come, now!"

"And sometimes utterly ruthless. This is not out of any brutality. It is because they cannot see the effect of their actions on any person except themselves."

Briefly Locke held up another mask before his face without putting it on. The features of a young girl, exquisitely tinted, as real as a living face, serene and innocent even to the long eyelashes, appeared in the glass.

"They are blind," the eyes in the mirror closed, "to any consideration except self-interest. They want something. They must have it. Point out to them that this is wrong; they will agree with you, perhaps sincerely, and in the next moment forget it. Youth is a cruel time."

The mask dropped.

"Now I will tell you, a stranger, what I would not tell my own wife."

"Monsieur," said the woman, "you frighten me."

"I beg your pardon. Most humbly. I will stop talking."

"No, no, no! I wish to hear! And yet . . ."

"Yesterday evening," said Locke, "when a group of us were being questioned by the doctor of philosophy in question, there occurred to me suddenly a new and unpleasant idea. I could not credit it. I cannot credit it even now."

"It occurred to me because of a question asked by this Dr. Fell. He suddenly asked, for no apparent reason, whether the lady who died—a handsome lady, in the full strength of her beauty—had visited my house on the afternoon of the twenty-third of December.

"I answered, truthfully, that she had. I did not add something else. I dared not add it. I will not add it. But shortly after she left my house I saw her, through my study window, walking in the frost-covered fields. There was someone with her."

Again Locke held up a mask to his eyes; and the face that sprang out of the glass was the face of a devil.

"I will deny this if I am asked. I can laugh at it. But the person in question handed to her something which I now half-believe to have been a small brown bottle. A bottle that . . ."

"One moment, monsieur," the woman said. "I believe the outer door of our shop is now open."

There was a jarring and blurring of the mirror. The devil mask slipped and dropped. Several things occurred with blinding swiftness.

Before Mademoiselle Frey could reach the front room of Sedgwick & Co., Holden was out in the passage. But he had no intention of flight, even if unobserved flight had been possible in that bare passage with its stairways up and down. In a split second he had made and discarded two plans, finding a third which was better for what he wished to discover.

As Mademoiselle Frey opened the door wide, he was standing in front of it with his hand upraised as though to knock.

Mademoiselle Frey was a slim, sturdy woman in her middle thirties. Though she was not pretty, with black hair and black eyes against an intense pallor and a vividness of lipstick, yet her vitality and sympathy made her seem so.

At the moment her eyes looked dazed, deeply immersed, in Danvers Locke's story; fascinated by Locke as so many people were fascinated by him. And, as Holden had hoped for, her complete absorption in a French-told narrative made her speak, abruptly and automatically, in French.

"Et alors, monsieur? Vous désirez?"

"I ask your pardon, mademoiselle!" Holden said loudly, in the same language.

He wanted Locke to overhear him, if Locke did not recognize his voice. And the best way to disguise your voice is merely to speak in another language, since the listener's ear is deaf to the accents it expects.

"I ask your pardon, mademoiselle! But I am looking for Madame Vanya."

"Madame Vanya?" The dark eyes looked blank.

"She is"—he made the accent deliberately clumsy—"she is a reader of the future."

"Ah! Madame Vanya!" cried the other. "Madame Vanya is not here. She is upstairs."

"I am desolated to have troubled you, mademoiselle!"

"There is nothing at all, monsieur."

The door closed.

Holden went quickly up the stairs to the top floor. It was very hot here under the roof. A dim little bulb burned in one corner. Leaning over the railing of the landing, keeping as far back as possible, yet staring very hard at the door of Sedgwick & Co. downstairs, he waited with tense expectancy for what he believed would happen.

CHAPTER XVII

WHAT the devil was Locke doing here?

It might be mere coincidence. He had said, at Widestairs last night, that he intended to come to town today. To find him buying masks in New Bond Street was not at all surprising. Yet in this particular building? In this particular building?

One thing seemed certain. If Locke knew that here upstairs was Margot's place of rendezvous with her unidentified lover, as Doris knew it, then no human restraint of curiosity could keep him inactive. Locke had just heard a man, speaking French with a strong English accent, inquire for Madame Vanya more than six months after Margot's death. And this at a time when the police were investigating.

Locke would come up here, on some pretext or other! He must come up!

So Holden waited.

And the seconds ticked by, and nothing happened.

Meantime, his eye measured the top floor for a possible way in. The same bare stretch of wall with its oak door and

Yale lock. Opposite, the same landing window open to a dingy air space between this and the next house. He went over and tried the knob of the door.

Locked, of course. No good at all without proper tools. But . . .

Low ceiling on this landing. No trap door to the roof, as there must be by law. Therefore the trap door to the roof is inside Madame Vanya's flat. Therefore the easiest means of entry is by way of the roof itself.

And still, from the floor below, nobody stirred.

You're off the track! he told himself violently. Danvers Locke doesn't know anything about this. Forget those notions that went through your head in the shock of seeing him! Forget it!

Pushing down both dusty leaves of the landing window, Holden stepped on the sill and put his head outside. The walls of the two buildings, black and scabrous brick, were not more than a couple of feet apart. Most windows in the house next door seemed either blind or boarded up. A mildewy smell drifted up from the ground some forty feet below.

He climbed to the outer sill of the window, his back to the house next door. With first one foot and then another on the joined sashes, he drew himself up still higher with one hand inside the window.

His right hand crept up to find the low stone coping round the roof above. Even at full stretch his fingers were still eighteen inches below the roof. Got to do a balancing act on these window sashes, and jump for it.

E-easy, now!

A bus rumbled in the street. From the corner of his eye, through the vertical opening between these two buildings as between high canyon walls, he could see far away the glitter of motorcars. Holding himself by a fingertip balance with his left hand now outside the window, he let go and jumped.

He was off balance, but his right hand caught and gripped. His left hand caught and gripped. With both knees drawn up, with the edge of one shoe wedged into the inch-wide projection of the window top, he swung himself up to the roof and landed on his feet like a cat.

The sun dazzle smote his eyes. It was a second or two before he realized that his own apparition, shooting up out of nowhere, had caught the attention of two startled workmen on the adjoining roof behind him.

The workmen were carrying between them a very long and heavy wooden signboard inscribed with the black-and-gold inscription, BOBBINGTON OF BATH. Their heads stared over it like heads over a fence. The mouth of one was open, and that mouth was about to say.

"Oi!"

Holden gave no indication that he had seen them.

He looked slowly and thoughtfully round the roof, studying it. From his pocket, in a leisurely way, he took out notebook and pencil. He frowned at the scarred gray surface of the roof, and made a note. He walked about, his footsteps creaking on tin, and made another note. He looked at the central chimney stack, one of whose chimney pots hung at an angle of nearly forty-five degrees, and made a series of notes.

It was only then that he addressed the workmen, in a tone of satisfied triumph.

"That'll cost 'em something in the way of a fine," he said.

" 'Strewth!" cried one of the workmen. The other did not speak, but his disgust must have reached up to the angels.

For again it must be emphasized that in this free England today you have only got to sound official, act officiously, or behave in general as though you were snooping to get the goods on somebody, and you will be accepted everywhere without question. The signboard, in wrath, executed a kind of dance. But suspicion was killed stone dead.

" 'Strewth!" repeated that disgusted voice. The signboard, maneuvering like an erratic quadruped, swung away toward the front.

Holden had already spotted the trap door leading down into Madame Vanya's rooms.

It was at the extreme rear of this narrow roof, close to the coping, well behind and to one side of another small chimney. There was also, near the chimney, a big sloping glass skylight, closely curtained on the inside; locked, immovable.

As for the trap door . . .

Most householders in this world, he was reflecting, cannot even tell you whether the attic trap in their homes is bolted or unbolted. Even if it happens to be bolted, its wood and tin are so rotted from long exposure to the weather that a sharp clasp knife will get you through to the bolt in a matter of seconds. His fingers clenched achingly on the clasp knife in his pocket.

But he could not act, dared not act, until those two men had finished hanging the sign on its metal posts facing the street.

So up and down that blasted roof he walked, up and down, concealing the coal-black palms of his hands, taking notes, while the men dallied and wrangled.

It was a bright, breeze-swept place, among a forest of chimneys. Far to the south, past blitz cavities, he could see a winking of windows in Piccadilly. To the north loomed the flags over Selfridge's. The sun was declining. God Almighty, couldn't those men hurry?

Smuts blew heavily here too, because—

Holden stopped short, his eyes fixed on the little chimney at the back. Unperceived until now, by a trick or shift of the wind, a coil of yellow-gray smoke gushed over the edge of that chimney, curled up, and was blown wide.

The dark, locked rooms of Madame Vanya, deserted since Margot's death, now had a visitor. The visitor had got there ahead of him. The visitor was burning something. It might be that vital evidence went up with that smoke.

Watchers, or no watchers, he couldn't wait. Holden went over to the trap door, and shook it gently. It was not a trap door, but a wooden-and-tin lid fitting over a hatch. Stuck, but not bolted. With a sharp heave he lifted it up, and a fraction of an inch to one side, showing darkness below. Whatever was down there, it couldn't be the room where the visitor had lighted a fire.

Pushing the lid to one side, Holden swung himself soundlessly down through the open space. While he held his weight with his right hand, with his left he pulled back the hatch cover until only a slit of light remained.

It showed him, underneath, a rusty gas range. He was in a little kitchenette; probably built out, with a bathroom beside it, at the back of the two rooms comprising this suite. Yes! There was a closed door facing front.

No noise, now!

He dropped to the top of the gas range, easing his muscles and landing with only the faintest of clanks. He slid off to the floor. The musty odor of a sink long dried, of premises given over to mice, seemed to heighten an intense stillness. That faint glimmer from the hatch showed him the sink, the cabinets, the linoleum, the door facing front.

When he softly turned the knob of that door, Holden smelt danger—violence, deadliness of some kind—as clearly as you sense the atmosphere of a quarrel in the room where it has just occurred.

He started to push the door open. It met a soft obstruction of some kind; probably a curtain. Still he could see nothing. With his body in the doorway, he groped along the wall to the left. Another door, with key in it; automatically he turned the key.

Groping, he found an opening in two dust-heavy curtains which masked the doors at back. He slipped through.

"You swine," whispered a voice.

Holden stood motionless.

Whether or not he had heard that whisper, he heard the crackle and pop of a fire. He saw flickering gleams of the fire, cut off a little by some low obstruction.

The fireplace was in the right-hand wall of the room as you faced toward the front. The obstruction seemed to be a large flat divan placed against the wall to the right of the fireplace. Of the room itself—airless, stuffy, muffled by carpet and curtain—he could make out nothing. But the fire, dying, must have been burning for some time; a heavy odor as of varnished wood in the flames, of cloth or canvas, made a reek and almost a haze.

Then it happened.

Beyond the divan, between divan and fireplace, silhouetted against the dying fire, was rising up a human head.

It rose slowly, unsteadily, into the dim silhouette of a man. There was about it a sick concentrated menace. The fire popped, flinging out an ember. The silhouette balanced itself. Suddenly its right arm went back.

Something flew at Holden, flew at his head out of the dark. The firelight struck a glassy flash from that object as it flew. Holden, dodging, heard it strike the curtained door behind him with a cushioned thud; it rebounded, thumped on the floor, and rolled slowly back toward the fire.

It was a fortune-teller's crystal.

Holden, his shoulders down, moved slowly forward toward that silhouette. The other man moved back. Not a word was spoken. A reek of burning poisoned the air. Step forward, step back. Step forward, step back. Holden began to circle as he closed in, to avoid the firelight. It seemed to him, straining his eyes in the dark, that the other man was trying to reach something on the wall.

So he was. But not for the purpose Holden anticipated.

A light switch clicked. Dimmed by a very small globe of frosted glass, a lamp on a desk in the middle of the room threw out feeble illumination. Holden, dropping his arms, stared in consternation.

Thorley Marsh, with one hand on the light switch, stood looking at him in a vaguely puzzled way.

Thorley's starched collar was torn open, his black tie dragged sideways into a tight knot. Dust patched his black coat, rucked up over his shoulders. His face showed pale, with a jellylike uncertainty; yet, as always, not a strand of his glossy black hair seemed out of place.

Then Thorley's eyes woke up.

"Don, old boy!" he said with a rush of friendliness and an attempt at a smile. He started forward, his hand extended to shake hands. He hesitated, stumbled, and pitched straight forward on his face.

That was where Holden saw the blood on the back of his head, clotting in the hair. And, as Holden's gaze moved along the floor, he could see blood smears on the fortune-teller's crystal as well.

"Thorley!" he shouted.

The bulky figure did not move.

"Thorley!"

He hurried forward, and tried to hoist Thorley up. With infinite labor, half-carrying and half-dragging him under the arms, Holden got him to the low black-velvet-covered divan.

"Thorley! Can you hear me?"

Half-supported under the shoulders, Thorley tried to speak. His lips twitched desperately, like those of a stammering man. But he could not speak. Grotesquely, two tears rolled from under his closed eyelids across his cheeks.

All the friendship Holden had ever felt for him—the memory of good nature, the memory of a hundred acts of disinterested kindliness—returned in a series of small lighted pictures with the haunting power of auld lang syne. If Thorley had tried to harm Celia . . . well, even so, you can't dislike a man when he's hurt and broken and crying.

For Thorley was badly hurt. How badly, Holden could not tell; but he didn't like the beat of the pulse. That big crystal, used as a bludgeon, would have made a murderous weapon.

Wait a minute! Telephone!

Dr. Fell had said there was a phone here, still connected. Rolling Thorley on his side, Holden swung round and surveyed the room.

It looked, he thought, like the quite genuine inner shrine of a fashionable seer. It was unrelieved black—black carpet, black wall curtains, black curtain over the skylight—except for a tall Jacobean chair, padded in scarlet damask, behind a carved desk in the middle. That would be the fortune-teller's chair; the client's chair stood opposite.

The dim little desk lamp showed ornaments disarranged on it, as though there had been a struggle there. Against one wall stood a carved cabinet, key in lock. But no telephone.

With a collapsing rattle, a gush of oily smoke, the last shreds in the fireplace tumbled down. They were simmering, fire edged; they might once have been sticks supporting bits of burned cloth, with broken lengths of varnished wood underneath them. Holden, yanking up the fire tongs and using his hands as well, raked it all out on the hearth.

But he was too late. He was too late! Whoever had been here, whoever had battered Thorley's head with the crystal, must have slipped away from here long ago.

On the divan, Thorley moaned. Telephone!

Another door in the front wall, Holden discovered, opened into a front room overlooking New Bond Street. The window curtains were not quite drawn. It was a waiting room: very much like the waiting room of a fashionable doctor, though overlaid with a more exotic tinge. There, on a little table against the wall, he found what he sought.

The only thing to do, he said to himself, is to dial 999 and call for an ambulance. That'll mean informing the police as well; it may wreck Dr. Fell's plans; but it can't be helped. Unless . . . wait; Better idea!

His right hand, which he had burned in raking out that fireplace, throbbed and flamed as he dialed another number. The buzz of the ringing tone seemed to go on interminably.

"War Office?" His voice sounded loud in that grotesque waiting room. "Extension 841, please."

Another pause, while a vibration of traffic shook against the windows.

"Extension 841? I want to speak to Colonel Warrender."

"Sorry, sir. Colonel Warrender is out."

"He's not out, damn you!" Holden could feel the startled A.T.S. girl shy away from the phone. "I can hear him rattling tea cups on his desk. Tell him Major Holden wants to speak to him on a matter of vital importance.—Hello! Frank?"

"Yes?"

In the adjoining room, Thorley Marsh began to laugh. It was a thin, vacant sound which crawled along the nerves; it was the laugh of delirium; it might be the laugh of the dying.

"Frank, I haven't got time to explain. But can you pull

strings to get me, *immediately*, an ambulance from a discreet private nursing home to deal with somebody who's been badly hurt: probably concussion? Can you?"

"That's absolutely impos—" Warrender began automatically. Then he stopped. "Look here. Does this concern the girl you were in such a flap about?"

"In a way, yes."

"Cripes! Have you been chucking her downstairs already?"

"Frank, I'm not joking!"

Warrender's voice changed. "There's nothing phony about this? You give me your word nobody'll get into trouble?"

"I give you my word."

"Right!" said Warrender. "What's the address?" Holden gave it. "Your ambulance will be there in ten minutes, and no questions asked. Tell me about it later."

And he rang off.

Holden sat back in the chair by the little table. His hand throbbed like fire. The sick taste of failure was in his mouth, of being too late and missing the murderer. What murderer? Never mind. He had been told to search; and, by the six horns of Satan, he *would* search.

He went back to the black-draped room whose small glimmer of desk light only weighted the shadows. There was nothing he could do for Thorley, who lay in a stupor, breathing stertorously. Beyond the desk loomed the scarlet damask of the tall chair. He inspected the desk.

Its disarranged black covering, he now saw with repulsion, was antique funeral pall. It breathed of more than mere hocus-pocus; it hinted at the abnormal. Crumpled back as though in a struggle, it was stained with one or two spots of drying blood.

Aside from the crystal holder, it bore only two other objects. One was an ibis head of green jade, rolled almost to the edge of the desk. The other was a flat bronze plaque, engraved with a design and a few lines of . . .

Familiar?

Yes! The design on that plaque was the same as the design on the lower part of the gold ring with which Dr. Fell had sealed the tomb. Holden bent closer to read what was underneath.

Here is a sleeping sphinx. She is dreaming of the *Parabrahm*, of the universe and the destiny of man. She is part human, as representing the higher principle, and part beast, as representing the lower. She also symbolizes the two selves: the outer self which all the world may see, and the inner self which may be known to few.

Disregarding this mysticism, Holden went swiftly through the drawers of the desk. All were unlocked and empty. Nothing: not so much as a coin or a discarded newspaper. He measured for secret compartments, but there were none.

The carved cabinet, then? The cabinet, with the key in its lock, against the wall opposite the fireplace?

Thorley moaned, and cried out in stupor, as Holden opened the cabinet. Inside he discovered a small but very modern steel filing cabinet, whose drawers rolled smoothly open. There were only blank index cards, but many gaps, and traces of cardboard adhering to the central rod where other index cards had been torn out. Those cardboard traces felt dry and harsh to the touch; they had not, he thought, been torn out today or even recently.

Gone were the names of Madame Vanya's fortune-telling clients; destroyed some time ago. Nothing here either. And yet . . .

He studied the outer wooden cabinet.

It was authentic Florentine Renaissance, scrolled with arms and saints. It might have come from Caswall. Whistling softly, he snapped on the flame of his pocket lighter and examined the lower part. To blot out from his own ears the noise of Thorley's breathing, now grown harsh and rattling like a man gasping for life, Holden spoke aloud.

"Now when an Italian craftsman of the great age makes his baseboard half an inch too high for proportion, it's interesting. When he decorates it with rosettes, and one of them has a center slightly larger than the others . . . Thorley, for God's sake be quiet!"

The unconscious man laughed.

"Be quiet, Thorley! I can't help you! The ambulance will be here in a minute!"

Holden had forgotten his burned hand now. The blood beat in his ears. He knelt down by the lower edge of that carved cabinet, and prodded at the rosette whose center was larger than the others.

There was a faint click. Feeling for the undermost edge, he drew out a very shallow drawer nearly filled with large sheets of gray note paper in Margot Devereux's rapid, clear, unmistakable handwriting.

Love letters written by Margot, the topmost one dated, Afternoon, December 22nd. He hadn't failed, after all.

Holden blew out the lighter flame, which was sizzling and scorching the wick. He knelt there in semidarkness, partly lifting the topmost letter, yet feeling an intense reluctance now to read it. Dead Margot, with her brown eyes and her dimples, seemed to walk in the room.

He got up, and dropped the lighter back in his pocket. He went back to the desk, where he spread out that letter on the funeral pall beside the dim lamp. The words lived again, the personality lived again, in what Margot had written:

MY DEAREST:

I'm not going to post this to you, or even give it to you, any more than any of the other letters. Is that silly? And yet it's the only way I have of being with you when you're not here, not here, not here. This time tomorrow, or two days from now, it will all be settled. Whether we marry, or whether we die. But—

Holden's eyes stopped. Here, in part at least, was ringing confirmation of a certain theory. The next part of the letter he dodged over. It was composed of intimacies explicitly described and set down. And then:

Sometimes I think you don't love me at all. Sometimes I think you almost *hate* me. But that couldn't be, could it? If you're willing for what we plan? Forgive me for thinking that! Sometimes I get pleasure just from repeating your name, over and over. I say to myself—

Holden raised his head quickly.

The outer door of this flat, the solid Yale-locked door giving on the passage outside, was in the front room. But the sound penetrated very distinctly. Someone was softly rapping on that door.

CHAPTER XVIII

IT MIGHT be the ambulance men, of course. He didn't associate that soft, hesitant, almost furtive rapping with any such errand. All the same, it might be the ambulance men.

Hurrying round the desk, Holden saw against the carpet the blood-smeared crystal with which, presumably, Thorley Marsh had been struck down. The people from the nursing home mustn't see it or hear about it—yet.

Regardless of fingerprints he picked it up, cradling it in Margot's letter, and carried it to the desk. When you straightened the pall cover, setting the crystal back in its holder and turning it round, the few blood smears were scarcely visible.

At the outer door, that soft rapping began again.

Holden set the desk lamp a little farther away on the table cover. Then, straightening his shoulders, he went into the front room. Drawing a deep breath, he twisted the knob of the Yale lock and opened the door.

Outside, with frightened faces, stood Celia Devereux and Dr. Gideon Fell.

Donald Holden could not have said whom or what he expected to find there: human being, beast, or devil. Yet certainly not these two. He backed away several paces, clutching Margot's letter.

"Are you—are you all right?" cried Celia.

"Yes, of course I'm all right. What are you doing here?"

"You look terribly rumpled up. Has there been a fight or something?"

"Yes. There's been a fight, right enough. But I haven't been in it."

Celia edged through the doorway. Her eyes, roving round this front room which might have been a fashionable doctor's waiting room, were furtive yet burning with curiosity. Dr. Fell, a wild-haired mammoth who had left behind hat, cloak, and one walking stick, breathed gustily as he lumbered in.

"Sir," he began, getting his voice level after a vast throat clearing, "our friend Inspector Crawford has discovered how the trick of moving the coffins was worked in the vault."

"Yes. I know."

"You know?"

"Danvers Locke told him. Locke's here now."

Dr. Fell's eyes flashed open. *"Here?"*

"Not in these rooms, no. He's downstairs, buying masks, at a place called Sedgwick & Co. Or he was. Anyway, he told Crawford."

"So it seemed advisable," grunted Dr. Fell, drawing a hand across his forehead, "to spirit the young lady away from police questioning until we could, or could not, prove something." He paused. "Mr. Hurst-Gore very kindly drove us to town. But he (harrumph) was compelled to drop us at Knightsbridge, and we have been more than an hour in getting here." Again Dr. Fell mopped his forehead, as though reluctant to approach what he must approach. "Well, my friend? What has been happening?"

Holden told them.

"Thorley," whispered Celia. "Thorley!"

"Celia! Please don't go into the other room!"

"A-all right, Don. Whatever you say."

Dr. Fell listened without comment. Yet, though he seemed no less grave, relief radiated from him like steam from a furnace.

"Thank you," he said, lifting his hand to shade his eyeglasses. "You have done well. Now will you please wait here for a moment: both of you. Er—better leave this front door open. In addition to your nursing-home people, I'm expecting our friend Shepton."

Holden stared at him. "Dr. Shepton?"

"Yes. I practically kidnapped the good gentleman from Caswall village. At the moment he is buying tobacco downstairs."

And Dr. Fell, without a word more of explanation, moved into the inner room. Holden and Celia were looking at each other in the hot, airless semigloom of the waiting room. Then Celia spoke in a low voice, dropping her eyes.

"Don."

"Yes?"

"That letter in your hand. Dr. Fell's been telling me a good deal about this. Is the letter one of Margot's?"

"Yes."

"May I read it?" Celia extended her hand.

"Celia, I'd rather you didn't! I . . ."

The slow smile, with the twitch of weariness or mockery at one corner of the lip, crept up into the clear tenderness of her eyes.

"Do you, of all people," she said, "think I mustn't be told about such things? I'm Margot's sister, you know. I can fall in love terribly too; and I have. Oh, Don!"

"All right. Here you are."

Now there were two persons to watch, in the silence that followed.

Celia took the letter and went to the window. She drew back one set of curtains with a wooden rattle of rings. Yet she hesitated, eyelashes lowered, with the letter pressed against her side, before she began to read.

In the adjoining room, the black-draped room with the crystal, Dr. Fell's tread could be heard all this time like the tread of an elephant. First he had blinked carefully down, through glasses that wouldn't stay straight, at the black fragments Holden had raked out of the fireplace.

Next he approached the back of the room, where curtains screened two doors set side by side. Billowing among the curtains, Dr. Fell opened the left-hand door, snapped on a light, and glanced into the kitchenette by which Holden had entered. Then he unlocked the right-hand door: a bathroom, as Holden could now see for himself as Dr. Fell switched on the light.

Celia began reading the letter. Her color rose and deepened, but her expression never changed and she did not raise her eyes.

Dr. Fell, after standing for some time in mountainous immobility at the door of the bathroom, switched off the light and closed the door. He wheeled round, his shaggy head lifted. And . . .

"No!" cried Celia. "No, no, no!"

Holden, who had been trying to watch both of them at once, felt his flesh go hot and cold at the suddenness of that exclamation.

"I'm sorry," said Celia, controlling herself. "But this name!"

"What name?"

"The man Margot was in love with." Amazement, incredulity (was there a slight disgust as well?) trembled in Celia's voice. " 'Sometimes I get pleasure just from repeating your name, over and over.' And here it is, about six times."

Celia stared at the past.

"But that explains—oh, that explains everything! Don! Didn't you read this letter?"

"I started to read it, yes. But that was when you and Dr. Fell knocked at the door. Who is the swine, anyway?"

Up the stairs out in the passage, with the effect of a competent quiet invasion, came a brisk young bachelor of medicine followed by two men carrying a folded stretcher. The young doctor made a feint of rapping on the inside of the open door.

"Emergency case?"

Holden nodded toward the back room. The deputation was met by Dr. Fell, who closed the door after them; and they could hear Dr. Fell's voice upraised in rapid speech as he did so.

Someone had followed the newcomers up the stairs. Old Dr. Eric Shepton, panting a little from the climb, his Panama hat in his hands and his white hair fluffed out round the bald head, loomed up big and stoop shouldered in the doorway. The kindly eye, the stubborn reticent jaw, had an air subtly different from his bearing in the playground.

"Celia, my dear!" he began.

Celia was paying no attention.

"At first it seems utterly incredible!" she said, taking a quick look at the letter and then folding it up into small creases. "And yet," she added, "is it so incredible? When you think of Margot? No. It's dreadfully *right*."

"Er—Celia, my dear!"

Celia woke up.

"You wouldn't speak to me," Shepton told her in a half-humorous tone, "all the way up in the car. And I hardly liked to speak in front of a stranger like Mr. Hurst-Gore. But I'm only a country g.p. I make more mistakes than I like to think, let alone admit. If I've made a mistake in your case . . ."

"Dr. Shepton!" Celia's eyes opened wide. "You don't think I'm holding that against you?"

The other looked startled. "Weren't you?"

"I told lies," said Celia, with a calmness which concealed misery. "What could you, or any decent person, possibly think? They'll probably arrest me; and heaven knows I shall deserve it." She put her hands over her eyes, and then flung them away again. "But why, oh, *why* couldn't you have told me about the other matter?"

"Because I was right not to do so," retorted the other, with a good deal of the kindliness vanishing under a hard shell. "And, London detectives or no London detectives, I still think I was right."

"Dr. Shepton, if you'd only told me!"

The door to the rear room opened.

Holden had no time to think about the meaning of the cryptic speeches he had just heard, though pain and anguish rang in Celia's voice.

Thorley Marsh, muffled to the head in a white covering, was gently and dexterously moved out on the stretcher. Thorley was still unconscious. But he was sobbing, in great gulping sobs which shook the white cloth.

The young physician from the nursing home, whose face was very grave, turned and addressed Dr. Fell.

"You understand, sir, that this will have to be reported to the police?"

"Sir," returned Dr. Fell, "by all means. You also have my assurance that I will report it myself. Exactly—how is he?"

"Pretty bad."

"Oh, ah! But I mean . . . ?"

"About one chance in ten. Gently, boys!"

I can't, Holden was thinking to himself, *I can't stand that sobbing much longer.* Thorley might know nothing; might feel nothing; he wandered mindless in some dim hinterland. Yet even in unconsciousness there is no sobbing without rooted cause.

Celia, her hands again pressed over her eyes, turned her back as that cortege went downstairs. Nobody spoke. Up the stairs after it had passed, moving softly, but gazing down at Thorley, came Sir Danvers Locke.

Locke, fastidious in an admirably cut blue suit, carrying a gray Homburg hat, gray gloves, and a walking stick, stood in the doorway in silence. The flesh was strained tight over his cheek bones; his mouth looked uncertain.

"If they'd only told me!" cried Celia. "If they'd only told me!"

Dr. Fell, so vast that he had to maneuver sideways through the door of the rear room and duck his head under it, now lowered among them. His face was fiery.

"My friend," he said to Holden, "this has gone far enough. We are going to end it. That contraption!" He pointed to the telephone with his cane.

"Yes?"

"It is (harrumph) erratic and unreliable. It never gets me the number I dial. Will you be good enough to outwit the blighter," intoned Dr. Fell, running his hand through his hair, "and get me the number I want?"

"Certainly. What number?"

"Whitehall 1212."

A stir, as of a very slight shock of electricity tingling the muscles, ran through the group at mention of that famous phone number. Seven times the dial whirred and clicked back. Then Holden handed the phone to Dr. Fell.

"Metropolitan police?" roared Dr. Fell, his several chins thrown back and his eyes villainously squinted at a corner of the ceiling. "I want to speak to Superintendent Hadley. My name is . . . oh, you recognize my voice? Yes; I'll hold on."

As though she could endure the atmosphere of this room

no longer, Celia raised the window by which she was standing. A gust of cooler air, grateful and cleansing, swept out the brocade curtains.

"Hadley?" said Dr. Fell, holding up the phone as though it were a jug from which he was about to drink. "I say. About this Caswall business."

The telephone spoke rapidly from the other end.

"So!" intoned Dr. Fell. "You got the order through and the post-mortem done in one day? What was it? Was it morphine and belladonna? Oh, ah. Good!"

Dr. Eric Shepton, staring at the floor, shook his head violently as though denying this. But Sir Danvers Locke was a picture of understanding.

"Well, look here," said Dr. Fell. "I'm now at 56b New Bond Street, top floor. Can you come over here straight-away?"

The telephone made angry protests, concluding with a single-word query.

"If you do," replied Dr. Fell, "I will present you with the murderer of Mrs. Marsh and the attempted murderer of Thorley Marsh."

Celia opened the other window, which ran up with a screech. Nobody else moved or spoke.

"No, of course I'm not joking!" roared Dr. Fell. His eye wandered round. "I have with me a group of (harrumph) friends now. Perhaps others will join us. I propose to begin now, and tell them the whole story.—When may we expect you? Right!"

He set back the phone with a clatter on its cradle, and swung round.

"One Hadley," he said, "one arrest."

Sir Danvers Locke, uttering a small cough to attract attention, moved forward. Of all the persons here, Holden wished most he could read the thoughts in Locke's head. When he thought of Locke sitting before a mirror, in the sympathetic presence of Mademoiselle Frey, and talking in a wild way about the "callousness and ruthlessness" of his own daughter (why Doris?), Holden could fit together no decipherable pattern.

"Dr. Fell!" said Locke. He paused for a moment. "Do you indeed propose to tell—the whole story?"

Nerve tension, under this studious politeness, was steadily going up.

"Yes," returned Dr. Fell.

"Do you mind, then, if I join you?"

"On the contrary, sir." Dr. Fell fumbled at his eyeglasses. "Your presence is almost a necessity." He paused. "I do not ask the obvious question."

"And yet," said Locke, "I will answer it."

Locke glanced sideways, through the doorway on his left, into the black-draped room where the crystal glimmered on the desk.

"I did not know," he spoke with painful enunciation, "that these rooms were here. Perhaps I suspected they might be somewhere . . ."

"Somewhere?"

"In London. We overhear our children speaking, just as they overhear us. But that they were *here*," the ferrule of his walking stick thudded softly on the carpet, "just over a place where I go two or three times a year to buy masks: this, on my oath, I did not know."

"Come into the next room," Dr. Fell said curtly. "Bring chairs."

As the group moved in, slowly and somberly, Celia hurried to Holden's side. She spoke in a whisper.

"Don. What's going to happen?"

"I wish I knew."

Celia reached out for his hands; and then drew back, her face whitening, as he flinched. She looked more closely. "Don! What have you done to your hand?"

"It's only a burn. It isn't anything. Listen, Celia: I quite honestly and sincerely mean it isn't anything; and I'm ordering you not to make a fuss. Because this is no round-table discussion. Something's going to burst with a hell of a bang."

This appeared to be the opinion of Locke and Dr. Shepton, each of whom had carried a gray damask waiting room chair into the shrine.

They were watching Dr. Fell.

Dr. Fell, as though silently urging them to note everything he did, made another inspection of the black-covered room. He motioned Holden toward the secret drawer, which contained Margot's letters, at the bottom of the Florentine cabinet.

Rightly interpreting this gesture, Holden took out the whole drawer, lifted it up, and put it on the side of the desk near the lamp. Into it Celia flung the letter she had been reading.

Dr. Fell picked up the letter, smoothed it out, and read it.

169

He glanced very rapidly through other sheets of blue note paper in the secret drawer. Then, after peering up at the covered skylight, and down at the carpet as though seeking something, he lowered himself into the tall Jacobean chair behind the desk.

"Those letters—" Locke began.

Dr. Fell did not reply.

In front of him gleamed the big crystal, against the coffin pall, with the small green-jade ibis head on one side, and the little plaque of the sleeping sphinx on the other. He reached out and picked up the plaque.

"'She also symbolizes,'" he read aloud, after a long pause, "'the two selves. The outer self which all the world may see—'" Dr. Fell stopped, and put down the plaque. "Yes, by thunder! That is the true application."

Slowly, while the others sat down, he fished out of his pockets an obese tobacco pouch and a curved meerschaum pipe. He filled the pipe, struck a match, and lit the tobacco with lingering care. The desk light, glimmering past the crystal, shone on his face.

"And now," said Dr. Fell, "hear the secret."

CHAPTER XIX

"You mean," Locke asked quickly, "the murderer?"

"Oh, no," said Dr. Fell, and shook his head.

"But you have just been telling us . . . !"

"That," continued Dr. Fell, blowing out more smoke, "can come later. I mean, at the moment, the carefully cherished secret which has sent so many persons wrong in this case."

Holden never afterward forgot their positions then.

He and Celia were sitting side by side on the huge velvet-covered divan, so sybaritic in that secret room. They saw Dr. Fell in profile, past smoke. Locke and Dr. Shepton were in chairs facing him, the former bending forward with his fingertips on the edge of the desk.

"It is all rooted," continued Dr. Fell, "in a tragic misunderstanding which has been going on for years. And it would all have been so simple, you know, if certain persons had only spoken out!

"But, oh, no. This thing must not be discussed. This thing was very awkward, if not actually shameful. It must be hushed up. So it was hushed up. And out of it grew pain and disillusionment and more misunderstanding; and, finally, murder."

Dr. Fell paused, dispelling smoke with a wave of his hand. His eyes were fixed with fierce concentration on Sir Danvers Locke.

"Sir," inquired Dr. Fell, "do you know what hysteria is?"

Locke, obviously puzzled, frowned.

"Hysteria? You mean—?"

"Not," said Dr. Fell decisively, "the loose, inaccurate sense in which all of us use the term. We say a person is hysterical or behaving hysterically when he or she may only be very much upset. No, sir! I referred to the nervous disease known to medical science as real hysteria.

"If I speak as a layman," he added apologetically, "Dr. Shepton will (harrumph) doubtless correct me. But this hysteria, the group of associated symptoms called hysteria, may be comparatively mild. Or it may require serious treatment by a neurologist. Or it may end, and can end, in actual insanity."

Again Dr. Fell paused.

Celia, beside Holden, sat motionless with her hands on her knees and her head bent forward. But he could feel her soft arm tremble.

"Let me tell you," pursued Dr. Fell, "some of the milder symptoms of the hysteric. I repeat: the milder! Each one of them, taken by itself, is not necessarily evidence of hysteria. But you will never find the true hysteric, who may be either a woman or a man, without all of them."

"And we are dealing here—?" demanded Locke.

"With a woman," said Dr. Fell.

(Again Celia's arm trembled.)

"The hysteric is easily moved, by small things, to either laughter or tears. She is always blurting out something before realizing its meaning. The hysteric loves the limelight; she must have attention paid her; she must play the tragedy queen. The hysteric is an inordinate diary keeper, with pages and pages of events that are often untrue. The hysteric is always threatening to commit suicide, but never does it. The hysteric is unduly fascinated by the mystic or the occult. The . . ."

"Wait a minute!" said Donald Holden.

His voice exploded in that group with the effect of blast waves.

"You spoke?" inquired Dr. Fell, as though there had been some doubt of this.

"Yes; very much so. You're not describing Celia, you know."

"Ah!" murmured Dr. Fell.

Holden swallowed hard to get his words in order.

"Celia loathes the limelight," he said, "or she'd have told her story all over the place instead of keeping it so dark. Celia never blurts out anything; she's almost too quiet. Celia can't even keep an ordinary diary, let alone the kind you're talking about. Celia admits she'd never have the courage to commit suicide. You're not describing Celia, Dr. Fell! But—"

"But?" prompted Dr. Fell.

"You've given a thunderingly accurate picture of *Margot*."

"Got it," breathed Dr. Fell. "Do you all see the tragedy now?"

He sank back in the big chair, making a vague gesture with the pipe. There was a silence before he went on.

"There, over the green lawns of the past, walked Margot Devereux. And how the outside world misunderstood!

"Because she was robust, because she was jovial, because she liked games, they laughed and approved and applauded. 'Strapping,' they called her. 'Uninhibited,' was another word. And if at times something seemed odd? Well! Only over-hearty, which was not a bad thing. Not only did the outside world misunderstand, but they got the position the wrong way round.

"Everyone here, I imagine, has heard the famous remark which Mammy Two made on a number of occasions. *'There's a funny streak in our family, y'know. One of my grand-daughters is all right, but I've been worried about the other ever since she was a little child.'* And, of course, that remark was applied to the wrong person.

"Suspect Margot, the hearty and athletic? In England, good sirs? Damme! Fie upon you! So they never guessed, any more than her own sister guessed, that Margot Devereux was a hysteric with the potentialities of a dangerous hysteric.

"But Mammy Two knew. The family doctor knew. Obey and Cook: be sure they knew. And they waited (with God knows what fear in their hearts; I am not looking at Dr. Shepton now) while Margot grew up into a very beautiful

172

woman. Even then stark tragedy might have been averted, if . . ."

Holden sat up straight.

"If—what?" he demanded.

"If Margot," replied Dr. Fell, "had not married."

Celia was trembling violently. Holden did not look at her.

"I will not," scowled Dr. Fell, "discuss the various physical causes which may bring about hysteria. Except to say this: that the hysteric becomes dominated by a fixed idea. She believes, let us say, that she is blind. To all intents and purposes, she *is* blind.

"In a case like that of Margot Devereux, it is plain that to marry almost any man would be dangerous. Except in the remote chance of finding the right man, it would be disastrous. For its root is sexual.

"Once married, she discovers (or thinks she discovers, which is the same thing) that physical intimacy with her husband is a matter of horror. She screams when he approaches her. His mere touch is nausea. And the poor devil of a husband, wondering bewilderedly what is wrong and why he has turned into a leper, is faced with a raging madwoman. And this may go on for years. And nobody ever knows."

Dr. Fell paused. Distressed and yet dogged, he would not look round; he kept his eyes fixed on the crystal.

And Holden, with a chill at his heart, recognized that his most poignant memory—the marriage in Caswall Church, with the colored dresses and the echo of music—must subtly alter in line. He must reinterpret the odd looks and tears of both Mammy Two and Obey. He must reinterpret, now he remembered it, the frankly dubious gaze of Dr. Shepton.

But above all (curse himself for being so blind!) he must reinterpret Thorley Marsh.

He must recognize why, in seven years, there had been changes in Thorley. Moods, expressions, whole sentences spoken by Thorley, crowded back to trouble him. Best of all he remembered Thorley being questioned by Dr. Fell in the Long Gallery last night. How do you know the door to your wife's bedroom was locked on her side? "It always was." And again Thorley's blank-voiced, groping cry: "Liquor always used to make me feel happy. It never does, now."

"Dr. Fell!" Holden said softly.

"Eh?"

"This plain speaking is right. It's got to be done. But do you think, in front of Celia—?"

"I know," said Celia, and turned suddenly and put her

173

cheek against his shoulder. "I heard about it this afternoon. But I never knew before. Dr. Fell! Tell them about . . . the seizures."

"Yes, by thunder!" said Dr. Fell in a different voice.

He put down his pipe, which had gone out.

"The hysteric, under these conditions, is afflicted with attacks in the form of physical seizures. They may be brought on by a word, a look, by nothing at all. The husband, on one occasion, may completely lose his head. To quiet that screaming, he may strike his wife across the face with a razor strap; or try to choke the cries in her throat with his hands.

"On other occasions, the attacks may be more severe. They may need medical aid. When the hysteric is afflicted like this, she has a tetanic attack—limbs rigid, body arched—exactly, to the eye of an uninformed person who sees it, like a case of strychnine poisoning."

Here Dr. Fell, wheezing angrily, looked at Danvers Locke.

"And then the hysteric, as hysterics will, admits to Celia Devereux that she has swallowed strychnine to end her tragic life! Archons of Athens! Can you wonder that another girl, perfectly normal but frightened half out of her wits because no one has seen fit to tell her, misunderstands all this? Can you wonder Celia Devereux thought what she did think? Good God, what would you expect?"

Dr. Fell controlled himself.

Breathing noisily, he wedged himself back into the chair. He was silent for a moment, one hand shading his eyeglasses. Then he addressed Dr. Shepton very quietly.

"Sir," he said, "it is not my place to question your professional conduct of this case."

"Thank you." Dr. Shepton looked back at him steadily.

"But why couldn't you have told Celia?"

Dr. Shepton, though he looked very old and very tired, kept the stubborn set of his jaw. He was bending forward, his big-knuckled hands holding the Panama hat.

"It's a pity," he murmured, shaking his head. "It's all such a pity!"

"I quite agree with you."

"But is it possible," insisted Shepton, "that you of all people still do not understand? I feared—we all feared—that . . ."

"That Celia, being Margot's sister, might be a hysteric too? And that to tell her all this might do her much harm?"

"In fact, yes."

("Easy, Celia!" murmured Holden.)

"Ah!" said Dr. Fell. "But, previous to Margot Marsh's death, had you ever any reason to suppose this about Celia?"

"It was always a risk. It was always a risk!"

"Sir, that was not the question I asked you. Had you any reason to suppose it?"

"No! No! I distinctly told Sir Donald Holden, two nights ago"—Dr. Shepton lifted his Panama hat and pointed with it—"that in Celia's version of what she called strychnine poisoning, there might have been room for . . . well! certain unavoidable misunderstandings."

"There *might* have been room?"

"Yes. And I would have told Sir Donald the whole story, too, if he had only come around to my hotel as I suggested. In reply to your main question: no! I had no concrete reason for suspecting Celia of hysterical delusions until . . ."

Dr. Fell bent forward.

"Until, in somebody's phrase, she began seeing ghosts all over the place? Is that correct?"

"Yes."

Unexpectedly, Dr. Fell began to chuckle.

It began, with slow earthquake violence, in the lower ridges of his waistcoat. It traveled up the tentlike alpaca suit in a spasm of uproarious amusement. Suddenly becoming conscious of Shepton's outraged look, Dr. Fell clapped his hand over his mouth and turned to Holden.

"Forgive me!" he pleaded. "I was guilty of another such unmannerly outburst, if you recall, when I met you in the Long Gallery at Caswall. But, as we clear away the poisonous nonsense, I think you will join in. Will you cast your mind back to Wednesday evening about dusk?"

"Well?"

"To the first time you went out to the Regent's Park house?"

"Well?" repeated Holden.

"Well," said Dr. Fell simply, "I shadowed you."

"You *what?*"

"I," Dr. Fell announced proudly, "shadowed somebody. Didn't I tell you you'd allowed me to accomplish something I never believed was possible? At first I didn't shadow you consciously, of course. Let me explain."

All the amusement faded out of Dr. Fell's expression. In that dim light his face looked grave and even sinister.

"Celia Devereux's letter to the police had been received two days before. It was handed over to me, who already knew something of the matter from having sealed the vault.

All the major events were outlined in that letter, including the ghosts of the Long Gallery. And I was disturbed. It seemed to me that in the elder sister we were dealing with a case of sexual hysteria—"

(For some reason, at this point, Sir Danvers Locke shuddered.)

"—and in the younger sister, perhaps, with nervous hysteria. I didn't know. I had to make sure. So on Wednesday evening, armed with the letter, I went out to the house in Gloucester Gate to ask questions.

"Ahead of me on the pavement," and again Dr. Fell nodded toward Holden, "I saw you bound for the same house.

"I had no idea who you were, or of your status in this affair. But you went in by the back way. I followed. I saw you go up those iron stairs to the balcony outside the drawing room. I saw you strike a light, and peer in through the window. I heard a girl scream (it was Doris Locke), and a man cry out. It seemed so extraordinary that I followed you up.

"And what happened?

"Outside those windows I heard more of the wretched, pitiable story. The tangled lives! The enshrouding misery! I learned who you were. I heard Thorley Marsh, who sincerely believed Celia to be mad just as she believed him a sadistic brute, I heard Thorley Marsh beg and plead with you to go away. And the door opened. And Celia Devereux walked in."

Here Dr. Fell looked very steadily at Holden.

"Have you forgotten," he asked, "that you were supposed to be dead?"

Holden started to get up off the divan, but sat down again. Dr. Fell nodded toward Celia, who had turned her head away.

"Here is a girl," he said, "supposedly so neurotic that she is seeing ghosts everywhere. She has had no warning this man is alive. She really believes him dead. All she sees, in one terrifying flash, is his face looking at her against the light of a single lamp in a dark room.

"And yet—she knows.

"I see her again, standing against that door in her white dress. The nerves tell the brain; the brain tells the heart. She does not even ask a question. She knows. 'They sent you on some special sort of job,' I hear her saying; 'that was why you couldn't see me or write to me.' And then, with a little nod, 'Hello, Don.'"

Holden would not have believed Dr. Fell's voice could be so gentle.

But Dr. Fell would not look at Celia. Ponderously he turned his head away. Removing his eyeglasses, he pressed his hand for a moment over his eyes before putting back the glasses. He addressed Locke and Dr. Shepton.

"Gentlemen," he said, "I write Q.E.D. and draw a flourish under it. If that girl is in the least neurotic, then I am the late Adolf Hitler. What does the prosecution say, what dares the prosecution say, in reply to that?"

There was a long silence.

"Well done!" said Locke, and struck his knee. "Write your Q.E.D.! Well done!"

"You talk," cried Dr. Shepton, "as though—" He stopped. "'Prosecution!'" he added. "You talk as though—"

"Yes?" prompted Dr. Fell.

"As though," he spoke in a quavering voice, "I wanted to harm Celia in some way!"

"Forgive me," said Dr. Fell. "I know you don't. And you were misled. Blame the girl, if you like, for telling lies. But in God's name let us have an end of these hush-hush methods which nearly did send her out of her mind and drove her to telling lies!"

"To—er—what do you refer by hush-hush methods?"

"The carefully cherished secret of Margot Marsh's hysteria, which ended in her murder. I am going on to explain that murder."

Dr. Fell picked up his dead pipe.

"Let's continue with the evidence of that same Wednesday evening. All this I heard and saw from the balcony outside the drawing room. Once (hurrum!) I was nearly spotted. You may recall, my dear Holden, that on one occasion Thorley Marsh thought he heard somebody out on the balcony? In very truth he did.

"However!

"Having begun this business of shadowing, I continued it. When you and Celia left the house (forgive me again!), I followed you. You may perhaps have noticed the shadow, too large to be any but mine, which emerged after you when you crossed the street toward Regent's Park? In any case, one side of the park playground had an open side with an iron railed

177

fence. Out of sight, beyond this, I heard the whole story," he nodded toward Celia, "from you.

"I heard it in blazing detail. In shades and nuances and hints which in their implications were staggering. By thunder, but it was a revelation!

"For if I postulated Margot Marsh as a hysteric, the approach of the storm could be seen with ugly clearness. About a year before her death, *she changed*. She became happy. Bright-eyed. Laughing and humming. Her own sister, not an observant person, says to her, 'You must have a lover.'

"The hundred-to-one chance had happened. The hysteric had met a man to whom she was suited. She was deeply and physically in love. The outward symptoms of hysteria disappeared, which is what always happens in such cases. But, instead of helping matters, it led inevitably to disaster.

"Why? Because she was bound to be thwarted! She wanted the person in question; wanted to marry him; and couldn't have him. For one thing, Thorley Marsh refused to allow a divorce."

"Dr. Fell, listen!" interrupted Holden. "That's the one part of the whole affair which doesn't seem to be reasonable!" He glanced at Locke. "Would you mind, now, if I did a little plain speaking?"

"I mind?" Locke's eyebrows went up. "Why should I?"

"About Doris, I mean."

"Oh. Doris. I see." Locke's hands tightened round the glove and walking stick that lay across his lap. "No. Not at all. Of course not!"

"In that case, Dr. Fell," demanded Holden, "where was the snag? If Thorley wanted to marry Doris, and Margot was violently in love with this other fellow, why couldn't there have been a compromise? Why did Thorley—of all people, in a situation like this—object to a divorce?"

"For the most powerful reason in the world," replied Dr. Fell, "which you will understand when you learn the whole truth. Let me emphasize this, though it may seem a bit cryptic to you now, by asking you a certain question. It is a serious question. Don't treat it lightly."

"Well?" prompted Holden.

"Well," said Dr. Fell, "are you still jealous of Derek Hurst-Gore?"

Dead silence.

In the quiet of that muffled room they could hear, from the outer room, the rustle and blowing of curtains at the open windows. Clean air crept even into the haze and smoke of this lair. Celia Devereux, startled, turned up pleading eyes.

"Don!" she cried. "You didn't *really* think that I . . . that Derek and I . . ?"

"Please answer the question," intoned Dr. Fell. "Are you still jealous of Mr. Hurst-Gore?"

"No, I'm not," Holden answered honestly. "When I only heard about him, and even when I first met him, he put my teeth on edge. But that passed very quickly. I think he's quite a decent sort."

"Ah!" boomed Dr. Fell. His eyes opened wide. "And why do you think that? Isn't it because you know, in your heart, that you're the favored suitor?"

Holden felt his cheeks grow hot. "I shouldn't like to put it quite . . ."

"Come, sir! Isn't it?"

"Very well. It is. But what application has this got to Margot and Thorley?"

Dr. Fell ignored the question.

"I need not stress the situation in the Marsh family," he went on, "since so much of it emerged in evidence yesterday. But think of the repressed violence, the hidden thunderbolts, crammed into it when that group went down to Caswall Moat House two days before Christmas!

"Many months before, the hysteric has met her lover. For a time all is serene. Then, in October, as we hear from Celia Devereux, violent rows break out between Mr. and Mrs. Marsh. They are heard behind closed doors. Thorley Marsh knows all about it, or has heard all about it. I think we are safe in postulating, at this stage, that Mr. Marsh knew who the man was."

"Why should you think that?" demanded Locke.

"Sir, your own daughter believes so," answered Dr. Fell. "She told Holden as much. If Margot wanted a divorce, she would obviously have told her husband who the man was.

"Then (mark it!) there is a space of dangerous quiet, while plans are being made. But it all boils up in tragedy when Margot and her husband, with Celia here, go to Caswall two days before Christmas.

"Follow the tensity of that scene, as described by Celia, before they set out for Widestairs in the evening to go to the party! Thorley Marsh, all that evening, so white faced that Obey thought he was ill: 'with furious dead-looking eyes.' And very polite.

179

"His wife all of a glitter, all in the mood which you, Sir Danvers, described to me. We can't get away from it. Late that afternoon or early in the evening—after going over to Widestairs to look for her husband—she had made one last appeal to him to arrange for a divorce. Thorley Marsh refused.

"She never guessed for a second that her husband was, to put it delicately, fond of Doris Locke. No! It was her affair, her affair; that was all she thought of. All the world was blotted out except for that. Margot Marsh *had* come to a decision. It was a typical hysteric's decision."

Dr. Fell paused. With his dead pipe he gestured toward Holden.

"Holden there," he said, "hit the nail bang on the head, or near enough, when he wrote two certain words on a piece of paper and gave it to me. He had worked out what Margot Marsh's decision—and her lover's decision too—apparently was. Tell these gentlemen what it was!"

"But . . ." Holden began.

"Tell them!"

The eyes of Locke and Dr. Shepton, which seemed unnaturally large, were fixed on Holden. Tension had grown to such a point that no one except Dr. Fell could quite sit still.

"If we decided this was murder—" Holden began.

"Go on!"

"If we decided this was murder, there was only one explanation of why it looked so much like suicide. Margot really had changed her gown in the middle of the night: dressing up (as Celia said) in the manner of someone going to a great dinner. Margot herself had the poison bottle, which we now know contained morphine and belladonna. The words I wrote for Dr. Fell were *suicide pact.*"

Locke started to get up.

"You mean . . ?"

"A suicide pact," retorted Holden, "arranged between Margot and her lover. At a certain time that night—she in one place, he in another—each of them was to drink poison. But he never intended to keep his side of the bargain. It would be a perfect method of murder."

Locke's immaculate hat, gloves, and walking stick dropped to the floor.

"Is this true, Dr. Fell?" he demanded.

"As far as it goes, yes."

"As far as it goes?"

"For if it is true," interposed Holden, "it means this was

a crime at long distance. The murderer needn't have been in the house at all."

"*Oh, yes, the murderer was,*" said Dr. Fell.

"In the house?" whispered Locke through dry lips.

"Yes."

"But . . ."

"Didn't I tell you," exclaimed Dr. Fell testily, "that the true hysteric never commits suicide? Margot Marsh passionately wanted a hysteric's suicide for love, yes. She believed she could go through with it, yes. She would even have drunk the poison, yes."

"Well, then!"

"But, when she felt the effects of the poison coming on, the true hysteric couldn't have held out. She couldn't have faced death. She would have screamed for help, and used it as a weapon, a lever, to force Thorley Marsh into granting what she wanted. She wouldn't really have died, unless . . ."

"Go on!"

"Unless," said Dr. Fell, "someone crept in and struck her down unconscious. Unconscious, you see! So that the poison could do its work. Oh, yes. The murderer was in the house."

"Thank God!" Locke blurted out the words. They could see the veins standing out in his neck. "Thank God!"

"Why do you say that?"

"It is villainous to say so. It is wicked to say so." Locke controlled himself. "But I do say it. The murderer was in the house! It must have been Thorley Marsh (no, that couldn't be). Or Celia Devereux. (No! That couldn't be either!) Or—Derek Hurst-Gore."

"Not necessarily," said Dr. Fell.

"For the love of heaven, man," exploded Dr. Shepton, "say what you do mean!"

"As you like," assented Dr. Fell. "Shall I show you the murderer now?"

"Where?" asked Locke, looking wildly round the room.

"From Celia Devereux's story, you see," said Dr. Fell, "there were certain blazing indications as to where to look for the murderer. When I went to Caswall on Thursday evening, I asked a number of questions and got the replies I wanted. By thunder, I got *more* than I wanted."

Slowly Dr. Fell hoisted himself to his feet, pushing back the big Jacobean chair.

"As to the murderer being in the house . . ."

"Whoever it was," said Locke, "couldn't have got into the house from outside!"

"Why not?"

"Every night," retorted Locke, "that place is locked up like a fortress front and back. Round it is a moat thirty feet wide and a dozen feet deep."

"Yes," said Dr. Fell. "That is what I mean."

"What you mean?—Where is this murderer?"

"He's here," said Dr. Fell.

Into the room, now, fell another shadow: the shadow of a tall middle-aged man who entered from the door to the front room. It was, in fact, Superintendent Hadley of the Criminal Investigation Department. But such is the effect of suggestion that every listener jumped up and turned toward Hadley as though . . .

"You are looking," observed Dr. Fell, "in the wrong direction."

"Wherever we are looking," cried Locke, "get on with this! You say the murderer is *here?*"

"As a matter of fact," said Dr. Fell, "he has been here all the time. That's why I had the nerve to call Hadley and force the issue. Our poisoning friend was rather badly smashed about in a fight with Thorley Marsh. He crawled in to get water, and collapsed."

"Crawled. . . ?"

"Into the bathroom."

Slowly Dr. Fell lumbered to the rear wall. Drawing back one of the black-velvet curtains, he disclosed the door of the little bathroom beside the kitchenette.

Dr. Fell opened the door. The light inside, which formerly had been switched off, was now burning.

And Celia screamed.

A man stood just inside, on shaking legs; and in his hand was the small, sharp blade from a safety razor. They saw it glitter as it went up to his own throat. Dr. Fell, lurching forward, cut off the view. But not before they had seen the white face, the staring eyes, the dark hair tumbled over the forehead.

For the murderer was young Ronald Merrick.

CHAPTER XX

IT WAS the following evening, in the big drawing room at Number 1 Gloucester Gate, that the whole of the story came to be told.

At the moment only Celia, Holden, and Dr. Fell were present. The room, Holden thought, looked just at it had looked when he stepped through the balcony window four nights ago: only the one table lamp lighted beside the large white-covered sofa, where Dr. Fell sat in vastness, frowning guiltily at a cigar.

Celia, facing him, was perched on the arm of Holden's chair.

"Ronnie Merrick," Celia said flatly, "was Margot's lover. And he murdered her."

"Oh, ah," grunted Dr. Fell, without raising his eyes.

"I think I guessed everything," Celia bit at her under lip, "when I saw his name in the note Margot wrote. But . . . Ronnie! He wasn't quite twenty!"

"That," said Dr. Fell, "is the whole point."

"How do you mean?"

"Merrick," said Dr. Fell, "was the vain, spoiled, unstable son of an eminent peer. He was too young, psychologically speaking, to realize quite what he was doing. But the law can take no cognizance of that. It's a good thing he—"

"Did away with himself?" supplied Holden. And then, with an effort: "Tell us about it."

"Dash it all!" complained Dr. Fell.

He reared back, so that the lamp rocked on its table and threw unsteady gleams across the green-painted walls and the marble mantelpiece with the great Venetian mirror. At Dr. Fell's knee there was a little table bearing a decanter of whisky, glasses, and a jug of water. But for the time being Dr. Fell did not touch them. He blinked round vaguely for an ash tray. Finding none, he tipped most of the cigar ash into his side pocket and let the rest float over his waistcoat as he settled back. Perturbed, he fiddled with his eyeglasses, took several puffs at the cigar and looked straight at Celia.

"Your sister," he said, "liked young people."

"I know." Celia nodded.

"That is the starting point," said Dr. Fell. "You stressed it in your own narrative. Your first thought, when you found Margot lying dead, was, 'She was so fond of young people.' I heard it ring in your voice when you said it. If we were looking for a man in the case, it was far more reasonable to look for a handsome youngster than anyone else. But put that aside, for the moment.

"Two points in that story of yours—both relating to the Murder game at Widestairs, and both concerning real-life criminals—struck me as perhaps of great significance.

"The first was that Margot wouldn't, in that game, play the part of Old Mother Dyer. No! On that particular night (strung up, having made her decision) she insisted on being Mrs. Thompson. You will recall, of course, that Mrs. Thompson was executed for connivance in the murder of her husband, because of her passion for her lover Frederick Bywaters: a boy much younger than herself?

"Coincidence? I hardly thought so.

"The other was that Ronnie Merrick (of all people) had been chosen to play the part of Dr. Robert Buchanan of New York. Are you familiar with the case?"

"No, no, no!" groaned Celia, shaking her head violently. From the arm of the chair she looked down at Holden and smiled.

"I understand," she added, "they were going to make out a terrific case against me for dreaming I was Maria Manning being hanged while people sang 'Oh, Susannah.' But really and truly I'm not guilty! Derek—Derek told me that bit, in the car on the way back home from the party!"

"Exactly!" boomed Dr. Fell.

"How do mean, 'exactly?' "

Dr. Fell pointed with his cigar.

"I agreed with Holden on Friday," he said, "that it was nothing, it was tuppenny-ha'penny evidence, it was a trifle which might be explained in half a dozen ways. But, if people pitched on that, it seemed amazing nobody had noticed the real howler which was made that night. Do you remember the Murder game?"

"Horribly well!"

"Young Merrick was cast as Dr. Buchanan. You desecribed him as 'dithering.' He said to you something like: 'My name's Dr. Buchanan; but I don't know who the hell I am or what I'm supposed to have done; can you help me?' Correct?"

"Yes."

"But I myself," pursued Dr. Fell, "went down to Caswall to ask some questions. In the Long Gallery (follow the line of attack here!) I put questions about the Murder game to Sir Danvers Locke, to Doris Locke, and Thorley Marsh. And I learned this from Locke:

"Locke hadn't anticipated his surprise game by telling anyone about it beforehand. But he had unobtrusively seen to it that every single person, with the exception of yourself, and necessarily the stranger Hurst-Gore, was very well read in his or her part. Got it? Very well read—he even presented them with his own file on each case.

"Now there seemed no earthly reason for Locke to tell a lie there. All other testimony corroborated it. He would be especially sure young Merrick, his protégé, the boy he hoped to have as a son-in-law, had read the case of Dr. Buchanan. Why, therefore, should Merrick have 'dithered' and blurted out that unnecessary lie when unexpectedly faced with this role?

"Well! Consider the facts.

"Dr. Buchanan, in 1893, poisoned his wife: a middle-aged hysteric. He poisoned her with a large quantity of morphine and a small quantity of belladonna, because the belladonna would offset the only outward symptom of morphine poisoning: contracted eye pupils. The belladonna would also, in morphia unconsciousness, produce hysterical symptoms. And the attending physicians would make no difficulty about certifying death from cerebral hemorrhage. That is what they did."

Dr. Fell bent forward.

"Just," he added, "as Dr. Shepton had no doubt about the cause of death in the case of Margot Marsh. Eh?

"In my interpretation, this lady's lover feared her horribly and wished her dead. At her own suggestion, they formed a suicide pact. Each, at a given time but in a different place, was to drink poison. And this was his chance.

"Incidentally, from certain letters to be dealt with in a moment, we now know something else. The morphine was provided by the lady herself, hoarded from various prescriptions, for her lover to make into a liquid solution. She thought it would be morphine alone, which is painless. The belladonna, easily procurable, he added to it. With full directions before him in the trial of Dr. Buchanan, even the callowest of criminals could not go wrong.

"But the murderer couldn't trust to that alone, even if

he had been dealing with a normal woman. Suppose she backs out? Suppose she swallows the poison and then shrieks for help? He must make sure; he must be there, on the spot.

"When I questioned Sir Danvers, Doris, and Thorley Marsh in the Long Gallery, certain evidence emerged with great clarity. Have you forgotten that on the afternoon before the crime Ronnie Merrick *fell into the water?*"

Celia stared down at Holden, and then perplexedly across at Dr. Fell.

"Oh, come!" Dr. Fell pointed his cigar at Holden. "You recall the episode in the afternoon, when Merrick fell into the trout stream. The fascinating point was not that Thorley Marsh walked across a log with his eyes shut. The fascinating point was that an agile young man rather clumsily fell in.

"But suppose, that same night, you intend to invade Caswall Moat House secretly. You can't get in by the front or back door; both are too heavily secured. Your only course it to . . . Eh?"

"To swim the moat," Holden said thoughtfully.

"Yes. The clue is water. It's not practicable to leave your clothes behind and invade the house naked, even if it weren't a bitter cold December night. Yet you must provide some explanation next morning, to hosts or servants, of why you have a suit of clothes completely soaked. And if you get it soaked beforehand, who will suspect it next day of a double immersion?

"Next evidence! Thorley Marsh, telling his detailed story of the night of the murder, walloped me in the eye with another bit. You recall his statement that Margot—in the middle of the night—must have taken a *bath?*

"He knew this, he said, because the floor of the bathroom was all wet and there was a towel thrown over the edge of the tub.

"But his interpretation wasn't feasible. For what had I overheard, on Wednesday night, from no less than two witnesses? That the hot-water system at Caswall was out of order. It did not get repaired until next day. Even the water for washing had to be carried up in little cans."

Dr. Fell looked at Celia.

"Do you, my dear, believe your sister would have taken a cold bath in the middle of a December night?"

"It's—it's absurd!" cried Celia. "Margot *loathed* cold. I remember telling you so myself, when we were in the churchyard."

"Ah!" grunted Dr. Fell. "And what else did you tell us?"

"What else?"

"In your original statement. You said, I think, that the bathroom window couldn't be locked?"

"Y-yes! It's a swing-together window that never would fit or latch properly."

"And what," inquired Dr. Fell, "is just outside that bathroom window?"

It was Holden who answered.

"A vertical terra-cotta drainpipe. A heavy one." He stared at the past. "I remember noticing it from the oriel window in the Long Gallery, just under that bathroom, when I was reading the note you gave me!"

"Should you (hurrum!) should you say that Ronnie Merrick, as a young man, is probably an agile climber?"

"He damn well *is* an agile climber. He can go all over Caswall Church."

"So we perceive," observed Dr. Fell, "that the wet floor wasn't caused by anyone taking a bath. But, unfortunately, Thorley Marsh put on his slippers before going on to his wife's bedroom and sitting room. Archons of Athens," groaned Dr. Fell, "if only he hadn't worn his slippers!

"For then, you see, he would have stepped in more wet tracks. The tracks of someone who came in through that unlocked window. The tracks of someone from the moat. The tracks of a desperate youth, half-screaming with hatred for his mistress, and bent on murder."

Celia slipped off the arm of Holden's chair and stood up.

"Dr. Fell," she breathed, "you really are a devil."

Dr. Fell, who resembled nothing so much as a perturbed Old King Cole, blinked at her over his eyeglasses.

"Hey?"

"You build up a case," Celia shivered, "bang, bang, bang, point after point, as complete and awful as—I was going to say, as a hangman's rope. But, please! Never mind your evidence. What I want to know is: why?"

"Oh, ah," said Dr. Fell.

"Why did they all behave like that? Why did Ronnie do such an awful thing? Why did Margot . . . oh, everything! The human motives!"

"Ah, yes," murmured Dr. Fell. "Ronnie Merrick."

He was silent for a long time, his thoughts far away.

"Here is a young man," he said, "Byronicaly handsome, very callow but admittedly of great talent, who has been indulged in every whim of his life. Everything he has wanted has been given to him. And now he wants Doris Locke.

"Please understand that. He was sincerely, blindly, ideal-istically in love with Doris. He exalted, of course, a girl who did not exist; but that is of no matter, because it happens to all young men. Very deeply he loved Doris; and hoped to marry her; never forget it; it is the mainspring of the murder.

"As for your sister . . ." Dr. Fell hesitated.

"Dr. Fell!" said Celia. "Please. No delicacy. I want to know."

"The story of their affair you may read in that long series of letters she wrote, and never posted; like a diary. I read them all today. But I suggest you don't read them. By thunder, it's a good thing they won't have to be read in court!

"As for the boy, he was at first flattered. Proud of being a conqueror! Captivated, too, for a time; because he was dizzy with the strongest of all stimulants in this world. But then—and it always will happen to immature people brought up in public-school traditions—he began to feel debased. He contrasted this with what he felt, or believed he felt, toward Doris Locke.

"And he began to hate Margot.

"On her side, the infatuation was only increasing. As he grew lukewarm, she grew more obsessed. To the boy's horror, she began talking about marriage.

"Thorley Marsh, who quite manifestly had learned of the whole thing, was only a little less horrified.

"Didn't you two ever wonder why Thorley Marsh always felt so intensely bitter toward young Merrick? When he was first giving you," Dr. Fell looked at Holden, "an account of his wife's death, he burst out into a tirade against Merrick in the middle of it. You may recall other occasions as well."

"Yes," agreed Holden. "Even when Thorley and Doris were telling Locke they meant to get married, Thorley noticed Merrick and got as black as thunder. Thorley as good as ordered him out of the house."

"Oh, ah? But why should he feel like that? Because of any jealousy he may have felt for Merrick as a rival in Doris's affections? Great Scott, no! He knew he was the favored suitor. Nobody could mistake that. When you are the one-and-only, you don't detest the fallen rival. You are more in-clined to think him an excellent fellow who is a little to be pitied. I (harrum!) indicated as much to you with a question about your own attitude towards Derek Hurst-Gore.

"Do you see now why Thorley Marsh wanted to keep

everything hush-hush, and would never have agreed to a divorce?"

"I think I see," murmured Celia. "It—it would have made him look a fool."

"A thundering fool, in his own eyes! Whether she officially divorces him, or he divorces her, the truth will be flying round for the amusement of all his acquaintances and friends.

"'Marsh's wife,' he could hear them saying at his club, with whoops of hilarity, 'is throwing him over for a boy not quite twenty. What *ho!*' If ever he tried to explain that his wife is a hysteric who can't stand his touch, at best it will sound caddish and at worst it will provoke more amusement."

Another scene returned to Holden in sharp colors of memory.

"'Show himself a fool,'" he repeated. "That was what Hurst-Gore said! It was when you were deviling Thorley to admit the whole truth, and nearly did get him to admit it. Hurst-Gore intervened, and shut Thorley up. Do you think our Derek knew everything?"

"That is my belief. He was Thorley's tutor in that gentleman's political ambitions. However, consider the situation just before Margot Marsh's death.

"To young Merrick, writhing, it had become simply intolerable. He is more than shying away from this older woman; he is frightened of her. She may do anything. *Doris will hear of this!* He'll never marry Doris! It will ruin his life!

"Youth, when frightened, can become insensately cruel. Merrick, as I met him later at Widestairs, was a likeable sort. But he was jumpy, unsteady (surely you saw that for yourself?) and blind to the matter in its right perspective. Like many another young man in a love affair from which he hasn't the experience to extricate himself, he could see only one way. He lost his head and decided to kill her.

"Margot suggested the suicide pact. And he, at the unnoticed suggestion of Locke, had been reading about another hysterical woman: Mrs. Buchanan. Mrs. Buchanan dies of morphine-and-belladonna poisoning, and the doctors call it a natural death.

"Could it be done? *Can* it be done? I see him gnawing his fingernails over the question, and deciding to try.

"So I attempted to discover just when Merrick might have given the prepared poison bottle to his victim. She had visited Widestairs that afternoon; but apparently she hadn't met Merrick.

"It was not until last night that I learned Merrick had been seen trudging back from the trout stream, with a greatcoat over his sodden clothes, meeting her in the fields near Widestairs . . ."

"And giving her the poison bottle!" interrupted Holden. "Locke saw him do it!"

Dr. Fell blinked at him.

"True," he grunted. "So I was informed by Locke last night. But how did you know it?"

"From overhearing Locke talking to a certain Mademoiselle Frey. Locke had been putting two and two together, with a suspicion which terrified him. Yes! And when he gave that fierce lecture about the 'utter callousness' of young people, he wasn't talking about Doris at all. He was thinking of Ronnie Merrick."

"But—Margot?" asked Celia.

"Your sister," returned Dr. Fell, "went back to Caswall with a plain (I repeat, a plain) brown bottle. She was going to make a last fiery appeal to her husband. And so she . . ."

"She printed a label," whispered Celia.

"A label," said Dr. Fell, "dramatically crying poison. I think I can see her holding it up before Thorley and saying, 'You see what this is? Let me go, or I'll drink it tonight. Let me have Ronnie; or I'll die.'

"And Thorley Marsh didn't believe her.

"She had cried, 'Wolf!' too often. She had threatened suicide too much. Here he saw a fake label clumsily printed on a toy press from the nursery. (You recall, I asked whether he knew about that printing press?) After her threat, she put the bottle more or less openly in the medicine cabinet. And, in an atmosphere of horrible strain, your party started for Widestairs."

Dr. Fell's cigar had gone out. He put it down on the little table with the decanter, the glasses, and the glass water jug. He eyed the water jug before continuing.

"We needn't recapitulate the events of that night, except for the actual murder. Ronnie Merrick got a bad fright when he was unexpectedly faced with the part of Dr. Buchanan at the party. But he had gone too far to retreat.

"The party was over. The hours went on striking. Widestairs was now asleep. Well before one o'clock, the time arranged for both of them to drink poison, Merrick slipped away from Widestairs to Caswall. Under a greatcoat he wore the sodden-wet clothes of the trout stream.

"He removed the greatcoat, swam across the moat, and

190

swung himself up the pipe. From outside he could see his victim, wherever she happened to be in her suite; as I discovered by questions, all the curtains were wide open and a ledge along the wall runs underneath them. He saw her in one of those rooms, now wearing a black velvet gown."

"Dr. Fell," said Celia, "what *is* the explanation of that gown? None of us had ever seen it! It was . . ."

"A black velvet gown," said Dr. Fell, "for a black velvet room."

"What?"

"You of course appreciate that your sister, before everything else in her life faded out under the stress of her passion for Merrick, had set up as a fortune teller as other women have done before her? It was an outlet for her hysteria, her frustration, her hatred of life.

"Once the affair began with Merrick, all that was forgotten. Madame Vanya disappeared. Her clients' cards were destroyed. The door was locked. The inner room became sacred to the love affair that destroyed her. But it was the dress she had worn as Madame Vanya; and in it Merrick painted her portrait."

Holden stared back. "He painted—?"

"Dash it all!" complained Dr. Fell. "Didn't you notice what was burned in the fireplace? Didn't you smell burning canvas?"

"Yes. Yes, I did!"

"And the burned sticks, arranged in a rectangle, with what might have been shreds of cloth attached? And the broken lengths of varnished wood, which had been the easel before he smashed it up? The room had a skylight, you know; a north light; an artist's light. That was why you saw me looking for the marks of the easel on the carpet. But that big velvet-covered divan . . . well, never mind."

Celia seemed about to comment on this last remark, but changed her mind.

"You—you were telling us," she said, "about the murder. About Ronnie crawling up out of the moat. And poor Margot getting dressed to die. What then?"

Dr. Fell pondered.

"For that," he said, "we have the testimony of no living person. Let me tell you what I think happened in those rooms.

"Merrick hasn't wanted to do this, you know. But he has got to the point of believing he must dispose of this woman, must take one last step, or he will never get Doris Locke.

"Clinging to the drainpipe outside, he peers through that never-quite-closed window into the bathroom. He sees his victim standing in front of the mirror, holding up a glass that contains an alcohol solution of morphine and belladonna. He sees his victim, with a swaggering gesture which does not quite mean business, lift the glass and drain it.

"But *he* means business. And he climbs through the window.

"He ran very little risk. The husband, drunk, can be heard snoring in the next room. Everyone else is far away. If she is startled by that specter, face twitching and sodden wet, then the hysterical brain will assume he has come to die with her and it will seem absolutely right.

"He stops only long enough to mop head and hands on a towel. She points toward the other rooms, her bedroom and sitting room beyond, and leads the way. He follows her. In the bedroom, while her back is turned, he can snatch up a weapon . . .

"Of course you guess what it was?

"It was a weapon from among the fire irons in the bedroom. It was the brass-handled poker which you, Celia, described as being in the sitting room on the following morning. A supernumerary fire iron, the touch of the murderer.

"As she steps into the sitting room, she collapses from a frantic blow across the back of the skull. Not hard enough to kill; not hard enough to leave a mark under that heavy hair. But hard enough to stun until the morphine can make her helpless.

"He drags that handsome, inert body over to the chaise longue, in the warm room with the lights burning. He must find and destroy her diary, that famous diary in the Chinese Chippendale desk. He finds the diary unlocked; he burns the pages.

"Young Bryon is freezing cold and nearly fainting. But he goes back to the bathroom, rinses out the glass she has drunk from, and puts the poison bottle in his pocket. He switches off the light in the bedroom and the bathroom. And down he crawls again into the moat."

Dr. Fell paused, wheezing heavily.

"But Margot Marsh, don't you see, still had the will to live? Now we can say 'did' instead of 'perhaps' or 'might have.' An hour later she struggled to semiconsciousness: morphine poisoned, dying, but calling for help. Thorley Marsh heard her. He stumbled into the sitting room—

"And, by thunder, but this man got a jolt! The moaning woman may be in a hysterical attack, yes. Of course! No doubt! But that brown bottle labelled 'poison.' My God, can she have meant what she said about suicide? Thorley Marsh rushed back to the medicine chest. The bottle had gone."

Dr. Fell drew a deep breath, puffing out the ribbon on his eyeglasses.

"That," he said, "was what I had to establish when I first questioned our friend Marsh. It had seemed clear from the first, by his incessant harping to everybody on the subject of a certificate of death from natural causes, that he at least suspected the possibility of suicide. So, to avoid scandal, he lied.

"But, if I could trip him up and get him to verify what I believed to be the truth, then I should be on safe and certain ground. And I did so. Will you concede that what I once told you was no paradox? It was because Marsh had been telling lies that I then knew he was telling the truth."

"And yet," Holden demanded, "Thorley didn't even tell Dr. Shepton he suspected Margot might have poisoned herself?"

"No. Because Dr. Shepton (if you recall) instantly told him it was a hysterical attack and probably not even very serious. Afterward it was too late. So he lied."

"I can't make Thorley out!" Holden said desperately. "I still don't know whether I ought to apologize to him or wring his neck!"

"And yet," said Dr. Fell, "he is the easiest person of all to understand. Thorley Marsh is a genuinely good-natured person, who likes his friends and will go to any amount of trouble for them, provided only his own self-interest is not seriously threatened." He paused. "There, but for the grace of God . . ."

There was a silence.

"Yes," said Holden. "There, but for the grace of God, go we all."

"And yet," Celia spoke softly, "I hate him. I hate him even when I know Margot was . . . was like that, and he never mistreated her. Maybe it's a dreadful thing to say, when he's—"

"Oh, ah?" rumbled Dr. Fell. "How is he?"

"They don't know yet. Doris is at the nursing home now. We're expecting her." Celia hesitated. "But I *hate* him," she said, "for telling you I was crazy and Margot died a natural death and there wasn't any poison bottle, when all the time he knew better! Don, dear! I know what I did was very silly. But do you blame me?"

"No! Of course I don't!"

"Nor I," said Dr. Fell. "But, by thunder, young lady, you gave me some very apprehensive moments!"

And Dr. Fell shook his head, massively.

"I informed you in the Long Gallery," he told Holden, "that this girl was in her right senses. Apparently she'd been seeing ghosts; but, when she saw you and knew you were no ghost, it was obvious she hadn't been suffering from delusions. At the same time, I had to make sure she wasn't . . ."

"Wasn't what?"

"Manufacturing evidence!" said Dr. Fell.

An expression of awe went over his face.

"When we went out to unseal that tomb," he continued, "I was frightened. Damme, yes! Not because I expected a supernatural occurrence, as you evidently thought. But, if this girl had been attempting to manufacture evidence, as seemed likely from that letter, then the police would be after her straightaway.

"At first glance, when we unsealed the vault, there seemed to be nothing wrong except the disarrangement of the coffins. And I was so relieved, so infinitely relieved, that Inspector Crawford noticed it.

"I had already, in case it became necessary, tried to put Crawford off the track with much hocus-pocus about the impossibility of entering that vault. Then, just when I was feeling better, Crawford's light picked up that infernal bottle where only Celia could have put it. Back I sank into the abyss."

"Dr. Fell," asked Holden, "how in blazes were those coffins moved?"

"Ah, yes." Dr. Fell looked guilty. "I (harrumph) fear my hocus-pocus talk must have deceived you as much as it deceived Crawford."

"Hocus-pocus talk nothing! Yesterday Locke cited a fact even more staggering. The two modern coffins, Margot's and that of a bloke named John Devereux, were airtight masses weighing eight hundred pounds each. Who could fling them about?"

"That, you see," explained Dr. Fell, "was the hocus-pocus. Flung was the word I suggested. But they were not flung. They were lifted."

"All right, then! How were they lifted?"

"Again," said Dr. Fell, "the key clue is 'water.'"

"Water?"

"The modern coffins were airtight. Therefore they were watertight. They would float."

Holden stared at him.

"The country around Caswall, as you've doubtless noticed," said Dr. Fell, "is watered by underground springs. The sort of thing the Germans call—"

"*Grundwasser!*" muttered Holden, with a sudden realization springing into his mind. "*Grundwasser!*"

"Yes. It rises nearly to the surface of the ground in the autumn and the spring, and sinks back quite quickly in the summer and the winter. Anyone who studied the countryside could make a small bet that during autumn and spring that vault would be flooded.

"It was four feet below ground level, as you saw. As you also breathed, it was distinctly damp. Crawford, when he walked there, left sharp finely printed footprints in the sand, which doesn't happen in completely dry sand; it was damp.

"The new watertight coffins, lifted up four feet and set drifting, were certain to move all over the place. It's not at all surprising that one of them, its head wedged against the back wall, should remain half propped up when the water subsided.

"But the oldest coffin, being sixteenth century and rotted, never moved at all; the water got into it. An eighteenth century coffin was only slewed round, partly moved and no more. You—er—you follow me?"

"Yes," said Holden in a dazed voice.

"Such an occurrence," grunted Dr. Fell, "had never happened before at Caswall. The vault was new. Aside from the old tomb, which was up in a hill and not likely to be troubled by groundwater, it was the only vault in the churchyard. But the phenomenon has been seen often enough in other places." *

"Then the sand on the floor. . ?"

"Naturally there was no footprint. Except for disturbances round the coffins, the effect of slowly rising and falling water on sand would be to make it smoother than before.

"Dash it all! I gave you a hint! The new lock, being far above the reach of the water, turned with a sharp clean click. But the lower hinge of the door, being well within slopping distance of rising water, squeaked and squealed. It was rusty. Water, water, water!"

* See *Oddities*, by Lieutenant Commander Rupert T. Gould, R. N. (London, Philip Allan & Co. Ltd., 1928, pp. 33–78.)

"And that's all there was to it?"

"That," agreed Dr. Fell, "was all there was to it."

"I'm the culprit, Don," Celia said in a stifled voice. "I—I found that in a book. I gambled on it happening. Do you hate me very much?"

"Don't be an idiot, my dear! Hate you?"

"But Dr. Fell must resent it."

"By thunder," said Dr. Fell, "I do resent it!"

"You've got every right to. I'm awfully sorry. I was looking for a fake poison bottle that resembled the real one; and in the cellar at Widestairs, where Ronnie must have hidden it, I got the real bottle without knowing it. I put it in there when you and I sealed the vault. You have every right to resent being victimized—"

"Nonsense!" said Dr. Fell. "I mean, you should have confided in me. Damme, my girl! I could have shown you far better ways of flummoxing the evidence than an ersatz supernatural story like that."

"I was desperate," said Celia. "There was Thorley smirking and calling me mad. So I thought I might as well be mad, and see how he liked it. But it only produced evidence against me."

"That, of course, was why you had to wait so long before getting in touch with the police? Until the water rose in the spring, and died back into the ground during the summer?"

"Yes. And it had been such a terribly rainy June I didn't dare gamble, in case there might still be water there. But July began baking hot, and continued like that, so I risked it. Thorley . . ."

She broke off.

The door to the hall opened. Doris Locke, a stanch little figure though with her eyes puffed from weeping, wandered in with a listless air. After her came her father. And the change in Locke was almost shocking; he seemed to have aged ten years in one day.

Celia, deeply concerned, hurried over and pushed out chairs for them. Doris, small and grateful, acknowledged the gesture with a pressure of the hand.

"Thorley's going to get well," Doris said. "And it's all my fault!"

"Your fault?" Celia asked.

"That Thorley and Ronnie went to the New Bond Street place," Doris burst out, "and had the fight." She looked at Holden. "It's your fault, too, Don Dismallo!"

Holden stared at the floor.

"Yes," he admitted. "I suppose it is."

"Never in my life," again the tears came into Doris's eyes, "will I forget walking back to our house on Thursday night, through those meadows, with Ronnie and Don Dismallo!"

Holden remembered it too, with an intolerable vividness now that he could see below the surface.

"Don Dismallo," Doris pointed at him, "asking me about That Woman's boy friend, and me telling him about the New Bond Street place, and saying please go and investigate it! And all while Ronnie was *there.*"

"Doris!" murmured the gaunt, fragile image of Sir Danvers Locke.

"I knew there was something wrong with Ronnie that night!" said Doris. "I could tell it by his voice, and the way his eyes sort of shone. But I never guessed *Ronnie,* Ronnie of all people, was That Woman's boy friend!" She looked at Holden as though a great oracle had let her down. "You, Don Dismallo!"

"My dear girl," protested Holden, "how could you expect me to guess it either? You kept talking about a 'distinguished-looking middle-aged man.' You said there was a friend of yours, Jane Somebody, who had seen them . . ."

"Jane didn't say he was middle-aged!"

"Didn't say—?"

"Jane Paulton said he was 'distinguished-looking.' It was Ronnie who caught that up, the first time I ever told him, and tacked on 'middle-aged.' He kept repeating it over and over. It was Ronnie who told you so that night. And it seemed all right," stormed Doris, "because you do think of somebody distinguished looking as being middle-aged."

"Come to think of it . . ."

"Y-yes, Don Dismallo?"

"The first time I ever met Ronnie," said Holden, "he unnecessarily dragged in a reference to Margot's lover and kept insisting on the middle-aged part."

How easy, he was thinking, when you have learned the truth! How easy to interpret the moods of young Merrick—whom he had liked, and liked very much—stalking dazed in the Long Gallery, or wandering wild-eyed across the meadows in the moonlight while Doris spoke to him about the murderer!

"She got on his nerves," Holden could hear Doris's voice saying, "so he killed her." And that, in sober God's truth, was the fact.

Sir Danvers Locke tugged at his immaculate collar.

"Dr. Fell!" he said.

"Sir?"

"Will you be kind enough to interpret one final point for me?"

"If I can."

"I take it," Locke was so white that Holden felt apprehensive, "I take it that Mrs. Marsh never really, in her heart of hearts, intended to die? And that was why she didn't give up the New Bond Street premises when the suicide pact was arranged?"

"That's my belief."

"But young Merrick never knew that?"

"Never. But he suddenly wondered, when your daughter spoke about it, whether the place might still be there. He had a key, of course. So he traveled up with you in the train next day. But he couldn't go directly to the same address, because you were going to the costumier's shop yourself . . ."

"Innocently, I swear!"

"And Thorley caught him," Doris said miserably. "I told Thorley next morning about what we'd said. So Thorley went haring up in the car, to see if there might be any evidence. He had a key too, now: That Woman's key. He was still—suppressing things. And there was a fight. Up there in that room, with only the fire burning, there was a fight."

She shivered. The vivid picture was in all their minds.

"You, of course," Locke glanced at Dr. Fell, "sent Holden after both of them when you realized. Yes. Yes. That is plain." He hesitated, a gray-faced shadow. "Let me," he added, "now make my recantation."

"Recantation?" exclaimed Celia.

"Doris," her father said formally, "I did not want you to marry Mr. Marsh. I confess it. I distrusted him. When we heard the first evidence, I believed he was a murderer too. It was only, on thinking things over late that night . . .

"Doris, your father's judgment is not good. I tried to force you into—never mind! I retract. If you now wish to marry this man . . ."

Doris, with absorbed and fierce concentration, was picking at the arm of the chair.

"But I don't think," she said in a small voice, "I do want to marry Thorley."

Locke sat up, shakily. "You don't wish to? Why not?"

"Oh, I don't know," Doris said. "I just don't. Celia!"

"Yes, dear?"

"You've always been in love with Don Dismallo, haven't you?"

"I don't like to say so in public," smiled Celia, and her eyes met Holden's across the back of Doris's head. "But—always and always."

"Well," said Doris, "it's not like that with Thorley and me." She paused. "He's not what I thought he was," she added. "He's just mean in the soul."

There was a long silence.

"I won't say, Doris," observed Locke, with a feeble attempt at a smile, "your decision displeases me. You are young; and we have the authority of an old saw that there are many fish in the sea. At least you have been delivered from—"

"Don't you say anything against poor Ronnie!" cried Doris.

While they looked at her, dumbfounded, Doris bounced up out of her chair. She walked to one of the windows, and stood looking out at the moonlit garden.

"Ronnie," Doris said, and there was a ring of reluctant admiration in her voice, "was a heller. An absolute heller! And I never knew it! I thought he was wishy-washy. I never guessed. Whatever's he's done, that's how I like a man to be! Oh, I almost wish I had married him, now!"

From the vastness of Dr. Gideon Fell's bulk emerged a murmur which might have been an ironic sigh. He shook his head. Bending over to the little table, Dr. Fell unstoppered the decanter, poured a very strong whisky into a glass, and added a very small amount of water.

The tolerant irony, the far-off twinkle of the eye, all radiated from him as he raised his glass.

"I drink to human nature," he said.

JOHN DICKSON CARR

The man many readers think of as the most British of detective story writers was born in Uniontown, Pennsylvania in 1906. After attending Haverford College, Carr went to Paris where, his parents hoped, he would continue his education at the Sorbonne. Instead he became a writer. His first novel, *It Walks By Night*, was published in 1929. Shortly thereafter, Carr married and settled in his wife's native country, England.

The Thirties were a highly prolific period for Carr, who was turning out three to five novels a year. Some of these were published under what became his most famous *nom de plume*, Carter Dickson. (Because the Dickson novels contain a great deal of a certain type of comedy, many of their earlier readers attributed them to P.G. Wodehouse. Could an American write like this? Never!)

In 1965 Carr left England and moved to Greenville, South Carolina, where he remained until his death in 1977.

In his lifetime, Carr received the Mystery Writers of America's highest honor, the Grand Master Award, and was one of only two Americans (the other was Patricia Highsmith) ever admitted into the prestigious—but almost exclusively British—Detection Club. In his famous essay "The Grandest Game in the World", Carr listed the qualities always present in the detective novel at its best: fair play, sound plot construction, and ingenuity. (He added, "Though this quality of ingenuity is not necessary to the detective story as such, you will never find the great masterpiece without it.") That these qualities are prevalent in Carr's work is obvious to his legions of readers. In the words of the great detective novelist-critic Edmund Crispin, "For subtlety, ingenuity, and atmosphere, he was one of the three or four best detective-story writers since Poe that the English language has known."